Baudelaire's Revenge

Baudelaire's Revenge

BOB VAN LAERHOVEN

Translated from the Dutch by Brian Doyle

PEGASUS CRIME

NEW YORK LONDON

For Caroline: patience, perseverance and a great heart for horses

———◦◦◦———

BAUDELAIRE'S REVENGE

Pegasus Crime is an Imprint of
Pegasus Books LLC
80 Broad Street, 5th Floor
New York, NY 10004

Copyright © 2014 Bob Van Laerhoven

Translation © 2014 Brian Doyle

The translation of this book is funded by the Flemish Literature Fund
(Vlaams Fonds voor de Letteren—www.flemishliterature.be)

Flemish
Literature
Fund

First Pegasus Books cloth edition 2014

Interior design by Maria Fernandez

Library of Congress Cataloging-in-Publication Data is available.

ISBN: 978-1-60598-548-0

10 9 8 7 6 5 4 3 2 1

Printed in the United States of America
Distributed by W. W. Norton & Company, Inc.

1

LIFE AND DEATH HAD TAUGHT Commissioner Lefèvre to love poetry and wenches, and in spite of his fifty-three years, he still wasn't certain which of the two he admired most. To him, poetry was an abstract emotion rooted in the primordial world, before the existence of language. The act of copulation skulked through the human brain like a prehistoric lizard, biting randomly.

The commissioner had decided to feed the reptile that evening and was in search of a warm haven. The prospect increased his sensitivity toward the aesthetics of a visit to the brothel. His burly frame, covered with coarse grey hair, had been washed and perfumed, reminiscent of years of abundance, handsomely oiled and gleaming. Lefèvre had trimmed his pubic hair as neatly as his short beard. He was ready to bear the burden of the flesh.

He had spent more money on *cocottes* in his life than he cared to remember. But he wasn't interested in expensive suits or alabaster-handled walking sticks. In exchange, he had memories: a lock of hair covering the eyes, ample dangling breasts *à la levrette*, trembling thighs in muted lamplight. They took him by surprise at times and soothed his restlessness.

The commissioner's favorite of the last six months was a faun-like creature, an outsider like himself. He thought it best not to get attached to one woman, even when it came to courtesans. The talons of a woman's heart are greedy and it was wise to avoid them. But the commissioner was fascinated by the wench's tender coquetry. She was a firefly trapped in amber. Compared with her, the other *cocottes* paled into insignificance.

An agreeable sensation in his chest inclined him to walk with a jaunt. What had started off as sexual necessity—Lefèvre was in his early forties at the time—had become more intoxicating than opium. The commissioner usually swaggered along the splendid Chausée d'Antin, brandishing his walking stick in the cool light of L'Opéra, which had been refurbished three years earlier in 1867 at considerable expense. But this evening, his rugged, stocky, yet well-tailored frame seemed agitated.

Lefèvre's gaze drifted toward the gleaming coaches bringing courtesans of name and fame to the inner courtyards of the city's palaces, where liveried servants waited to escort each to her *aimant*. The "skulls and Pickelhaube helmets"—a designation much favored by *Le Moniteur*—of the Prussian troops advancing toward the border appeared to be having a significant effect on the aristocratic libido.

Lefèvre had read in the same *Moniteur* a couple of hours earlier that Baudelaire was now considered one of France's greatest men of letters, a mere three years after his death. The article also claimed that Baudelaire had predicted this disastrous war. Lefèvre had only witnessed a single performance of the deathly-pale poet, a genius if many were to be believed. But traces of the poet's words—rumor had it he was already suffering from syphilis at the time, which explained his bulging eyes and their metallic lustre—had left their mark on the commissioner, like the tracks of a vineyard snail. Typical of the French bourgeoisie to cherish a poet years after his death, when they had loathed and persecuted him while he was alive.

Lefèvre involuntarily mouthed the words of *Les Deux Bonnes Soeurs*, as strophes of the poem with their vigorous timbre invaded his mind.

His head told him he had garbled the lines. His heart told him that a few shreds of the poem contained everything he wanted to know about life.

> *Debauchery and Death are pleasant twins (. . .)*
> *Both tomb and bed, in blasphemy so fecund*
> *Each other's hospitality to second,*
> *Prepare grim treats, and hatch atrocious things.*[1]

The last line rubbed against the commissioner like an invisible satyr when he heard a woman scream behind the chic facade of one of the Chausée d'Antin's sumptuous bordellos.

PAINTINGS BY BOUGUEREAU DECORATED THE vestibule, a sign of opulence given the hefty fees the artist commanded for his work. As Lefèvre charged up the thickly carpeted stairs, he cast a fleeting yet disapproving glance at the painter's classical panoramas, which had come to symbolize the strict guidelines of *L'Académie* on realism in painting.

The woman's scream resounded once again somewhere above him. Lefèvre held his revolver in his left hand, his police badge in his right. An older woman in a turban, *en vogue* among the more fashionable whores, awaited him on the landing, wringing her hands. Lefèvre guessed she was the concierge, held his finger to his lips when she was about to open her mouth, and showed her his police badge. He brought his lips close to her neck, pointed to the doors on the landing, and whispered, "Which one?"

She pursed her lips. There was a look of uncertainty in her eyes, but she was neither surprised nor disapproving. Lefèvre could see she had lived a life of secret encounters and smiles behind lace napkins. She pointed to room twelve.

Lefèvre approached the room with caution, but the door swung open to meet him. A young lady in a lavishly fluffy negligee, filling the air with the scent of absinthe and a hint of musk, came running from the room. "Inside?" the commissioner inquired. He had had plenty of experience dealing with romantic intrigues. As *officier du paix*, he had to keep an eye on the city's moral reputation. Lefèvre preferred discretion to good morals.

That was why he remained disapprovingly tight-lipped when he discovered a corpse in the room instead of a disappointed client demanding his money back because an excess of wine had affected his ability to rise to the occasion. The body's twisted expression reminded him of Dr. Guillaume Duchenne de Boulogne's electrophysiological experiments, photographs of which Lefèvre had recently been privileged to see. De Boulogne, according to many a dangerous madman, applied electrodes to the human body to chart muscular reactions. He was convinced that electrical pulses could suggest immense agony on a patient's face without him suffering real pain.

But the dead man had clearly felt something: the horrific cramps of one or another poison. Strychnine? He missed the odor of bitter almonds. Lefèvre cursed under his breath. His plans for a night snuggled up against his mystifying Claire de la Lune had gone up in smoke.

He leaned over the body and noticed a scrap of paper with fragments of a poem scribbled wildly, as if the holder of the pen had been drunk or had fallen prey to violent emotion.

Debauchery and Death are pleasant twins (. . .)
Both tomb and bed, in blasphemy so fecund
Each other's hospitality to second,
Prepare grim treats, and hatch atrocious things.[2]

It was as if a needle had pierced Lefèvre's left eye. He shook his head in amazement and a faint smile appeared on his lips. A mind-reading murderer. How appropriate on a night like this.

But there was more to this, the commissioner thought, unable as yet to put his finger on what it might be. He examined the handwriting.

The slightly sardonic smile on his face disappeared. It was strangely familiar.

He examined the corpse at closer quarters and observed the tattoo of a mythical animal on the left wrist.

The subdued light of the boudoir's sparsely distributed oil lamps started to play games with his powers of perception.

The tattoo appeared to change color for a moment.

3

THE CHAUSÉE D'ANTIN? ACCORDING TO the coachman, something had happened in one of the street's fancy bordellos. Inspector Bernard Bouveroux grimaced. No wonder the commissioner had made it to the scene of the crime so quickly. Bouveroux was familiar with Lefèvre's predilection for ladies of ill repute. In such circumstances, a coach was warranted to have his assistant brought to the scene.

As he put on his jacket, Bouveroux glanced outside at the coachman, oil lamp in hand, waiting for his fare to arrive. The vehicle seemed out of place in the darkness of the Rue du Jardinet. The inspector lived on the left side of the street, where wealthy eighteenth-century merchants had built unimaginative yet spacious buildings, which had since been divided into apartments for people who found it difficult to make ends meet. The people on the other side were a lot worse off: a hodgepodge of tiny, dingy, low-built houses, inhabited by labourers' families with hordes of children, who emptied their potties every morning onto the street from their bedroom windows. As he searched for his coat, the inspector rubbed his stomach, which had been troubling him for the best part of twenty years.

It was the end of August and already hard to get by without coal for the fire or a warm coat and hat outside. But the fire wasn't burning. The war with the Prussians had sent coal prices soaring. The room was cold and damp. Bouveroux shivered, but not because of the approaching autumnal chill. He had read somewhere that those who study the human mind were convinced that nightmares had meaning. He made his way down to the coach, still perplexed by the symbolism of the dream from which the coachman had awakened him. The stairwell reeked of chicken casserole. All that had remained was an overpowering sense of misery, a loneliness that dangled round his neck like a rope.

His dead wife Marthe had appeared to him again, but not in her usual angelic radiance. This time she was a beacon of affliction. Bouveroux hoped that this oppressive vision was the result of an excess of wine diluted with vinegar he had downed the night before. *Marthe, when will it all end?* he thought, as he left the building and observed a vague shadow of himself cast on the rain-drenched cobblestones by the light of the coachman's lamp.

4

LEFÈVRE HAD ALREADY QUESTIONED MOST of the ladies before the coach arrived with his assistant Bouveroux. The inspector's nose was gleaming from the cold when he entered the boudoir, his small perceptive eyes streaked with red.

Bouveroux looked at the corpse, snapped his fingers, crouched, and traced the contours of the tattoo on the dead man's wrist with his index finger. He looked up at Lefèvre.

"A *rakshasa*, commissioner."

When both men were on duty, Bouveroux addressed his superior as commissioner, although they were old friends who had saved each other's lives on more than one occasion.

Lefèvre removed his hat and rummaged in his jacket for his chewing tobacco. "Looks like some kind of exotic Japanese demon."

"It's an evil spirit from Indochina," said Bouveroux. "My nephew just returned to Paris with a similar tattoo. He had it done during a drunken night on the town when he was stationed in Tonkin. He didn't know at the time that the image was actually a curse, and now he's worried about his future. Tattoos like this are usually done by women. They call it a *khout*. Take a look: part man, part hawk, standing on a magic square."

"So where did you pick up your knowledge of Indochinese mythology, Bouveroux?" Lefèvre already knew the answer. Bouveroux was an ardent collector of useless information. Anything even vaguely related to the supernatural made him laugh, but curious facts from exotic places drove him wild. In spite of his caveman exterior, Lefèvre was more sensitive to moods and impressions than his gaunt assistant.

"After we spent the night in the palace of the Dey in Algiers, where we sipped better wine than we'd ever tasted at home and found parchment scrolls that appeared to be older than the Qur'an, I developed something of a passion for scholarly research into foreign peoples and their history," said Bouveroux.

"Scholars fill the newspapers with nonsense these days just to butter up the public." Lefèvre realised he sounded a little stale. During that memorable night in the palace in Algiers to which Bouveroux had alluded, Lefèvre had done things that had little to do with knowledge or wisdom, things of which Bouveroux was unaware. His assistant was only three years his junior, but the inspector was better equipped to deal with the feverish pace of change characteristic of the times in which they lived. Paris had become one enormous building site. Conflict between the rich and the poor was close to boiling point. The emperor was a simpleton with an inflated ego, who was determined to lead France into a war it could never win. Little wonder people were prepared to listen to scholarly humbug or believe in the devil.

What was a man to do in such circumstances? His duty "to the last," as prefect of police Banlieu had prescribed.

"Get the concierge in here. It's time we had a word."

Bouveroux obediently disappeared. Moments later the concierge was standing in the doorway. She had taken off her turban to reveal silver-blond hair as dry as straw. Her slanted eyes and ample mouth suggested she was once an exceptional beauty. Lefèvre glanced at her shoes, which had clearly seen better days, and then her delicate shoulders, which had once borne the burden of a covetous, faithless love. "I saw nothing, sir," she said, before Lefèvre had the chance to ask her a question.

He tried to concentrate on the task at hand. The unfortunate murder had cast a shadow over his evening. His mind's eye was working fast and furious, leaving his senses far behind. He could picture the prostitute he called Claire de la Lune in every corner of the boudoir. Her smell, a potpourri of oriental memories, her husky laugh, the look in her eyes of a startled mare, the danger that appeared to lurk beneath her quivering limbs, were more tangible now than when he was with her.

"Tell me it was about jealousy, and we can both get on with our day," he said, gesturing toward the courtesan from room twelve who was still snivelling into her lace handkerchief. Her eyes were red and her shoulders lifted, as if some invisible figure was holding her under the arms.

"Natalie is well-suited to her profession. She has a weak character, but self-preservation has made her sweet," said the concierge, walking over to the fragile nightingale and caressing her hair as one would pet a poodle. "I can't imagine her committing murder. She might be pushed into stabbing a man in the eye with a pair of scissors out of fear or repugnance. But Master Albert was a regular customer and Natalie often spoke highly of his manners, discretion, and generosity." The woman she referred to as Natalie looked at her with timid gratitude and nodded gently.

"Albert who?"

"It's not our custom to ask our guests for their surnames, sir," the concierge replied reproachfully.

The whore started to sob again and produced a second handkerchief from her low-cut bodice; this one had even more lace.

"If you ask my advice, Natalie's not the one you're looking for," the concierge concluded.

"You'll have to come up with more than that if you're to convince me," said the commissioner. "The girl told me her client had suddenly taken ill, started to wave his arms around, and collapsed to the floor, foaming at the mouth. For no apparent reason? Sounds a bit fishy to me."

"I know nothing about the circumstances," said the concierge, "but this looks more like the work of some tormented soul."

"What makes you think that?"

She pointed to the tattoo. "An old lady like me has few small pleasures left, commissioner. I have seen Master Albert stripped to the waist on previous visits and I can assure you that this is the first time I've noticed any form of bodily decoration."

"Young men are prone to such whims, even when they're aesthetically questionable," said Lefèvre dryly.

"Right you are, commissioner, but that decoration gives me the shivers."

Lefèvre glanced over at Bouveroux, who was on his knees in front of the body and not really listening to the conversation. The inspector leaned forward and sniffed the man's wrist. He then carefully touched the tattoo with his gloved righted hand.

"It's not a tattoo," he observed. "The image has been painted on."

"Don't touch it, Bernard," said the commissioner. "Take off that glove and wrap it in a cloth."

Bouveroux raised his eyebrows, but did as he was asked. His old friend's occasional intuitive outbursts—which he liked to call "danger signs"—were best obeyed.

Lefèvre turned once again to the concierge, as if the short intermezzo with his assistant had never taken place. "Did anything unusual happen today?"

"No."

"Take your time."

The concierge struck a pensive pose, which only lasted a few seconds. "A couple of hours ago, one of the Ursuline nuns knocked on the door. She said she wanted to pray for the souls of the ladies who work here. She then visited each of the rooms to introduce herself. I didn't see her leave. So many people come and go in this place."

"Had none of the other pious sisters ever come up with such an idea?"

"No. But it's not really surprising for a nun, if you think about it."

"What did she look like?"

The concierge sighed, raised her hands, and shook Natalie by the shoulders. The girl turned her tear-stained face. "She wanted to pray with me, but I didn't have the time."

"Did you see what she looked like?"

The girl looked at the commissioner with dismay. Lefèvre grunted. "A hooded figure. Religion is a beautiful thing, don't you think?" The commissioner's military service in Algeria had eroded his faith in religion.

Bouveroux coughed impatiently. Lefèvre restrained him with a glare. The commissioner knew that patience could be rewarding in some situations. If only he could count on the same patience when lust drove him to the *cocottes*.

"Do you have anything else to say, madam?" Bouveroux inquired.

"Actually I do, sir," said the concierge, "but I'm not sure if it's relevant."

"This is a murder inquiry, madam."

"The nun was extremely beautiful. She had a face like one of those porcelain dolls that are supposed to look like Japanese women, do you get my drift? Please understand, commissioner. I've been in this business for a long time. Ladies who receive men and are well-versed in the art of lovemaking take on a particular appearance after a while. The thought went through my head that the nun might once have been a courtesan."

Lefèvre raised an eyebrow.

"And if I'm right, she practised her profession not so long ago," the concierge concluded with a vague expression on her face, as if she were reminded of something in her own past she would have preferred to forget.

5

THE COMMISSIONER'S OFFICIAL PLACE OF work at the prefecture had heavy curtains, a desk, a pipe stand, and two woollen carpets he had brought back from his military service in Algeria. A portrait of Napoleon III, which made *l'empereur* look like an escapee from a lunatic asylum, graced one of the walls, while his desk, which connoisseurs would describe as Classicist, was a little out of the ordinary with its countless drawers and extraordinary ornamentation. Most of the drawers contained weapons. Lefèvre had a predilection for heavy-gauge pistols. His collection included a Basque front-loader and a Richards–Mason .357. Lefèvre considered the Mason more reliable than the Colt of the same calibre Bouveroux used.

The commissioner blew his nose and browsed through his notebook. He had spent a restless night in his apartment on the Rue de Nesle. After organizing the removal of the corpse to the morgue, where a police doctor could examine it, he had considered continuing on his way to Claire de la Lune after all, but a curious listlessness had prevented him. The demon on the wrist of the murdered young man, which had changed colour while he was looking at it, continued to preoccupy him.

He put the optical illusion down to the Algerian love potion he had downed before getting dressed. The commissioner was aware that drinking the watery solution of *Scilla Autumnalis* was not without its risks. The Berber from Sidi Bel Abbès, who taught him to make the potion long ago, had told him about the Roman legend of the beautiful nymph Scilla who had begged Circe for a love potion. Instead of drinking it, she had bathed in it to be sure her satyr lover Glaucus would remain faithful.

"Too much passion, *sidi*, can turn a person into a monster. Scilla was transformed into a woman with two serpent's tails and six barking dog heads. She threw herself into the sea, and since then she has murdered every unfortunate soul who comes near her." The Berber produced the sinister, piercing smile of someone you would prefer not to meet in a dark alley. But his potion worked and Lefèvre had come to trust its properties down through the years.

He had noticed the need to increase the dose every now and then to maintain the effect. The love potion produced a burning sensation like hot fiery coals in his lower belly, running from his navel to his testicles. But *Scilla Autumnalis* sometimes made him see things that were not there. Did he really see the *khout* change colour? The commissioner decided to reduce the dose next time.

Bouveroux entered the office without knocking. "You look as if you did more last night than interrogate the *demoiselles*," he said in good spirits.

Lefèvre could smell wine on his old army comrade's breath. He had stopped reprimanding Bouveroux for his alcohol consumption years ago. The commissioner accepted that everyone needed their own secret poison to make life liveable. He had advised his assistant to rinse his mouth with a *digestif* made from crushed mint, to freshen his breath after drinking serious amounts of alcohol. The inspector had answered that his memory was like a sieve. By the time he had downed his first glass, the thought of mint-flavoured concoctions had vanished.

When they were alone, they treated each other as friends. In 1842, twenty-eight years earlier, they had spent three years in Louis Napoleon's Algerian army. The man insisted on being referred to as Emperor Napoleon III, in spite of the fact that Otto von Bismarck—the "Iron Chancellor"—had sworn he would humiliate the "puppet emperor" if he continued to resist the presence of a German Hohenzollern prince on the Spanish throne. Twenty-four-year-old Lefèvre and twenty-one-year-old Bouveroux had fought in Algeria against *Sufi* who were convinced that death in the name of Allah was a man's proper and only destiny. They had reclined in the arms of *houri*, highly skilled at satisfying a man's needs yet dangerous nonetheless. Esoteric contacts with *djinns* sometimes drove these veiled creatures to relieve the Frenchman they had just fondled at their welcoming breasts of his testicles, hacking and cursing like women possessed.

Nostalgic by nature, Bouveroux had gradually drowned the realization that he would never be the great historian he had dreamed of becoming in gallons of wine. His syntax may have been pedantic at times, but it concealed an industrious and analytical intellect. The inspector was a fervent library visitor with an encyclopaedic disposition. While Lefèvre was interested in the subterranean twists and turns of the criminal mind and often followed his instincts, Bouveroux was a gatherer of facts. In contrast to the commissioner, whose bulbous cheeks were reminiscent of an English bulldog, Bouveroux had an elongated ascetic look, in spite of his alcohol consumption.

"We have the victim's identity," he said triumphantly, as if it was the result of peerless detective work. "His name is Albert Dacaret. An artist." Bouveroux placed a wickedly large pile of snuff on his thumb, snorted it deep into his nostrils, and grinned blissfully. "The motive was probably money. Artists are always short of cash and end up borrowing from the wrong kind."

"Dacaret?" said Lefèvre. "Interesting. A promising young poet, the papers say."

Bouveroux's grin turned to a frown. The commissioner maintained an interest in the press, in spite of his well-publicized conviction that it was full of lies and foolishness, but the inspector preferred not to make a point of it. "Your knowledge of French literature continues to amaze me, Paul."

Lefèvre looked at him with a smile. He knew his friend better than he was willing to admit. "I presume you also know the cause of death. Otherwise you wouldn't look so self-satisfied."

Bouveroux took a seat and placed his hat on the chair next to him. "That's what makes the case so remarkable," he said. "The painting on the man's wrist contains an exotic poison. The natives of French Guiana use it to kill giant lizards." Bouveroux appeared to be hungry. In spite of his thin frame, he could eat as if there was no tomorrow. "The deadly tincture needs time to take effect. Once the colossal reptiles are dead, they cut them up and cook them. They say their flesh is as tender as a baby's."

He started to pat his jacket and trousers and after some searching produced a crumpled piece of paper from his inside pocket. Bouveroux was in the habit of scribbling down the things his investigative mind was likely to forget and ferreting them out later from various openings in his clothing. "Albert Dacaret. Caused a furor six months ago with the collection *Le Fièvre du Diable*. Was hailed by newspaper critics as 'the new Baudelaire.' Became seriously angry at this response and wrote a letter to the editor of a newspaper in which he annihilated his deceased predecessor. Just three weeks ago, the Spanish poet Gustavo Adolfo Bécquer predicted that Dacaret would 'tear the staggeringly conceited romanticism of French letters to pieces'."

Bouveroux started to pat his pockets again, this time in search of his tobacco box, which turned out to be empty. Lefèvre tossed his own tobacco at Bouveroux, who caught it with gratitude. "Where do you get all this information?"

"You know me, Paul," said Bouveroux. "I have plenty of journalist friends. Let me tell you something. In less than a century, the journalists will be bigger stars than the sopranos at the opera!"

Lefèvre, who was standing at the window with his back to Bouveroux, could see the church of Saint-Germain-L'Auxerrois a couple of blocks up the street. The gothic edifice was constructed on the site of an ancient Merovingian sanctuary. Simpler souls believed that light could be seen inside in misty weather, giving the deep-blue stained glass windows an unearthly glow.

Once again he felt a stabbing pain in his left eye and imagined, for a split second, that he was leaning against a curtain that had once concealed a wall, but not anymore. He glanced over his shoulder. It was a grey morning. The gaslight in his office made Bouveroux's cheeks appear pallid and the sockets of his puny eyes black. The sky above Paris was restless and darker than the cloak of a servant girl waiting in a doorway for her lover. It was the end of August and the summer had been a disappointment. Rain, thunderstorms, a plague of mosquitoes, howling dogs and agitated cats.

The commissioner's broad face, which betrayed his roots among the fishermen of Brittany, was grim and dour. Bouveroux was convinced that an air of melancholy had been hanging 'round his old friend of late. Perhaps the commissioner was worried about approaching old age. It was better to drown such worries in wine than to face them eye to eye, the inspector thought.

"Artists have explosive temperaments," said the commissioner pensively. "They hate one another with a vengeance."

Bouveroux fluttered his eyelids. "I'm no great follower of art, Paul. Overstated trickery, if you ask me. I prefer to stick to the facts in the newspapers and in books. Art is the same as spiritualism. Did you know that there are more than six hundred soothsayers and mediums in Paris at the moment, all of them earning huge sums of money from people who believe that their futures can be read in a crystal ball?"

Bouveroux produced a neighing sound, interrupting the commissioner's concentration. He hadn't been paying his assistant much attention. The prickly atmosphere of the previous night and the apprehension in his stomach left the commissioner with the impression that he had missed something important.

Lefèvre tried to sort out the evidence thus far: an exotic poison introduced into the body of the deceased via a painted tattoo. What did this have to say about the murderer's methodology? Had he learned the technique during a visit to Indochina? Or had he picked it up from an island dweller living in Paris? Dark-skinned foreigners had been popular in the city of late. It was hard to avoid hearing about the furor caused by Creoles, Indians, Patagonians, and Spice Islanders at the salons held daily in the capital, as if the danger posed by the advancing Prussians was a mere fantasy.

"How long does the poison take to work, exactly?"

Bouveroux looked contritely at his boss. "I'll have to check that with Doctor Lepage. You won't get an answer right away, I'm afraid. Lepage will have to track down a colleague who served in French Guiana."

"Fine. And check whether Dacaret ever visited any exotic destinations, although the man's simple background doesn't point in that direction. If he's never been abroad, then we should concentrate our inquiries on tattooists in Paris . . ."

"It's not a real tattoo, commissioner."

"Perhaps some tattooists are familiar with the technique you were talking about."

"Rakshasa tattoos?"

"Precisely, that demon of yours. Which of them is talented enough to paint such creatures on the skin? Try to find out as quickly as possible."

The commissioner's demeanour told the inspector that his boss wanted to be alone. Bouveroux made a couple of trivial remarks and left the office.

The corridors of the prefecture were old, winding, and poorly lit, reminiscent of the wine-coloured light illuminating the bazaars in Algeria. The memory sharpened Bouveroux's senses. As he headed mechanically toward the stairs, he muttered under his breath about the séances that were all the rage. An Enlightened Empire? Not a bit of it! The French were either stupid, frightened, or unfortunate—mostly a combination of the three. Bouveroux counted himself among the unfortunate. The rooms he rented in the Rue du Jardinet were poorly maintained, had curtains the color of rotting gums, and were furnished with junk delivered by cart sometime in the distant past.

But his apartment provided the anonymity he needed when he was away from the prefecture. He liked to compare it with the lair of a wounded animal. Since his Marthe's death, the only thing that could relieve his melancholy was a visit to the public library. While his wife was alive, Bouveroux had only succumbed to the distraction of cheap women when the need was greatest, when certain memories of Algeria returned to haunt him—memories he had to expel. He had never told his colleagues that he had remained monogamous in his heart, not even Paul Lefèvre. If he had confessed that he was attached to his wife like a homing pigeon, they would have accused him of betraying the true Frenchman's pride in his national flag, flown by preference "in his trousers."

His name resounded against the walls. Bouveroux looked back to find the commissioner standing in the doorway of his office. A different image took its place. Lefèvre at an outstation in the Sahara, covered in blood, standing in the doorway of the brightly-lit waiting room of a whitewashed fort, illuminated by the frosty stars of the desert night. Bouveroux remembered the excitement on his friend's face.

Almost thirty years later, he saw the same expression. The commissioner had been on the prowl for a long time, and he wallowed in the confusion and hunger in his soul. Lefèvre was waving the piece of paper that had been found on the corpse. "The same handwriting," he said. "Identical! I knew I had seem it somewhere before. Take a look."

In his other hand the commissioner was holding a book, which he held out to Bouveroux. As a fervent library visitor, the inspector registered both title and author in an instant: *Le Peintre de la Vie Moderne* by Charles Baudelaire. He took hold of the book and followed Lefèvre's index finger. The volume contained a dedication: *For a man of the law who obeys the laws of poetry above all else. Charles Baudelaire, 1857.*

A single glance at the scrap of paper in the commissioner's right hand was sufficient.

The handwriting was indeed identical.

6

GRANIER DE CASSAGNAC WAS SO excited about his recent trip to Nouméa, and the impeccable travelogue he planned to write about it, that he didn't pay the slightest attention to the picturesque cloudscape hanging over Paris. He turned into the Rue Saint-André-des-Arts and strutted boldly past the *estaminet* run by the moustachioed Jean-Claude, who almost certainly had a good bottle of wine at the ready to kindle his ardour. But not today! His writing desk was waiting, polished and fragrant with beeswax.

He passed a newspaper kiosk on the Rue Dauphine where they sold *La Patrie* and *Paris Journal*. It wouldn't be long now before *Paris Journal* was begging for the right to publish his story about the French penal colony on New Caledonia. Gautier, a literary jester who imagined himself to be the French Thackeray but was little more than a small-minded nobody who constantly grumbled about money, was going to vomit with jealousy. The last time de Cassagnac had seen the parvenu, Gautier was in the company of the de Goncourt brothers, perfumed vampires and the bane of every promising young artist. With enough pathos to make a third-rate Greek theatre jealous, Gautier had thrown himself on the sofa and announced that as far as he was concerned he was dead, and that everyone should rejoice in the fact. Death, after all, was the highest form of existence. A poet capable of producing such nonsense deserved nothing better than to have to make his living as a vulgar journalist. Gautier considered the latter a plague to which he frequently dedicated lengthy and whining laments.

De Cassagnac chased the conceited dandy from his thoughts and replaced him with sonorous sentences that drifted through his mind as coaches clattered past on the rutted cobblestones. He stopped to admire the gloomy side wall of Jean Mangin's restaurant, which was decorated with fashionable paintings advertising his wares. He paid no attention to the conspicuous cluster of clouds above the pointed edifice, but saw in his mind's eye the crude huts of New Caledonia, populated by young men caught stealing or committing some other crime and shipped to the colony to serve as cheap labour. The miserable brutality he had witnessed on New Caledonia had given his writing an exceptional élan.

One of the rascals was a particularly effeminate individual, referred to by the others as the White Bitch. He would put on a turban, make up his eyes with black powdered kohl, and parade himself among the workers until the bidding started. The colony's guards took their cut of his profits and provided him with henna to color his hair, and natural oils used by Polynesian women to keep their skin smooth.

De Cassagnac had never encountered the kind of moral depravity he had witnessed in the Malaysian, Chinese, and Polynesian quarters of Nouméa. He suspected that the task of describing the natives, who were prone to humping one another at every opportunity, day and night, would likely stretch his syntax beyond its usual elegance. Many an author would be unable to rise to the occasion. The brothers Edmond and Jules de Goncourt, for example, would turn such an immense subject into gutter prose and emboss every disgusting detail onto pretentious medallions with fancy writing. De Cassagnac had decided to use a naturalistic style, which he was sure would cause the book-loving ladies in the most infamous salons to faint. He couldn't imagine a better expression of appreciation. He had even taken note of a couple of sayings in

Ajië, the local dialect of the Polynesian tribes. Their opulent resonance would grant an extra dimension to the innovative literature that was lingering in his mind.

As he turned right at *Petin's Bronzes d'Art et Pendules* on the way to his rented study, a coach with drawn curtains stopped immediately in front of him. De Cassagnac saw its occupant step out onto the street and automatically stood aside. He was surprised when the person spoke to him, but he responded nevertheless with a gallant bow. He suddenly felt a hefty stabbing pain in his neck.

7

GRANIER DE CASSAGNAC RECOVERED CONSCIOUSNESS when someone held a cloth soaked in ammonia under his nose. The penetrating odor confused his senses. The feeling that he was having a nightmare was reinforced by the lack of light. De Cassagnac hoped this was a dream, like the horror stories of that hysterical American Edgar Allan Poe. But the cold, hard floor beneath his body and the stench of brackish water that had gradually replaced the smell of ammonia were all too real.

His body stiffened involuntarily when he realised he was in a cave, a feeble smoking torch in a corner its only illumination. The light flickered against the walls, revealing stacks of human skulls and other bones, black with age. De Cassagnac instinctively looked away. A figure dressed in a hooded cloak crouched to his left, silent, motionless.

"Gracious God!" The words were out before he had the time to regret them. He already knew that his prayer would go unanswered. His breathing accelerated and he broke into a sweat, in spite of the cold humidity of his catacomb prison.

"*Arrêtez! C'est ici l'empire de la mort.*" The whispered words echoed around the cave. They were familiar words, words used by Baudelaire years before as the title of an article.

De Cassagnac realised that he had not been tied up. He wanted to get to his feet, push his assailant out of the way and flee, but his limbs refused to move.

"You are familiar with more exotic climes," the voice continued. "It should please you that I set aside an exotic poison for you alone. It's made from Pseudo-nitschia, algae found only in far-off waters. The natives of Mauritius use it to commit crimes of passion. The algae renders the victim powerless, but has no effect on the mind. The symptoms all have ritual value: the sacrifice is forced to watch in silence and fully conscious as the machete cuts a graceful arc through the moonlight on its way to the neck. No raucous screaming, no pig-like death throes, just elevated torment, precise, meticulous, poetic."

The figure leaned forward.

"An enemy eliminated in such a fashion furnishes the perpetrator with magic powers. Magic, my dear Mr. de Cassagnac, is a talent, equal to writing. With your phenomenal literary talent, you should be able to appreciate such a death, am I wrong?"

De Cassagnac tried to scream, but was forced to watch in silence as the flicker of light that had appeared in his murderer's hands moved precisely, meticulously, and poetically towards his throat.

8

DEEP IN THE CATACOMBS, BERNARD Bouveroux cleared his throat, making a noise that sounded as if the piles of skulls behind him were grating together.

"I thought I had seen the dirtiest filth God's creation had to offer in Beni Abbes," the inspector muttered, "but I was wrong."

Lefèvre crouched over the body and said nothing. His face appeared pale and sickly in the light of the oil lamps placed around the cave by the uniformed police. The commissioner's gloved fingers fumbled with the lines of verse lying on de Cassagnac's belly.

He read the text out loud with a lilting tone, which the inspector found completely inappropriate given the situation and, indeed, the words themselves:

> *Men scheme each night and hope each morning,*
> *Yet no man grows one moment riper*
> *But suffers, at each turn, the warning*
> *Of the insufferable viper.*[3]

"Our killer must have been a sizeable viper," said Bouveroux. "He's taken the man's head off with a single bite." The inspector retrieved a perfumed handkerchief from his pocket and held it under his nose as he knelt down, although the corpse was still fresh. He ran his hand with the utmost care over the naked torso and hesitated above the two mock breasts that had been roughly stitched to the man's chest.

"Is that human skin?" the inspector asked. He cleared his throat once again.

Lefèvre nodded, but said nothing.

"What do they contain?" Bouveroux coughed. The cold air of the catacombs was not good for his weak lungs.

"Candle wax."

Bouveroux's eyes strayed towards the man's naked crotch. "There must have been a lot of blood with such a wound," he observed.

"He cleaned up after himself." The commissioner rubbed the dust from his gloves. "A tidy murderer."

"He removed the man's genitals. Has he taken them with him?"

"So it would appear. But if he hid them behind one of these piles of bones we'll never find them."

"The wound has been stitched together, commissioner."

"Yes, I noticed."

"There appears to be a protruding layer of frayed skin, like female genitalia . . ."

"I noticed that too, Bernard."

"What is the murderer trying to tell us?"

The commissioner heard his knees crack as he got to his feet. Lose weight, resume his fencing lessons, recover his fitness. Too much red wine in mediocre establishments, wine that stuck to the glass like tar and added extra layers of fat to his waistline.

"We can't be sure if the killer was also responsible for Dacaret's demise."

"There is one obvious similarity: verses from Baudelaire," the inspector observed.

"True, but the method is completely different. The poison tattoo suggested extraordinary preparation, almost artistic talent. This murder was a ferocious deed. Even the symbolism is unrefined. There was a great deal of blood. He took the head with him as if it had insulted him. He attached false breasts to the man's chest and castrated him, sowing up the wound in a manner suggestive of a vulva. In short, he turned the man into a woman." The commissioner looked down at the body. "An ugly, repulsive woman."

"Both victims were young and had slightly effeminate features," Bouveroux chipped in. "Mr. de Cassagnac's long curls and bizarre wardrobe made him look womanish. Police physician Lepage discreetly informed me that young Dacaret's genitals were . . . eh . . . not the normal size for a man of his age."

"Do you think we are dealing with sex-inspired killing?" said Lefèvre, "committed by a sodomite, perhaps?"

The inspector coughed delicately into his handkerchief. He was used to his boss's boorish character. Bernard Bouveroux had often heard his friend say that women were worse pigs in the bedroom than men, especially when they pretended to be bashful and prudish in company. "Perhaps the killer is raging against his own gender?" said the inspector.

"You sound like that half-wit analyst who's always on about human urges and desires," said Lefèvre, who wasn't much impressed with such new-fangled tendencies.

"Charcot?" said Bouveroux, unconsciously strutting his encyclopaedic intellect. "'We look up to the heavens, but the heavens are empty. That's why we look inside ourselves.'"

The commissioner grumbled angrily.

"And what do we see then, commissioner?" Bouveroux continued cheerfully. "That we lie to ourselves day and night. We talk about love but want to copulate like ordinary riff-raff. We talk about friendship yet stab one another in the back. We hate humanity and we hate ourselves. We're pitched into this world alone and die without making an inch of progress. All that's left, after a bout of tragic lucidity inspires us to clear the table of our little house of cards, is the universal power of desire."

The commissioner said nothing for minutes on end.

"Let me put it in analytic terms, Bouveroux. The corpse tells me we are indeed dealing with the same killer, but he's getting angrier and is coming closer and closer to the heart of your infamous desires. But it's not because of some insight into his inner existence, as you so eloquently explained, but because it's making him suffer and his soul has broken adrift. He can no longer communicate with words and is forced to use slaughtered flesh instead."

"He also uses Baudelaire's poems to communicate," said the inspector dryly. "Haven't you noticed the handwriting, commissioner?"

Lefèvre looked at the piece of paper. "Indeed, again the handwriting of Baudelaire himself." The commissioner sounded like someone gasping for air after waking from a frightening dream. "The handwriting of a dead man."

9

CAROLINE ARCHENBAUT-DUFAYIS, *LA VEUVE AUPICK*, was sitting in the
bay window of her rundown house in Honfleur. The letter from Madame
de Cassagnac containing news of the death of her husband—a promising
young writer with the affable characteristics of a dreamer combined with
Flaubert's passion for innovation—lay beside her on the floor. Charles
Baudelaire's mother quivered from head to toe.

She fumbled with the collar of her dress. The sagging skin around her
chin and neck revolted her. This same flesh was once wild and foolish,
and it had brought forth a shadow that could never be erased. Joseph-
François had called it *the curse*. Her husband had never said it out loud,
but the words "God's punishment" had always hung between them.
Caroline Archenbaut-Dufayis knew that her husband had died in the
conviction that "God's punishment" had rained down on him because
he had turned his back on the priesthood.

Baudelaire's mother tried to concentrate anew on the letter. Madame
de Cassagnac had provided a veiled description of the horrendous circumstances in which her husband had been found. A boorish policeman
had tried to intimidate her by suggesting she herself might have something to do with the killing. She had quoted the impudent individual

word for word: "When the genitals are mutilated, we usually start with the victim's nearest and dearest. If it's a man, we'll want to know if he's been true to his marital obligations. Women often lose themselves completely when he hasn't."

Madame de Cassagnac had shown the barbarian the door and registered a complaint at the prefecture. It was not followed up. With the trumpets of war blaring in the background and the emperor delivering pompous declarations about the grandeur of France, all sorts of things were apparently permissible, including the moral decline of the police.

Caroline Archenbaut-Dufayis was familiar with the grief of the recently widowed de Cassagnac, who appeared to identify her pathos with martyrdom. Madame de Cassagnac was evidently unfamiliar with the ways of the world, but this time the young woman's words touched her deeply. She had concluded her letter with the lines of verse that had been found on her husband's body together with a couple of questions from the arrogant policeman who had left her in such bewilderment.

Did your deceased husband ever allude to Charles Baudelaire as alive or dead after the official registration of the poet's death three years ago?

Did your husband ever wear women's clothing or show signs of an inclination to sodomy?

Widow Archenbaut-Dufayis sensed a sadness well up within her as she read those final lines, a sadness mixed with rage, disgust, and grief. Since the death of her second husband General Aupick thirteen years earlier, she had dedicated herself completely to her gifted but fragile son Charles. She had financed everything: the sexual cravings that took hold of him like a whirlwind, medication against softening of the brain that had crept up on him so unexpectedly, and expensive tropical concoctions to fight the disease that had plagued his loins since his liaison with "the black imp" Jeanne Duval. Some insisted that Baudelaire had picked up "lust's little demon" from common street whores, but mother knew best. He had acquired the crippling malady from the black witch with the red Creole eyes.

Caroline opened a leather folder containing a photograph by the magnificent Nadar, a leading light in the renewal of the photographic arts who had made several portraits of Baudelaire ten years earlier. She stared long and hard at her son's quicksilver eyes, his thin, pursed, and repelling lips, and the enormous buttons on his coarse linen jacket.

The folder also contained a letter from General Aupick, years old, written in Madrid when he was ambassador to Spain. In all those years she hadn't reread the letter. Baudelaire's mother pulled herself up from her chair. She looked out at the craggy rock on which her little house was built. The agitated, rust-coloured mass of clouds on the horizon made her think of her dead son's tormented soul. She could hear his hesitating voice, feel his timid sidelong glances on her shoulders. *The beautiful is bizarre by definition.*

Her son had spent his entire life in a state of anger at being born.

The jagged grey-brown rock, so close to the house that it appeared to be stalking it, reminded her that death was approaching, hard, cold, and indifferent.

She turned from the window and took the letter from the folder.

She felt a tingling sensation on the back of her neck.

As though the devil peered over her shoulder.

10

Madrid, June 17th 1850

Madame,

My devoted wife,

In spite of the years that have passed, I still ask myself: Am I really a man of bad moods and negative disposition, the kind of man your son Charles sees in me? Was it wrong of me to expect discipline from your recalcitrant and unstable son? Why did he make us all unhappy? I'm not saying he neglected his studies, far from it, nor was I upset by his desire to become un homme de lettres—given his considerable talent, which even an old war-horse like myself was able to detect—no, what drove a wedge into my heart was his wild and indecent behaviour.

Forgive me if I seem unkind, but I suggest you spoiled your son excessively after the sudden and unfortunate death of his father. A young man riddled with such noxious contradictions, with such a pensive temperament, and with such passion in his heart needs a firm hand. His moods verge on hysteria at times and hallucinations engulf his mind. Charles's weak nervous system requires regularity, industry, and iron-rich nourishment. Instead, he prefers to indulge his pedantic *flashes of wit, his useless day-dreaming, and his feverish excursions into a world of fantasy that absorb him more and more by the day.*

Forgive this stiff old soldier's curtness of manner. My heart is bound to yours in an inseparable bond and I revere your gentle character, your admirable maternal affection, and the eminent tranquility with which you bear your lot. You have tried to mediate between Charles and myself. But I sensed his bitter defiance toward me from the outset, and observed the measureless pride that skulks behind his otherwise impeccable manners. His eyes, madame, are pools of veiled contempt. His body, at first sight strong, conceals a spinelessness that poisons his mind by conjuring up visions of power and glory.

But more than your complex and conflicted love for your son, your life has been disfigured by the shadow cast over you by what you choose to call "the curse."

I have witnessed your nightmares, madame, when you wept in your sleep. I have heard you gnash your teeth deep into the night. Your suffering, which you imagined was invisible to me, touched me deeply. In my youth I was a man of weapons. If an enemy attacked, I was ready to fight, and win if it pleased God.

You on the contrary had nothing to defend yourself against the invisible enemy that tormented you. There can be no victory without weapons.

I realised all this twelve years ago. In an effort to understand your affliction I visited the Ursuline convent without telling you. With the help of your name and the fact that I am your husband I was granted an audience with Mother Superior.

She was reluctant, but she finally agreed to my request.

I have seen the creature you call "the curse."

It was small and seemed good-natured, although her clouded eyes appeared to see more than the walls of the lunatic's cell in which she had been incarcerated.

Mother Superior informed me, with her wimple shrouding her face, that lust made the creature howl at night and moan. But it could also be docile and flirtatious. As you had recommended, the Ursulines had taught it to read and write, and it had developed a particular predilection for courtly novels recounting exotic journeys in far-off lands. According to Mother Superior, the creature was intelligent and sharp-witted, but her intellect was clouded at regular intervals by unbridled and predatory passions.

As I tried to analyze the introspective face of the wretched creature through the bars of its cell, it lifted its nightdress with a gesture of mockery and I saw something God's creation had never foreseen. I saw a hand wander down to the protuberance below her belly, groping for . . .

Mother Superior had to gently pull me away from this dismal sight. I felt as if I had been nailed to the ground.

As you are aware, madame, men can be tempted to make crude remarks about a woman's anatomy, especially when they are far from home and family. They do so because the female anima has such a potent function, close to absorbing, which instills fear in the male of the species.

What my eyes witnessed can only be described as a travesty of that anima.

Since that day the creature has followed me in my dreams, and I know that the enemy that torments you cannot be defeated.

That enemy, my poor wife, has a name.

It is guilt.

That enemy, my poor wife, has a weapon.

It has your blood.

Through my unplanned convent visit, my uncontrollable curiosity, the recklessness that made me think that I, as a man of influence, could find a solution to your suffering, I have inherited a portion of the guilt that fate cast on your shoulders.

I have concealed one thing in the intervening years. I continued to visit the creature on occasion and I succeeded in conversing with it. To my surprise it was able to carry on a normal conversation for quite some time, until inevitably, and always unexpectedly, a grand mal took hold of it that scared me so much I stole away like a soldier turning his back on the battlefield. I don't remember when the creature started to talk about Charles. It happened before I was aware of it. After all, ma'am, your son was a millstone around my neck, and that is the reality of it. It listened, it asked questions, it demonstrated enormous interest in human interaction.

Its intense eagerness to learn was terrifying.

But on Tuesday, January 8th, 1839 I received an urgent message from Mother Superior. It was addressed to you. You were not at home. The good sister who delivered the letter had seen me with her superior a number of times. She gave me the letter without hesitation.

When she left I read the letter and tore it up.

Mother Superior had informed me that you had severed all personal connection with the sisters when you left "the curse" in their care. Each month you had a courier deliver six gold francs to the convent in continuance of the agreement you had made with the Ursulines. You had charged them to meet the creature's wishes where possible.

I did not want it to become known that I had regular contact with the one you had rejected. You would have experienced such a revelation as painful treachery. When I had read Mother Superior's account of the creature's escape, vanished from the convent as if it had never existed, I sought a solution to my problem in the sort of strategy a general would deploy in war.

You should know, madame, that the bloodiest of wars are fought within the intimacy of the family.

I replied to Mother Superior in your name, saying that you were deeply indebted to the sisters for their discretion and dedication and that you intended to pay the monthly sum for the rest of your life, although the money was no longer required.

I signed the letter in your name.

Without knowing it, you fulfilled your obligation for years on end. As head of the family, I instructed our housekeeper to continue to hand over six gold francs at the convent door, every month without fail.

Please understand me, my dear wife. I wanted to spare your soul further anguish if you had learned that the creature had escaped. You had suffered enough. I perfectly understood why you acted as you did. My fascination for "the curse" has its roots in a sinister amalgamation of my own character, the terrible things I have witnessed as a soldier, and the years I have spent searching for an explanation and perhaps a cure for your son's eccentric behaviour. I have long asked myself whether the source of Charles's malady is in some way related to the fate of the piteous creature locked away in the convent of the Ursulines. I wanted to understand it better, in order to understand him.

I confess, however, that I have failed in my intention.

I have carried this secret with me for years. But time has taught me with a heavy hand that secrets of such magnitude should not be allowed to exist between husband and wife.

Each time I saw Charles, the shadow of "the curse" clung to him. Each time I saw you, "the curse" crept closer and closer.

Now that Charles has emerged as a poet capable of stirring the minds of the French population with the audacious subjects he broaches in his writings, I can no longer conceal the fact that I know your secret, and I understand your anguish.

Rest assured, my dear wife, your secret will go with me to the grave.

Nonetheless, there are moments in the night when my heart races, I gasp for breath, that barren cell appears before my eyes, and a shiver runs through my soul. At such misbegotten moments the creature's fathomless loneliness takes hold of me and I sense a sadness that hisses like a snake ready to strike.

At such moments, and of this I am convinced, I feel the insane hatred coming from—

Years earlier, when Caroline Archenbaut-Dufayis received the letter from her husband, her left hand had convulsed with such intensity as she read the last line that torn snippets of paper bearing the creature's name fell to the ground at her feet. She did not even notice at first.

The letter from her husband had caused a pain more vigorous than the cramps that had announced the birth of her beloved Charles.

11

LA PREUVE OPTIQUE ET CHIMIQUE des Esprits adorned Jean Bavière's calling card in a mass of exuberant curlicues. Bavière, in his early thirties, identified himself as a *photographic medium*, and in spite of his modest years he wore a monocle and an old-fashioned worsted suit.

His visitor was certain Bavière had financial reasons for dressing as he did. Despite the pretentious calling card, the man was just one of the many photographers who plied their trade on the streets of Paris. They barked loud and proud about their talents, but most of the lucrative work was reserved for the masters: Carjat, Nadar, and Fix-Masseau.

Bavière rented rooms in the narrow Rue Fresnel, in a dubious neighbourhood where Turks and Mohammedans were aplenty. Tea sellers scuttled back and forth, their water pipes like hideous bagpipes. Knife fighters with bushy eyebrows and curly moustaches sized each other up. The city authorities had talked about clearing the neighbourhood to make way for a grand avenue leading up to the abbey of Sainte Geneviève. But in the meantime, the spirit of Balzac's Paris, of his *Comédie Humaine*, continued to drift over the bumpy cobblestones, the open sewers, and past the house facades, crudely tiled to protect them from passing coaches.

The facade of the tenement in which the medium had found lodgings was monolithic and lacking the least architectural adornment. The rooms had once been inhabited by a woman. The mildewed walls were still decorated here and there with semolina advertisements. The marble sink was cracked and discolored. The ash bucket in the fireplace hadn't been filled in many a year. A couple of voltaire armchairs in torn and threadbare red damask stood side by side against the wall. The room's only window gave out onto a depressing inner courtyard that looked for all the world like a massive oubliette.

The young crank, who claimed he had learned his craft in America, carefully examined the photo provided by his visitor. He closed his eyes, pressed it theatrically to his forehead, and swayed back and forth as if he had been stricken by a minor stroke. The visitor remained calm and pursed his lips. There was something hard about his eyes, Bavière cunningly observed, in spite of the delicate eyebrows that framed them. He sensed a vague threat.

"The gentleman would appear to be dead," said the medium.

"Correct." The visitor's face remained motionless.

"What would you like to know about him?"

"His death was caused by a ghost. I need evidence to prove it."

The medium smiled discreetly and with an air of self-satisfaction. "And I have to provide the evidence you seek, I presume."

The visitor's eyes narrowed. "You're smarter than I thought, sir, if you don't mind my saying so."

Bavière graciously inclined his head. If one ignored the puffy facial features, which pointed to meals in soup kitchens with large amounts of tapioca, and concentrated on the eyes, there was a degree of charm in evidence, and even a hint of spirituality.

The visitor continued: "If I tell you the name of the ghost, then you can make it visible in the photograph with your 'magic', so I've been told."

The medium fluttered his eyelids in slow motion. A rapport had evolved between them in the damp and dingy room. Kindred souls, almost. "If you have a picture of the phantom you wish to create, I'll see what I can do."

The visitor's hand disappeared into his finely embroidered jacket. "Will this suffice?"

Bavière frowned unobtrusively when he examined the photo. "I know this man. He had talent, unmistakeably, but not as much as he himself imagined. And I can't say I agreed with his opinions."

"I'm aware of that," the visitor responded. "I also know that you had a serious exchange of words with him five years ago." An almost inaudible tension had wormed its way into the visitor's voice, a tightening of the vocal cords.

The photographer seemed less sure of himself. He tried to recover his calm with an impertinent remark. "Your knowledge of my life surprises me. Perhaps you are the medium and I . . ."

"He challenged you to a duel. He was the irascible type. They say the opium drove him insane. Anyway, you didn't show up."

"I didn't want to be the cause of his premature death on account of a ridiculous difference of opinion," Bavière answered curtly. "Alas, my concern was wasted. He died shortly thereafter and . . ."

"Modernity is the transitory, the ephemeral, the accidental," the visitor interrupted. "That was his hypothesis. And this is yours: 'How can these three principles—which are after all alike and thus represent nothing more than a few words in a meaningless pile—how can these three principles be applied to photography or painting, which ought to immortalize things, establish them, make them available for future generations?' Think about it, Monsieur Bavière. If I'm not mistaken, your own three principles are also alike."

Bavière got to his feet. "It wasn't a banal difference of opinion, but a fundamental misconception of the meaning of art," he said, blushing.

The visitor made a reconciliatory gesture. "We're not here to rake up the past, Monsieur Bavière. Can you see to it that this 'ghostly phenomenon' despatches the soul of the person in the first photograph to the kingdom of Charon? I'm told you're a master in your craft."

Bavière relaxed a little. He carefully examined both photographic images. "Photography is a child of our age. It makes the invisible visible.

First there was the magic lantern; now with certain salts, chemicals, and developing trays, an experienced psychic hand like my own can conjure up demons and the dead."

"Even in life, this dead man had taken the place of another," said the visitor. Once again there was an elusive quiver in the voice, like the tightening of a violin string.

Bavière coughed. "It will cost you one hundred gold francs."

"A great deal of money."

"You should visit the market halls of a morning. People are fighting for space to sell cauliflower and celery. The best butchers have nothing to offer but horse scrapings. The air is filled with absinthe and war."

"What value is money in time of war?"

"You twist reality. War revolves around money more than any other social circumstance."

The visitor's lips curled into a discrete smile and he nodded approvingly. Bavière was slightly taken aback, in spite of his initial pluck.

"So you agree to my price?"

"I do."

"Come back tomorrow. For such an intense séance I need to be alone."

"I understand. But make sure the results are satisfactory."

Bavière peered into the eyes of the creature sitting opposite him and laughed self-assuredly. He showed the visitor out and withdrew into an adjacent room where a penetrating smell of chemicals filled the air. He closed the door and darkness embraced him, only to take a step back when he lit a red candle.

While Bavière went about the business he had learned in a photographic laboratory in far-off America, he was overcome by a feeling that his visitor had not left but was standing at his back, following every step of the process.

He tried to banish the unpleasant sensation by concentrating on his totem spirit, which he had brought with him from America's wildest state. He asked his totem why the visitor had made the hair on his neck stand on end, in spite of an outer appearance that some would have described as infantile.

12

WOMEN ARE BEAUTIFUL WHEN THEY MOURN.

The perfume of wounded passion engulfed the recently widowed Madame de Cassagnac, with her chubby frame and curls twisted by hot tongs into the latest fashion. Commissioner Lefèvre, who tended to prefer women from the Levant because of their sinister unpredictability and uncivilized morals, was impressed by her sad demeanor.

He had summoned Bouveroux to his office, intent on reprimanding him for the arrogant tone the inspector had used with the young woman during the interrogation. Bouveroux withdrew into his shell like a tortoise. He offered his apologies without complaint. Madame de Cassagnac could not have known that the staged interaction between the two men was a matter of routine. Lefèvre was taken by the approach after reading a couple of stories by Edgar Allan Poe, translated by Baudelaire. Those charged with upholding the law both strike and salve in the hope that a suspect might betray himself by his words or with his posture, the flutter of an eyelash, a twitch in the muscles around the mouth, the hesitant way he touched himself.

This time the procedure had not worked. The young lady departed with a vague air of satisfaction, although still deeply pained by her husband's terrible death. Lefèvre already knew why. Madame de Cassagnac had blushingly confessed to the charming commissioner that she came from a family of merchants. Her father had had a bad year.

"If that woman killed her husband, then she's dumber than a rabid dog," said Bouveroux despondently when the scent of lilac blossom perfume had finally evaporated. "De Cassagnac comes from a wealthy family. She's lost her husband and her livelihood in one fell swoop. There also doesn't appear to be a will. You don't think about such things when you're that age. Perhaps the dead man's father will be kind to her. But fathers can be unpredictable, especially when their sons meet such a ghastly end."

The commissioner nodded absentmindedly. "I'm beginning to suspect that the murderer had a personal motive, a motive we cannot see."

"What about the handwriting, commissioner?"

Lefèvre seemed reluctant to broach the matter. His broad face even appeared slightly ill at ease. "It doesn't take much to mimic someone's handwriting. A little talent and patience, nothing more."

"But even then it's still evidence we shouldn't ignore. If the murderer went to so much trouble to imitate Baudelaire's handwriting, then he must have had good reason."

Lefèvre was pensive. His hand groped intuitively for *Le Peintre de la Vie Moderne*, the book Baudelaire had inscribed when Lefèvre visited him in jail thirteen years earlier and expressed his admiration for the man's poetic artistry. The first edition of *Les Fleurs du Mal* had just appeared. France had been turned on its head by the audacious themes with which the poet had confronted his public. Baudelaire was arrested while a judge decided whether the collection was to be considered blasphemous. The court finally decided that six poems should be subject to censorship. *"Un outrage aux bonnes moeurs"* was the self-satisfied headline in *Le Moniteur*. Baudelaire was fined three hundred francs, something that annoyed him more than the couple of nights he had spent in jail. Even Victor Hugo's published conviction that Baudelaire had introduced *un nouveau frisson* into the world of French literature wasn't enough to make him forget the injustice that had been done to him. He lamented at length about the disastrous fine, a fatal blow to a penniless poet such as he.

Bouveroux could see that the commissioner was troubled. "Perhaps the murderer is doing something Charles Baudelaire wanted to do his entire life but was unable?"

"Baudelaire told me that of all life's pleasures there was only one that he loved," the commissioner mused as he lit his pipe.

"His beloved Jeanne Duval, the black panther?" Bouveroux grinned as if a seedy figure in a café had just told him an inappropriate joke.

"I didn't know you were a devotee of the lives of artists," said the commissioner. "Most of the time they're insignificant or sentimental and melodramatic." As he spoke he drew circles in the air with his pipe, the agility of his wrist surprisingly feminine for a man of such heavy stature.

"I'm a devotee of encyclopaedic knowledge," said Bouveroux conceitedly, ignoring the fact that he had already told the commissioner about his preference countless times. "Knowledge excites me, even if it has no practical value."

Lefèvre returned to his thoughts. Bouveroux tried to gauge his superior's mood. Behind a surprisingly playful and yet often brusque facade, the commissioner had a troubled and unusually sensitive personality. The man's vigor occasioned physical greed, extraordinary mood swings, a repressed relentlessness that was often held in check by compassion, and, paradoxically enough, a powerful craving for detachment. Behind Paul Lefèvre's forehead, hermit and whoremonger were engaged in a perpetual battle and neither could claim to have won victory.

"If it wasn't Jeanne Duval, then it had to be money," said Bouveroux. "Artists are only interested in two things, 'cash and cunt', as they so eloquently call them on the street."

Lefèvre took his pipe from his mouth and said resolutely, "Death. Baudelaire told me there was only one thing in life he respected. The end."

"Of course, his flirtations with the end," said Bouveroux, slightly affronted. "Romanticism's ardent adversary and misanthropist *par excellence* secretly cherished a romantic notion of death." The inspector, whose slim stature and abrupt gestures hinted at neurasthenia, jumped to his feet and proclaimed in an irritatingly nasal voice: *"And I will bring you, brown delight/Kisses as cold as lunar night/And the caresses of a snake/Revolving in a grave. At break/Of morning in its livid hue/You'd find I had bequeathed to you/An empty place as cold as stone".*[4]

Bouveroux looked as if he had just tasted something bitter. "The man saw himself as a snake on a tombstone doling out cold kisses. But that's not the way people die, Paul. Some drop dead on the street, stricken by heart failure or a blood clot in the brain. Their faces are twisted with tortured surprise because their lives are suddenly no more. Others perish in hospitals where the sisters mince around their stinking beds like huge black crows, and when their time has come, their minds are dull with opium or deranged by the pain."

There was a knock at the door. A beat policeman straightened his cloak and entered the room. "Another dead body, commissioner, on a grave in Montparnasse cemetery."

"Work for the city's garbage collectors," the commissioner barked.

"Er . . . we have reason to believe that a murder has been committed, commissioner. First, the dead man's face is hideously twisted, and second, we found a snake on the grave. The creature resisted arrest and is probably hiding somewhere in the cemetery."

The commissioner and the inspector looked at each other in astonishment.

"The black arts!" said Bouveroux. "Either the culprit can read our minds, or one of us is the killer." He was trying to be witty, but his words seemed somehow misplaced. The policeman tugged at his moustache as a subtle reprimand for his superiors.

"And there's a third," said the commissioner. "I can see it in your face."

Bouveroux peered at the policeman as if he was some kind of exotic animal, but he was unable to read anything in the man's face.

The policeman pursed his lips. "You're right, commissioner. The corpse was found on the grave of Charles Baudelaire."

"*Mon Dieu*," said Bouveroux. "Now our killer's offering sacrifice to dead art."

The commissioner's eyelids fluttered. "Or to a loved one."

13

A STUBBORN MIST MADE MONTPARNASSE cemetery appear endless. In the poor visibility, the trees on Rue Emile Richard, which ran through the middle of the cemetery, seemed like giant spiders' webs. The graves seemed on the verge of sinking into the musty earth. Stone birds and statues of women, their bodies chiselled by grief, dominated the two policemen's field of vision. Lefèvre's attention was drawn to a statue of an eagle with crown, perched on a pedestal and covered in black mould. The bird pointed its commanding beak westward, for all the world like an emissary from the dark abysses of the Ancients, where the soul laments its fate. Most of the female statues had a twisted neck, their stone faces turned away, their shiny bodies oozing chagrin.

"Look at the way they hug the tombs, like mistresses begging one last kiss from their beloved," said Bouveroux, inadvertently lowering his voice. "Some are wearing veils over their heads, others have wilted flowers in their hands. They mourn until the end of time. That's the way women are. Don't you think Death must be a woman, commissioner?"

"Human sorrow is ambiguous," said Lefèvre absently. He groped for his watch chain. "Wouldn't you like to leave this world behind and everything in it, to meander as pure soul through unknown dimensions?"

"Aha, so you admit that spiritism has you under its spell. I thought it was the preserve of powdered caterwauling ladies," Bouveroux quipped.

"Undoubtedly, you will be dispatched to hell, Bouveroux," said the commissioner, still distracted.

Bouveroux smiled. "If I don't lose my taste for absinthe, I'll prove you right one of these days." The humor in his voice was in contrast to the air of sadness on his face.

The commissioner examined the stone on top of a simple grave. It was as if it had set out to give birth to an adult woman, had given up the battle, and settled for the silhouette of a child searching the heavens with empty eyes.

Baudelaire's mother had buried her son next to her husband General Aupick, although neither of the men could stand each other when they were alive. The gravestones had something oriental about them and were of brightly colored stone. The text asked the living to pray for the general and for Charles Baudelaire. A body was lying in front of the stone, its contorted shape suggesting that death's last agonies had been horrendous. The two policemen stood still. Lefèvre looked back at the black eagle brooding over the hour of its death with folded wings.

"It must be terrible to die like this," said Bouveroux. He knelt by the body, carefully examined its drawn-back lips, flared nostrils, twisted hands. The snake's venom had caused the body to swell up, making it appear hunchbacked.

"How many times did we pray self-concocted prayers to be allowed to die a true soldier's death as the Bedouin crept up on us, curved knives between their teeth, in the desert near Beni Abbes?" Bouveroux rubbed his eyebrows with his gloved hands. "The very idea of being emasculated and then thrown to the desert vultures even inspired us to cry out to the god of the Mohammedans."

"You're very talkative today," said Lefèvre calmly. His hands carefully explored the victim's clothing. "Or at your wit's end," the commissioner continued. "What can we do, confronted with the rage of this murderer, Bernard?"

Bouveroux looked up. "Fatalism doesn't suit you, commissioner."

Lefèvre pointed to the body. "If we are dealing with a sick mind, someone who kills for reasons only he understands, then the case will never be solved."

"The works of your beloved Poe will no doubt have taught you that even the insane need their *moment de gloire*. Sooner or later they'll want to let the world see what they're made of, or they'll begin to imagine themselves invincible . . . then they make mistakes. What was that?"

A shout echoed between the graves, followed by a gunshot.

The commissioner straightened his back. "The serpent among the graves. It would have made the perfect title for a Baudelaire poem. I think our colleagues have found the creature."

"Paul," said Bouveroux, his intonation suddenly changing. "Remarkable." The inspector removed a piece of card from beneath the dead man's jacket.

The commissioner recognised it as a *carte-de-visite*, the new photographic rage that allowed dandies to have a self-portrait with them wherever they went. Lefèvre saw the image on the card and gritted his teeth. He glanced at Bouveroux, who was standing up. His subordinate did not look him in the eye but stared at something behind him.

"There are moments, Paul, when I count myself lucky I never reached your rank," his friend said in a gentle tone of voice.

Lefèvre turned. Prefect Banlieu, an impetuous young magistrate with a tousled lock of hair dangling over his left eye and a narrow moustache, a man of good birth who had used his political connections to make a rapid career for himself, came storming toward him waving a copy of *La Gazette de France*.

Without knowing exactly why, the commissioner stuffed the *carte-de-visite* in his jacket pocket.

14

"Don't lie on top of me," Claire de la Lune cautioned. "You have the build of a Japanese wrestler and you would break my ribs." The evening was filled with the aroma of resin and turpentine, engulfing them with the rarefied air of childhood dreams. Claire de la Lune wore a skirt and a Hungarian blouse. She didn't need hot tongs to create the waterfall of curls that cascaded down to her slender waist.

Claire de la Lune was drawn to countries with deserts, prairies, and wild horses. Her boudoir in the Rue de Lappe on the edge of the Saint Antoine suburbs, a neighbourhood full of scrap merchants and revolutionary artists who competed with one another in excesses of every kind, was a haven for the exotic. Charcoal drawings from Japan, demonic statuettes from French Patagonia, a lion skin from Africa, a sketch of the composer Berlioz by the Belgian artist Charles Baugniet—everything mixed together. The result was intoxicating, confusing, controversial.

"And just like a Japanese sumo wrestler, you look as if you're planning to tear someone apart this evening," the whore continued.

The commissioner sat naked on the edge of a bed that could easily have been plucked from the harem of one or another sultan's palace and looked at his belly. Claire de la Lune laughed and grabbed a roll of fat.

It was surprisingly hard and stiff. Her hands glided over his enormous shoulders and massaged his hirsute back, formidably strong under an evenly distributed layer of fat, the result of too much wine, pastry, and red meat.

"Those bloody papers," said Lefèvre. "Journalists are scavengers. Dung flies. Excuse my language, *ma chère.*"

"I never read the papers."

"Wise idea. It helps you stay sane. But my sanity is gone forever. One of my men must have spoken out of turn. *La Gazette de France* published details today of the murder of Albert Dacaret. The headline read: *Ghost of Murdered Poet Takes Revenge.* I talked to the editor. He found an anonymous letter in his mail with details of the killing, including the poison tattoo. Paris is no longer talking about the advancing Prussians, but about an article in the paper insinuating that the police are lax, lazy, and incompetent. Am I mad, or is it the times we're living in?"

The young woman smiled. The commissioner found her tranquil and serious nature pleasant, although she could also be secretive, sometimes verging on devious. "We live in a world of ghosts, commissioner."

"Exactly," said Lefèvre. "A haunted hall of mirrors. This afternoon I had that hysterical young prefect Banlieu on my neck, and *darling*, he wasn't in a good mood." Claire de la Lune smiled. The commissioner's English was dreadful. "And he wasn't only up in arms about that bloody article. The third victim, the one we found in the cemetery, Monsieur Pinard, was a senior magistrate. Perhaps I should have shown that unbalanced snob Banlieu the photograph we found on the corpse. He would probably have choked on his own spit."

The commissioner rummaged in his jacket and produced the calling card Bouveroux had found on Pinard. Claire de la Lune's oval face remained calm as she examined the photo.

"Ghosts exist, but they're generally not vulgar enough to let themselves be photographed." She sounded serious.

Lefèvre asked himself why he had kept the *carte-de-visite* from Prefect Banlieu and not from his mistress. A sense of recklessness had plagued him the entire evening, as if he had drunk too much wine.

"Bouveroux says you can concoct all sorts of effects on photographic plates using chemical baths. But he's missing an important detail. Your mind is sharp and analytic. Can you identify it?"

"Who had the time to take a photograph of young poet Dacaret?" said Claire de la Lune as if it was evident that she should answer immediately. "A photographic image requires time. Cameras are cumbersome things, and hard to disguise. Besides, the way you described the death of the young poet, it must have been impossible to photograph the dead body, with all my competitors fluttering around." She tugged teasingly at the tufts of grey hair above his nipples. "I hope you behaved yourself with all those fancy whores."

Lefèvre smiled. Banlieu would have a stroke if he knew that the commissioner had discussed the details of a judicial inquiry with a *cocotte*. The very idea neutralised his reservations and freed him to indulge the indiscretion. "I would be happier with you as my prefect. I would gladly lay my ignorance—as that dandy so eloquently calls it—at your feet."

Claire de La Lune laughed. The commissioner was aroused by the naughtiness of her smile. "As your prefect, I would have to punish you, commissioner."

"But the fact remains, I thought the same as you." Lefèvre placed his hand on his nocturnal companion's left breast. The pleasure of touching such young resilient flesh stirred the wolf in him. "There was talk of a nun who visited the establishment to save souls," he said. "Perhaps she hid the camera under her habit." The commissioner grinned at the idea and continued straight-faced: "If you interrogate people at the scene of a crime, you always encounter extraordinary figures who usually have nothing to do with the case. Murder sensitizes people to the mysteries that lurk behind everyday life."

Claire de la Lune shrugged her shoulders. Her collarbone reminded the commissioner of the willowy skeletons of tiny mammals on exhibit at the city's natural history museum. "Perhaps the influence of an unnatural death that struck a victim in their surroundings makes them see things that aren't there," said Claire de la Lune.

"Is that influence powerful enough to make the ghost of a dead poet visible?" The commissioner pointed to the photograph. "The discovery of the portrait of Dacaret in the clothing of the last victim Pinard complicates the mystery and at once simplifies it. The photograph makes it clear that we're dealing with the same killer, a killer with a message. But why use such a modern technique to communicate with us?"

Claire de la Lune narrowed her eyelids and let her blouse glide from her shoulders, reminiscent of the ladies in the Japanese prints that adorned her room. "Perhaps he wants you to understand him. Or maybe he's simply mocking you. And what if he alone can comprehend the sick world he lives in? But the most important question remains: How did he take the photo?" Her voice was deep, like the first notes of the choir of nuns that once filled Lefèvre's Sundays with purgatory and hell in a far distant past.

"The solution to the mystery has to be with the poet," Lefèvre mused. "Are you familiar with Baudelaire's work?"

"Women read poetry too." A certain intonation in her voice caught his attention without him knowing why or what it meant.

A vestige of sadness crept up on him unexpectedly. He knew its source well enough and also knew that his *mal de vie* was incurable. He tried not to think of it, but for a moment he was again a boy of thirteen, on an incline near a river, watching a scene unfold that was to change his life forever.

"A penny for your thoughts, Paul? You look as if you want to kill someone."

The commissioner dispelled the memory in the way he knew best. He tore open Claire's blouse completely and pressed his thumbs against her breastbone. "There are unexpected moments when I think about death, and the world around me seems like a dream, a bubble that can burst at any second. You, at least, are solid."

"Men usually save such outpourings for after the deed, when they've spilled their seed in a woman's womb, and she sighs and hopes that no child will come of it."

Claire de la Lune lifted her skirts and sat in front of him with her legs wide open. Her genitalia were delicately formed. The opening, with slightly fanned labia, was small and resilient. The commissioner wormed his plump forefinger into her delicious warmth. The *caroncule* on top of the vulva, which many doctors still solemnly styled the *verge feminine*, was pert and light brown. The commissioner was endeared when it turned red and stood bravely to attention when he drew circles around it with his moistened finger.

That was the moment at which Claire de la Lune turned around and slipped cushions under her belly so that his penis, its head the size of a plump radish, could penetrate her anus, which she had cleansed the classical Japanese way with an enema syringe, a shallow bath, and lavender vapours. The deed gave the commissioner enormous satisfaction. As he took her from behind, he sensed a dominance, the enjoyment of power. Claire de la Lune made pleasurable noises like a purring cat, shifting to a gentle sigh when Paul Lefèvre's robust penis swelled up and he thrust his belly forward, breathing deeply in and out, to ease the sweet pressure in his loins and prolong the moment. Sometimes he would seize her thick tresses of hair, tug them and make her groan. The last move was for Claire. She would grab his penis and stick it in her vagina to let him come as she cooed. Her natural acceptance of her own body and his climaxed in a moment of gluttonous delight.

Afterwards he would lie against her back, grunting in drowsy contact with the pounding of his heart.

"Why do you always attack as if it's your last time?" asked Claire.

"When a man pairs, the devil steers," said the commissioner. "A man thinks about his mother's milk and compassion, but he sees the softness and innocence of a young woman and wants to destroy them."

"That's why an orgasm for a man is always *la petite mort*. No wonder you wage war, stab women in the belly, write poems and novels."

"So you think the killer is a man?" the commissioner teased.

Claire de la Lune didn't respond immediately. "Women use poison, women use snakes."

"You're right, the murders could have been committed by a woman. But do women cut off a man's testicles and make breasts from the skin of his scrotum?"

The young woman smiled. "In the old days, perhaps, when there were female warriors. Now we're squeezed into corsets and we're too fainthearted for such dreadful outrages."

"In Algeria, the women were crueller than the men."

"A woman should confine her cruelty to her tongue, commissioner. If she has blood on her hands, her children inevitably pay the price. It's different with men."

Both fell silent, and just as Claire thought her client had fallen asleep, the commissioner spoke. His voice sounded absent, as if his thoughts were elsewhere. "Now and then, when I'm alone in bed and unable to sleep, I try to picture the moment that my heart stops beating. It has worked so long, day and night, unremitting. It would almost make you think there was a God."

It took a while for the boyish woman in his sturdy arms to respond. "I think only the devil exists, Paul. I can feel the devil. I can't feel God."

The commissioner grinned broadly. "True, true. The devil has captured many a soul in the name of God. When I was young I despatched hundreds of Levantines in his name to hell and damnation, while they roared at the top of their voice that Allah would make them invincible."

"And what was the result of this?" Claire asked.

"That I live a lonely life, filled with anger, in a permanent state of unspeakable panic."

"Without love, or the illusion of love?"

"Love is for women." Paul Lefèvre's voice sounded resigned. He repositioned his heavy body. The whore, trained in interpreting body signals, sensed no irritation in his movement.

"Men kill for love," she said. "At least that's what they claim. That means they must believe in it."

"Love is like God," said Lefèvre. "We all say we believe in Him, but deep in our hearts doubt jeers at us."

"Modern life is too complicated, commissioner. There are contradictions everywhere. People would be better off with a more tranquil existence, with life's more simple pleasures."

"I am a simple man. The flesh and the taste buds are my only two pleasures."

"Was what I just dished up simple enough for you, Paul?"

His hand glided over her belly. His palm was so large, and Claire de la Lune so delicate, that it covered more than half of the distance between one hip and the other. "You're far from simple, nor is the pleasure you give."

"I'm only a whore."

"There's poetry in your body."

"The body of a whore is the devil's rocking chair, nothing more." Claire de la Lune spread her legs and fingered her clitoris. "Look, my profession has made my *caroncule* grow larger. I'm almost a boy."

The commissioner wasn't sure if she was joking or not. He decided to make light of the matter. "Then you'll have the body of the future. Men and women will one day merge into one single being and overcome death."

Claire smiled. "What an imagination. Most men aren't capable of such thoughts."

"Most men are animals. They let themselves be led to the slaughter-house because they don't want to think about death," said the commissioner. "I think about it every day. I resist, I puff and pant and stamp my feet. When I'm able, I toss death into the air with my horns. But sooner or later he'll take hold of me by the ring in my nose."

Claire de la Lune pressed her buttocks against him. "I have words that can comfort you, my brawny bear."

"Words conceal and lie. They sound pretty if you have talent, but they're as powerless as the emperor in the face of death."

It's Death comforts us, alas! and makes us live.
It is the goal of life, it brings us hope,
And, like a rich elixir, seems to give
Courage to march along the darkening slope.
Across the tempest, hail, and hoarfrost, look!
Along the black horizon, a faint gleam!
It is the inn that's written in the book
Where one can sleep, and eat, and sit and dream.[5]

Her voice sounded airy and melodious in the darkness.

The commissioner's eyes were almost closed. The shadows in the dark room were massive yet strangely furtive. "If you talk of the devil, you'll see his tail," said the commissioner.

Claire de la Lune laughed heartily. "Appropriate indeed, my dear commissioner."

"I met him shortly after he wrote those words."

"Really?"

"He was in jail. I had read some of his essays on art and literature. I admired him as a writer. But as a person? He was sitting on his wooden bed, hunched up, dispirited by a court of law that had found his poems offensive and worthy of punishment. He complained about his debts and threatened suicide. He was a tormented man, plagued with anxiety. He was as touchy as a hysterical woman, but there was also something bestial about him, like a cornered animal ready to pounce. Baudelaire, my sweet, wrote no words of comfort. Rather, he subjected fear to the incessant resonance of sounds and syllables until it acquired handsome yet sickly colors."

"Your attraction to death is enough to make me shiver," said the woman at his side. "Death is the lover who only visits once."

The commissioner repositioned himself. An overwhelming sense of pity engulfed him. An echo from outside seeped through the walls of the tapestry-lined room, which always made him feel he wasn't there, he was somewhere else, in a no-man's-land.

Just like me, the echo whispered.

The commissioner opened his eyes. Had he dozed off? Had he really heard the rustle of a thin wispy voice? "The message," he said, taken aback. "The dead Pinard had no verses of poetry on him. I let myself get carried away by Banlieu's anger. You should have seen the commotion he made when he found out who the victim was. He made me miss something, a sign."

Claire de la Lune lay beside him, luminescent like a moonstone, and pretended to be asleep.

$\boxed{15}$

THE MORGUE, WHERE CORPSES WAITED with indifference to be examined by police physician and notorious drinker Dr. Lepage, was only a couple of hundred meters from the *Vierge de la Grand Mer* hospital. Every day at six in the morning, the district's horse-drawn hearses delivered their cargoes. In the summer, when the heat refused to dissipate and drove the population insane, the corpses were numerous. Only the serious drunks and the few ladies on their way to the morning market with fully laden vegetable carts saw the hearses pass. The women would quickly bless themselves, the drunks shake a fist or laugh inanely.

Lefèvre was standing in a tiled, well-lit room, with Dr. Lepage at his side in a nonchalantly unbuttoned white coat. The place stank of formalin. The corpse was on a low plank and covered with a white sheet.

"Not exactly a cause of death to put my expertise to the test, commissioner," said the police physician as he snorted two ample portions of snuff from an old-fashioned tobacco box. "Deputy Pinard died as a result of a snake bite. The venom of the Malaysian adder took his life."

"Such reptiles don't tend to be common household pets," said the commissioner dryly, "not in Paris, at least."

Lepage shrugged his shoulders and sneezed. "The ports are full of ships from exotic climes nowadays, and there are enough oddballs around pretending to be fakirs who can easily help you lay your hands on such an agile assassin."

"You need to know how to treat snakes properly."

"If I may be so bold, commissioner, I suggest you interrogate every snake charmer in Paris. I'm told there are certain establishments where women dance naked with snakes around their necks . . . vulgarity at its utmost." Dr. Lepage winked. "If you come across any in the course of your investigations, let me know. My scientific curiosity is particularly open-ended. I also collect butterflies, you know."

The commissioner crouched and closely examined the right side of the corpse. Lepage looked down at him and sneered. "What now, commissioner? Does the corpse of the magistrate who landed Baudelaire with a hefty fine thirteen years ago deserve the commissioner's kisses?"

The commissioner didn't respond, but inched rather toward the corpse's legs and pointed at the soles of the dead man's feet. "It had to be there," the commissioner muttered. "I just knew it had to be there."

Lepage was curious and moved closer. "Aha," he said contritely. "Perhaps the only place on a body a doctor's likely to miss." With a melodious voice he read what was written on the sole of the dead man's left foot: "*Would I had whelped a knot of vipers—at the worst . . .*" He hopped to the right foot like an enormous bird: "'*Twere better than this runt that whines and snivels there!*"

The police physician stared archly at the commissioner. At such close quarters the pores of the man's nose glowed like those of a young boy. "That sounds familiar, my dear commissioner. Give me a moment!"

In a fit of activity he raced round the room, which was in a lamentable state of chaos. During the day, a copyist registered the death announcements in a logbook. Lepage left his notes lying around all over the place, giving the clerk hours of extra work trying to organize things before he started copying the forms. The police physician rummaged through the papers in his rolltop desk and produced a book.

He winked at Lefèvre. "I managed to get my hands on a copy with the infamous forbidden poems," he said in a roguishly conspiratorial tone. "I broke the law, *monsieur*. Do you have to arrest me now?"

"Let me guess," the commissioner groaned. "You have an uncensored copy of Charles Baudelaire's notorious collection."

"Exactly!" Lepage crowed. "People who spend their days working with the dead aren't averse to a bit of racy reading on the subject. And our Baudelaire doesn't disappoint. Look, here's the verse, it's from *Bénédiction*. Ah, such refined and bitter cadences. The burning breath of jealousy, hatred, fear, and love . . . all tossed together in a single venomous pile. Life in a nutshell, yes? Sublime! Read for yourself."

Lepage handed the commissioner the book, but continued without taking a breath: "Read the last lines of the preceding stanza. *The Poet is brought forth in this wearisome world, His mother terrified and full of blasphemies.*"

Lefèvre read the lines, his lips forming the words without a sound. He then crouched at the dead man's feet once again and studied the writing. "The Berbers use this technique to tattoo a dead man when they want to curse him," he said slowly. "The mystery is widening, Lepage. Or is it narrowing? The killer is evidently fascinated by all things oriental."

"And by Baudelaire," said Lepage. "The victims are all people who were critical of the man. If you ask me, he also uses Baudelaire's unsurpassed oeuvre as a source of inspiration." The police physician sniggered. "He's probably an artist himself. Those strange fools think the sun shines out of their . . . er . . . rectums."

"Who has been killed so far?" Lefèvre mused, without paying the slightest attention to the doctor's secret amusement. "A young poet, praised as Baudelaire's reincarnation while he in fact despised the man; a writer who didn't agree with Baudelaire's ideas on art; a magistrate who had him fined."

"The next victim might bring us even closer to the dead poet," said the doctor, a roguish glint in his eye. He tugged excitedly at his pomade-rubbed moustache. "But there's a lot worse out there, my dear commissioner. What if we're dealing with one or more amoral criminals imbued with the spirit of the age? I've heard mesmerists screaming from the rooftops that the world is going to be struck by giant meteors in a couple of months. What help are morals and a conscience when you're facing doom and destruction?" His right hand drifted absently toward his crotch and the enormous fly of his tattered loose-fitting trousers, which were in sharp contrast to his expensive printed-cotton jacket.

"Amoral murders?" said Lefèvre. "Possible, I suppose, if it were not for the fact that they appear to be symbolic."

"A sick mind, my dear Paul, can be both symbolic and amoral at one and the same time."

The commissioner realized that this discussion might cost him time. "And there's another strange phenomenon. In both instances, the message was written in the poet's own writing. The handwriting on the deputy magistrate's soles looks more like the work of a Moorish tattoo artist. What do you think of that?"

Lepage shrugged his shoulders. "A lapse, a mistake, slovenliness. Indifference to prior motives. Impetuosity. A habit from the past rearing its ugly head once more. Who can say? We're living in miserable times!"

The commissioner changed course: "The killer's resentment would appear to be completely unforgiving. The fine of three hundred francs imposed on Baudelaire by Deputy Pinard was later reduced to fifty francs because the poet couldn't afford the initial sum. Fifty francs is hardly a reason to kill someone."

"Perhaps the serial killer murders because he feels guilty," said Lepage, suddenly taken by a new line of thought. "It might be one of Baudelaire's friends, someone he begged for money after he almost died of hunger in Belgium. The hypothetical friend ignores the poet's appeal and loses his mind after Baudelaire's death. Guilt! Guilt, my dear commissioner, is a fiend that should never be underestimated . . . Hey! Where are you going?" The commissioner was already standing in the morgue doorway.

"I think the time has come for a word with Madame Archenbaut-Dufayis."

16

THE WAR HAD MADE PARTS of France inaccessible by rail, but the brand new steam train to Le Havre was still running. Paul Lefèvre took off his overcoat. The compartments were heated. It was cold for the end of August and the heating was hardly a needless luxury. The summer had been a disaster and the autumn didn't promise to be much better. The commissioner was struggling with contradictory thoughts. He was reminded, on one hand, of the climate in the Orient that had left him listless at lunchtime, but then had filled him with a feverish reckless-ness after supper. He also thought of Prefect Banlieu's arrogance when he had listened to his hypothesis concerning the killer with an excess of scepticism.

"People who call themselves poets and artists are in reality derailed and unproductive individuals, commissioner. They're capable of breaking the law, but only in minor ways. As a rule, their neurasthenic inclinations tend to make them incapable of committing murder."

Lefèvre had unwillingly been forced to agree with the prefect, if only in part. Most killers he had hunted down were primitive types who killed in response to irrepressible urges. The primary motives were jealousy and greed. The *poetic killer* was a rarity. In his heart, Lefèvre included himself in this elusive category. He was a killer in the service of his country and the law, and that made him a protector of innocent citizens. But he was quite familiar with the murderer's primal drive, his lust for blood. While watching a performance of Gounod's *Faust*, Lefèvre had absorbed every gesture and every word at the moment when Mephistopheles captured the soul of Faust. The scene had a special significance for him, one he had still to fathom completely.

A man dressed in what looked like a peasant blouse from an earlier century, with golden-blond hair and a round face with friendly if absent bovine eyes, lugged a painter's easel and a couple of hefty knapsacks into the compartment. In fluent French, but with a strong accent, he asked if the bench opposite Lefèvre was free. The commissioner responded in the affirmative. The traveller clumsily stowed his baggage and flopped onto the bench with a sigh. He started to fill his pipe.

An observer by profession, Lefèvre noticed that in spite of his robust frame the man had finely formed hands. "You're not French," he said.

The man smiled diffidently. "Is it so obvious? My name is Johan Bartold Jongkind, a Hollander. I'm on my way to Honfleur to paint some landscapes."

"What a coincidence."

"You're an artist?" The Dutchman sounded a little too eager, as if he was an aspiring and ambitious artist in search of an entourage of admirers.

The commissioner smiled and shook his head. "I mean that I'm also on my way to Honfleur. I once hoped that I would develop the soul of an artist, but that was a long time ago."

The painter seemed to be an agreeable man, judging by the sympathetic expression on his face. "I hope your talent wasn't nipped in the bud by one or another buffoon posing as a critic. They're all over the papers these days. Thoroughly uncivil."

"No," Lefèvre reassured the Dutch painter. "I craved talent in my youth, but I had none."

"None?" said Jongkind. "We all have talent in one form or another." The Hollander smiled disarmingly. His blond curls had preserved an air of boyishness about him.

The result of naivety, the commissioner presumed, gesturing toward his materials with his head. "You're planning to go painting in the country?"

"Yes indeed, sir, but not in a manner the salons of Paris would understand. The painters of the Barbizon school, with all due respect, are like peasants among peasants. I, on the other hand, am an impressionist."

"And what's an impressionist?"

"We no longer live in a natural environment. Nature has become a decor that has to be painted *en plein air*, in fine weather, when its beauty elevates townsfolk like us into higher spheres, or fills us with melancholy. The painter has become as important as his object. We impressionists have an eye for human realizations: stations filled with trains and steam, people leaving the city behind at the weekend for a picnic in the woods. Emotion, sir, is our future."

"Nature as antidote for animal lust and mental aberration, the maladies of our time," said the commissioner pensively. He had intended to be sarcastic, but realized that he had not succeeded. "And the war? Aren't you afraid?"

The Hollander shrugged his shoulders. "Modern warfare has no place for heroism. War is soulless."

"And what about suffering?"

"Banal. Modern human beings are tired and weary. Contemporary art should soothe the boils on their souls," said Jongkind excitedly. "Or expose them . . . it depends on the temperament of the artist. I belong to the former school. Visual representation becomes art's primary task, especially when you look at the naturalistic novels being written these days, without a single clear idea about life or the soul, so flavorless, so lacking in lofty intentions. Just representing."

"I once met a poet who wrote much the same," said the commissioner in a slightly mocking tone. "He hated the fact that our world today endeavors to explain mysteries by declaring them 'disorders of the senses'. He was determined to encapsulate the vestiges of our passions in robust language."

"Smells of spiritual naturalism," said the northerner with a pensive finger on the side of his nose.

"Precisely!" said the commissioner, relieved. He asked himself why he had started a conversation with a complete stranger about a topic he knew very little about. From the carriage that brought him to the station he had seen the military police violently suppress a workers' demonstration. Lefèvre had studied their determined faces, could smell their repressed rage, feel their hungry eyes penetrate his skin. On the other side of *Les Halles*, the coffin of a *franc-tireur* was being carried to its final resting place. Had he fallen in the war against the Prussians, or was his death the result of a duel with a hot-headed rival? The latter was more likely. Paris had reached its boiling point. The people were on the verge of revolution, the mob ready to plunder.

"And might I ask the name of the poet to whom you refer?" said the painter after a lengthy pause.

"Charles Baudelaire."

"I'd be more inclined to call him decadent, sir."

"Indeed," said Lefèvre, scowling slightly.

"But a great artist," said the Dutchman. "On that I agree wholeheartedly."

Three young men, two armed with modern hunting rifles and one with a muzzle-loader that was probably three times older than himself, clambered noisily into the compartment. Their flushed faces led Lefèvre to presume they had taken one or another intoxicant, perhaps the highly popular opium. They parked themselves a couple of benches away from Lefèvre and Jongkind and whispered to one another with the fervor of newly recruited sect members.

They were followed by an exceptionally small man with a bowler hat and a moustache that hung over his upper lip like a curtain. He clambered onto the train with an excessive display of exhaustion, in spite of the tiny suitcase he trailed behind him. In his doll-like right hand he was holding a couple of white roses that had clearly seen better days.

"*Messieurs!*" he said with a peculiar screech when he caught sight of Lefèvre and Jongkind. "Damned factories! The air in Paris is simply ghastly. Before long it'll be mixed with gun smoke, mark my words! Let's hope the fresh Norman air of Honfleur will revive our spirits." The man's accent was soft, his vowels rounded. His cape was bright red and didn't match his suit. "Camille Poupeye, from Brussels, pleased to meet you."

The diminutive Belgian held out his beggarly bunch of roses in Lefèvre's direction as if he was offering hay to a horse. "Money, good sir, flows mostly to scoundrels and not to honest upright merchants like myself. That's why I give it away with such generosity, even to the gypsy children who sold me these pathetic flowers." The Belgian flopped onto the wooden bench next to Jongkind. The contrast with the tall and pale Hollander was nothing short of comical.

The commissioner observed his new travelling companion. He asked himself why strangers on trains were so tempted to unburden themselves, especially in this day and age. The train's piercing whistle sounded their departure and they left the station.

Paris looked like a tin engraving from the previous century under the thick layer of cloud, but the commissioner could sense the raw energy of the new era that had manifested itself in broad avenues designed to accommodate the rising flood of coaches seeking access to the city. Recent newspaper reports even spoke of a certain German by the name of Benz who was working on a coach not drawn by horses, but driven rather by an engine, like a train without tracks. Such vehicles were set to populate the cities of the future. Some journalists had become obsessed with figments of their own imagination. Perhaps Napoleon III was paying them to publish such nonsense to keep the public's mind off the war.

"You bought the roses from gypsy children?" The Dutch painter glared disapprovingly at the cheerless bouquet. "They steal them from graves, good sir. The thorns are symbolic of the vicissitudes of life and death. The flowers themselves are reminiscent of the chalice that received the blood of Christ."

Lefèvre noticed a head turning toward them a couple of benches away.

The Belgian stared wide-eyed at the flowers in his hand. "What you say, good sir, reminds me of the time I was in the Orient. They don't have the same view of death as we do. The Indian gurus have no fear of it. They're convinced they'll receive a new life time and again until they've reached a state of mental perfection."

A compactly built *franc-tireur* with a hint of a moustache and plump cheeks leaned closer, an unpleasant smile on his face. His brand new carbine was hanging in the fold of his arm. Lefèvre was a connoisseur and could see it was a *chassepot* made in Saint-Etienne. He aimed the weapon at the Belgian, and Lefèvre noticed that he had an unusual forked scar on the left of his jaw. "A dwarf from Brussels with flowers from a grave. What does that tell us, gentlemen?"

"That we're young and drunk and stupid and looking for trouble," said Lefèvre in a gentle tone. He opened his jacket with his left hand.

The young man peered at the commissioner from the corner of his eye, but kept his attention and his rifle focused on Poupeye. Jongkind was glued to the spot and looked like a lamb being led to the slaughter.

"That tells us," the *franc-tireur* continued with the affectation of a stage actor, "that we have a spy in our midst in the pay of *les Prussiens*. We *franc-tireurs* have no time for such—"

Lefèvre's foot shot out and kicked the rifle from the young man's hands. He stood up before the boy had regained his balance and tugged at his jacket. The young man's head thumped against the wooden bench. His two comrades jumped to their feet.

Lefèvre drew his police revolver and gestured to the *franc-tireur* whose nose was bleeding heavily. "Take him with you, sit down, enjoy the journey, and be as silent as death knocking on your mother's door."

They looked at him. They looked at each other. They did what they were told.

A lengthy silence followed.

"Why did you say that?" said Poupeye. The Belgian seemed cheerful, as if he had just enjoyed an entertaining spectacle. "Death knocking on your mother's door? What a strange comparison!"

"Bull's-eye," said Jongkind quietly, before Lefèvre had the chance to respond. Lefèvre noticed a tremble in the corners of his mouth. "I had a premonition last night about death. I was floating above an open shaft in the ground and was slowly sucked inside, where I encountered a strange figure that gave me a sign: a slow beating sound, barely audible, like the beating of a heart ready to give up the struggle. I shall not even try to describe the terror that took hold of me."

Lefèvre kept an eye on the young men. They were sitting like wax statues peering out at the passing landscape. The young man with the forked scar pressed a handkerchief to his nose and looked over his shoulder. Their eyes met. The corners of Lefèvre's mouth curled downwards into a frown. Another new enemy. Oh well, he had so many.

Poupeye smiled indulgently at his travelling companion. "Artists like you yearn for immortality. As a result, your brain has difficulty accepting the fact that you will one day cease to exist. A man like myself, on the other hand, has days he wishes it was all over."

The painter seemed perplexed. "That means you are a sensitive soul, good sir."

"May I ask you something?" The diminutive Belgian turned to the commissioner with a questioning look on his face. Lefèvre observed powder and theatrical greasepaint. He found it hard to estimate the dwarf's age. "You are a man of action, but deep in your soul the budding fauna of your fantastic dream world is much more powerful than your beggarly everyday existence. Do you ever dream of bells?"

Lefèvre smiled evasively. "You're not one of those visionaries, I hope? They're everywhere these days, and only too willing to demonstrate their skills."

"No, but I've travelled far and wide and I've observed people. The supernatural? I saw things in the Orient that are beyond human comprehension. I'm convinced that the mysteries of the east will one day reach our shores. It's only a matter of time." The Belgian gestured toward Paris. The city seemed to be moving, the train standing still. Lefèvre gazed into the comical little man's eyes, but there was nothing amusing to be found there.

Bells? In recent months he had often dreamt of a tower atop a measureless plateau of ice. The peal of its bell made him shiver when he woke. He put it down to age. He had comforted himself for years with the conviction that he was a skilled bloodhound in the service of his country. But in reality, modernity's many derailments were nothing for him. He had held onto his bloodhound reputation, though, not afraid to weigh in against the insane, against killers. Once he dug his teeth in, he refused to let go. His body bore the scars of pitiless duels. He cherished them.

When had the transformation taken place? The shift from bloodhound to civil servant looking forward to retirement, yet afraid, at the same time, of the pathetic soup kitchens, poorly heated lodgings, and the stench of old age that awaited him? He often sat alone in his room at night with a loaded *Lefaucheux* at his right hand, staring at the door as if he was about to face his final confrontation. Such moments left him with the ever-increasing feeling that he would point the pistol at his own head should the door fly open. Then came the reaction: a frenzied recklessness that drove him into the night and into the arms of whores.

"You're clearly a lover of mystery," said the commissioner to the Belgian, rummaging in his overcoat for the photograph he had found on the corpse of Deputy Pinard. "What do you think of this?"

The Belgian produced a monocle from his jacket pocket, propped it into place, and carefully examined the photograph.

"A ghost coiling out of a corpse," said Lefèvre. He realised that he sounded aggrieved.

Jongkind had difficulty containing his curiosity and blushed when he noticed Poupeye's penetrating eyes suddenly peer back at him over the top of the photo. Poupeye handed Jongkind the photo. "Tell me, good sir, do you believe in ghosts?"

The painter looked at the photo and scowled. "They say photography is the new art, but all I can see is smoke and trickery."

"Your answer is an emotional one," said Poupeye. "But you're right nonetheless." He turned to the commissioner. "If you ask me, the 'ghost' in this photograph is the product of chemical reactions in a developing tray, manipulated by someone skilled in the creation of such illusions. But I have another, more important observation to make."

Lefèvre raised his eyebrows. The rotund little man paused, enjoying the dramatic effect. "You mentioned that the man in this photographic image from whom the spirit is apparently emerging is dead. Well, I challenge your findings: the man is not dead."

Before the commissioner had the chance to respond, the Belgian leaned forward. "My work obliges me to keep a close eye on technical advances, to look precisely and to think. Do you see the fine shadow and the lines around the body? As I'm sure you are aware, modern bellows cameras require a much shorter exposure time than they did twenty years ago, when the only cameras available were those of Monsieur Daguerre or the Englishman Talbot. The new-fangled calotype process has made portraits of this small size possible, but it still requires a couple of minutes of exposure time. And in those couple of minutes, *monsieur*, this gentleman moved. That explains the lack of sharpness around some of the contours of his body."

Lefèvre studied the photograph carefully. The little Belgian may have been right. The commissioner sensed his hunting instinct stir within him, a flicker of anticipation, the feeling that fate was spinning its thread and he could see it. "The man was definitely dead when I saw him, but your observation is astute, I'll give you that."

Poupeye smiled. "Thank you, good sir. May I ask what you do for a living?"

"It has to do with the dead." The little Belgian nodded guardedly, his sense of humor ebbing by the minute. Lefèvre noticed Jongkind's artless eyes glaze over. "And yours?"

Poupeye announced without shame: "I made an important erotic discovery in Syria, a technique taught me by a *gazelle*. Forbidden in many a civilised country, I can assure you of that. And vulgar to the extreme, needless to say! Ideal for the male imagination!"

Jongkind leaned forward, slightly shy.

"A lady in some sheik's harem, no doubt," said Lefèvre, pretending to be unfamiliar with the Orient. "Some countries in the east have turned the erotic into an art. Here it's common or garden."

"What you say is true," the Belgian replied. "It was a Circassian, a genuinely noble specimen, who welcomed me into her arms. She first danced for me to the elegant rhythm of drums and tambourines. She then subjected herself to a centuries-old ritual with an artificial phallus, the size of which was enough to cast a shadow over the majority of men. I was extremely aroused as a result. During that night in Antioch, an idea started to ripen in my mind, an idea I dare to call brilliant, and I have been working on it for the last two years. Good sirs, I have combined the latest miracles of technology with a centuries-old erotic ritual! I will soon stun all of Paris with my discovery. And it will inspire the man of the future to praise the pleasures of voyeurism above his more primitive sexual urges."

"The only orgy Paris is likely to see in the near future is an orgy of death," said Jongkind diffidently.

The little man stared at him caustically. "Men are men, whether they're Prussian or French. They're governed by the same urges and they'll be fascinated by my invention. In their droves!"

The Belgian dwarf handed his calling card to Lefèvre with a flamboyant gesture. "Had he known about my discovery," he said, "Baudelaire would have written the most exquisite poem he was capable of writing about it."

17

MADAME ARCHENBAUT-DUFAYIS'S LIVING ROOM EXHIBITED all the characteristics of bourgeois taste. The commissioner observed traces of negligence nevertheless. The damask on the table was dusty and there were patches of mould on the curtains. The woman sitting on the sofa exuded the same allure, the serene listlessness of a flickering, faltering flame when its time has come.

Baudelaire's mother raised her hand to her bosom. Lefèvre detected an inclination to the theatrical, something she had clearly passed on to her son.

"You can't be serious, commissioner," said Caroline Archenbaut-Dufayis.

"When I asked if your son was still alive, ma'am, I meant in the mind of someone who loved him, someone who might be confused enough to think he should seek revenge in your son's name." The commissioner waited a moment and then added: "Or be Charles Baudelaire's reincarnation?"

He had presented the widow with the various elements associated with the three murders that alluded to her son. Her reaction had been evasive and curt. She had complained that Paris was full of hysterical second-rate lowlifes pretending to be artists. The norms of morality no longer governed the times we lived in. Insanity had become ordinary. She didn't sound particularly clear-headed, but Lefèvre had noticed something in the corners of her eyes that had set his senses on edge. His intuition told him, albeit in a whisper, that the widow was hiding something.

"My dear Charles enkindled a great deal of jealousy throughout his dramatic life," said Baudelaire's mother. "If anyone should be avenged, it's him. But I can't think of anyone who would have the courage to do such a thing. Today's cowardly pen-pushers? No, commissioner, you should look for a mind shrouded in darkness, someone who found comfort in my son's sombre poems. If you ask me, it's the emperor himself. He claims to be a misunderstood genius, doesn't he, who would rather write poetry than wage war. A miserable failure in both disciplines, alas."

"Have you received letters from anyone in recent months?" the commissioner insisted, determined to push his point. "If we're dealing with one or another sickly soul who claims to have a link with your son, then perhaps he tried to contact you."

The woman shook her head in silence. She was like a wounded bird unable to fly, closing its eyes at the approach of the fox.

"Did none of his friends, drunk or under the influence of opium, ever swear they would seek revenge for the injustice done to him?"

"No, no, no. Commissioner, I fear your dangerous and tiring train journey was for nothing. You must be desperate."

"Not desperate," Lefèvre bluffed. "Rather a bundle of suspicions."

"Honfleur is not the place to confirm them. Have you other possibilities in mind? Perhaps the murderer is using my son's work to mock him posthumously by drawing your attention to him."

Lefèvre could not deny that the widow had a point. But her poorly camouflaged anxiety was still visible. "You could be charged with complicity if you withhold information and there's another murder."

The fragile woman blushed red. The whites of her eyes were yellow. A cat stirred in a basket in the corner, its green eyes full of sleep.

"Complicity? What do you know about complicity?" Caroline Archenbaut-Dufayis snapped. "I brought a genius into this world, a genius and a monster. And you cannot imagine the price I have had to pay. The artistic soul does not confine itself to the conventions of bourgeois society that would have us believe in the existence of order and law. In reality, death, chaos, and eternal lust govern our lives. You consider yourself a servant of Justice, but pain and revenge count more nowadays than a blindfolded trollop with counterfeit scales, who lets herself be raped by the powerful of this world."

The widow reached for the lace collar of her dress and stared out the window as if she had suddenly opened her eyes in an unfamiliar place.

"I'm not concerned with official justice," said the commissioner in a soft tone of voice, "but with the victims."

For an instant, a mere flash—perhaps an illusion—he saw naked terror in her eyes.

"Do you have children, commissioner?"

"No."

"You have no idea what children are capable of."

"No."

"They devour you." A coarse shrewdness filled her face. "They start with your innards. Every hour of your existence they gnaw at you."

The cat had jumped onto the windowsill and was looking outside, its head crooked. A bird fluttered past the window. The cat let out a tortured shriek of desire.

The widow was startled by it. "Who can I expect to see when I die?" she muttered, as if the commissioner was an oracle she had finally been able to consult after years of hardship. She was sitting opposite Lefèvre, but she was far away, in a place where death was on the verge of settling its bill.

18

"HE'S IN A BAD WAY, poor bastard," said the policeman. He straightened his kepi. "Looks as if he's been scalped by a bunch of savages from the jungles of America."

"Not jungles, but prairies," said Bouveroux with a frown. He liked people to use the correct word.

"Jungles, prairies, what does it matter, inspector?" the policeman grumbled. "We're worse than those American savages. Slitting each other's throats is common these days. And I haven't been paid for two months."

Bouveroux sighed and turned to the corpse against the wall. The house on the Rue Mouffetard was under construction. On completion it was to offer accommodation to the hard-working day laborers who earned fourpence a shift at one of the new mills or forges.

On his way to the scene of the crime, Bouveroux had crossed the Place Saint-Pierre, where a crowd had gathered around "science's latest miracle." Bouveroux had dallied a little, hoping to catch a glimpse of the tiny airship that was about to embark on a trial flight. The newspapers had been full of it the last couple of days. He had read that the miniature prototype was full of hydrogen and was propelled through the air by a clockwork engine. Now that he had been able to see the thing in real life, it didn't impress him. One and a half meters of scrap, he thought.

The crowd jeered when the inventor, a watchmaker by the name of Julien something, announced that the wind was too changeable for a trial flight. The man had trumpeted far and wide for weeks on end that his invention would help force the Prussians to their knees. He predicted that France would assemble an invincible fleet of giant airships with engine-driven propellers and awe-inspiring weaponry. In recent months, any diversion that ended in nothing was enough to drive the Parisians hysterical.

Bouveroux was convinced that the emperor—who had worked as a simple policeman in London prior to 1848, the year of the revolution—would be better advised to show his face more on the streets of the capital. Instead he had ensconced himself in Châlons after the humiliation at Metz and spent his time haranguing his generals with pointless commands while his empress Eugénie ran Paris. Had the unstable emperor, who suffered from countless physical ailments, lost touch with the street to such a degree that he was unaware of the tensions in the city, that unrest had reached fever-pitch? The menacing echoes of the First International resounded through the city's workers districts, stirring more support with every passing day. The Second Empire was crumbling, the republican Gambetta gaining in popularity. The man himself favored the Prussians, as long as they brought down Napoleon III. Flaubert referred to him openly as Clodhopper the First. Did Gambetta not understand that the Universal Suffrage he supported with such vigor would spell the end of the social order?

Bouveroux had a tendency to look down on the plebs and their obsession with the satisfaction of their primary needs. On the other hand, as a servant of the law he had frequent contact with the wealthier classes and had experienced their boundless arrogance more than once. The inspector preferred to see himself as a hard-working citizen determined to climb the social ladder. It was his conviction that the middle classes would form the backbone of France's future.

The uproar surged. Hats flew into the air. A number of *franc-tireurs*, who had just returned from one or another daring maneuvers, fired into the sky. Taking the shots to be a signal, the crowd stormed the unfortunate inventor. The military police charged in to liberate him.

Bouveroux shook his head and continued his journey, passing the empty shop windows and eateries with poor quality offal on their menus. Poor France. Its national guard was good for nothing except marching up and down, ready for the scrap heap.

The inspector sighed again. The poor bastard at his feet didn't look the type to warrant much of the prefecture's attention and manpower. In light of recent events, Bouveroux had taken time to review the life of Charles Baudelaire and he remembered, with a hint of bitterness, that the poet had written a number of arresting "in memoriams" in his day, odes to the wealthy to help pay for his addiction to opium and laudanum. The mutilated creature at Bouveroux's feet was beyond recognition and Baudelaire would surely have had nothing to say about him. But the conceited poet had not the slightest difficulty proclaiming the virtues of the affluent deceased, and himself *en passant*.

Where had he read these words of criticism? Bouveroux enjoyed putting his memory to the test at appropriate moments. It irritated him—as it did now—when he was unable to trace the source of the facts that fluttered though his mind. *L'Hibou Philosophe? Le Salut Public?* Bouveroux hadn't read any of Baudelaire's poems, but he had developed a fascination for the poet's capacity to turn things to his own advantage, and the opinions on art he had aired in journals and newspapers.

"Sad days for the likes of us," said the policeman. He looked like a man who enjoyed a glass of local wine and the sight of what his wife revealed beneath her skirts when she polished the floor.

"Sad days for everyone, my friend," said Bouveroux as he crouched closer to the mutilated corpse. "I have a second cousin in Belgium. He knows the Prussians and what it means for us to concede defeat to them time after time. I think we . . ." He had carefully turned the body in the meantime and he suddenly fell silent. The dagger that had slashed the man's face in a wild rage and had transformed his lower belly into a stinking mass of entrails was protruding from his back as one final humiliation.

It was a Moorish dagger, and Bouveroux thought it vaguely familiar. He had probably seen something similar during his military service in the hands of one or another Algerian combatants.

"A hot-tempered Maghrebi settling a score, no doubt," he said. "And all for a whore or the spoils of a theft. Who can say? The prefect isn't likely to be very interested. Identification? Close to impossible with a face like that. The clothing suggests working class. Have them collect the body for burial in a pauper's grave. No need for an autopsy."

The policeman nodded and heaved a sigh of relief. Bouveroux got to his feet and was about to walk away when something made him stop a couple of meters from the body. He turned, retraced his steps, took the man's right hand and held it to his nose.

19

DEATH? LEFÈVRE HAD ENCOUNTERED DEATH in a variety of guises. And each time he had asked the same question deep inside: *Have you come for me this time?* Death was never pleasant company, but its grim determination made it a potential ally.

When had the commissioner started to long for death? Lefèvre had lost count, like a lover trying to forget his rejections.

On afternoons like these, with changeable winds, a sky the color of pewter and with enormous swan-like clouds, a walk along the Seine usually helped him organise his thoughts. But he was distracted by the Parisians and their outfits as they paraded past the river's troubled waters, mocking the war. The wind on this first of September was blustery and capricious, tossing brightly colored parasols into the air and whipping up lace collars. On occasion it flirted under a lady's skirt, exposing a frivolous ankle boot.

Lefèvre tried to concentrate on the problems at hand, especially the demeanor of widow Archenbaut-Dufayis, who clearly knew more than she was willing to reveal. But the contrived joviality he encountered along the city's riverbank—with its recently installed gas streetlamps— made it difficult for him to focus. Perhaps Prefect Banlieu was right and he was "insignificant." And if the situation in the capital continued to deteriorate at the same tempo, who would give a damn about the murders in a couple of weeks? When the commissioner walked through the vast vaulted entrance to the *Bureaux de la Préfecture de Police* that morning, large groups of people had assembled outside, citizens from the wealthier neighbourhoods insisting on police protection from the threat of revolution that was swelling in the working class districts. He had read in the papers that all the laborers from the *Seine-Inférieure* would have to resort to begging. The number of rat catchers was increasing by the day. And the rich, in the meantime, indulged their anxious passions with almost hysterical intensity.

Lefèvre straightened his hat and tapped the riverbank energetically with his walking stick. Its bulbous handle was shaped like the head of a lion and had cracked more than a few skulls in its time.

One day, or so he hoped, he would be confronted by an adversary with the same fighting spirit as himself, but with a younger, faster body. Then his time would come. He preferred such a death to the thought of pining away in a bed, surrounded by nuns trying to keep his crumbling body alive with cool hands and soup made from rotting vegetables. Lefèvre was determined to avoid the latter fate, come what may. And in the meantime he had to get on with life, although stoicism wasn't easy in a century inclined to extremes.

In recent years, the commissioner had found it hard to stay apace with the technical advances of his day and had grown convinced that they coincided with the decline of civilisation. So many wondrous things had become commonplace in such a short period of time, but the people had lost their heads and some considered themselves above morality. Daguerre and his photography, the Lumière brothers and their moving images—*cinema*, they called it—electric trains, mysterious pianos that played tunes using cogwheels and ingenious clockwork mechanisms, typewriters that made the need for practiced penmanship redundant and fired the imagination; there was no end to it. One or another new contraption appeared every day, accompanied by a clamour of rumours and gossip. Visionaries like Jules Verne, who wrote about trips to the moon and submarine ships, had become idols. Genuine scholars went even further than the storytellers and their ravings. A couple of months earlier, Bouveroux had made a remark about a certain Babbage and a thinking machine he was said to have invented years ago. He had called it a computer and no one had paid much attention at the time. Now everyone was talking about it.

Lefèvre had difficulty with the vanity of such eccentricities. The commissioner, who remembered his early years in Lorraine wondering where the next meal was going to come from, saw more advantage in practical inventions such as the current fad for transporting vegetables in ice-cooled carts to keep them fresh and crisp. How many times had he been forced to eat stringy meat and limp vegetables, which an enterprising chef had attempted to disguise with a revolting layer of béchamel sauce? Lefèvre had grown up in Lunéville, an old garrison town in a region full of castles, crucifixes, convents, rolling forests, and the remains of ancient Roman roads, not far from the village of Dornrémy where Jeanne d'Arc was born. He had spent his youth on the banks of the river Meurthe, which the *oualous* used to transport enormous flotillas of tree trunks to Metz. The hardy lumberjacks called the river *l'eau sauvage* and he remembered the old songs they would sing as they followed their wares downriver. Many of Napoleon's former soldiers had been unable to turn their backs on the garrison town and their stories fired the imagination of the well-built but sensitive lad. Many a worn out war-horse had shown him his *Médaille de Sainte Hélène*, awarded by the empire for services rendered. Just as often they had told him stories bristling with fear, pride, nostalgia, bitterness, and warning. The young Lefèvre couldn't get enough, and dreamed of a life of heroism. His father, a formidable wrestler in his free time, was a teacher at the local school for boys, a position rewarded with more respect than salary.

The commissioner had been fashioned by a youth full of dreams and five years of military service in the desert. Lefèvre's faith in God had slowly dissipated during his time in Algeria. The soldier's life had instilled a profound admiration in him for the strength of the beast in each of us. He had sought beauty in the desert's majestic sunrises that had kindled a fire in his heart. But he had also murdered and raped with a passion that amazed and horrified him all at once. Like a half-starved ascetic, he had begged for a sign of forgiveness from the Divine.

When he returned to France, he encountered a world that was even crueller than the Orient in many respects. He found work with the police, climbed the ladder, and was ultimately given charge of security whenever a *Grand Bal* was thrown in one of the palaces on the right bank of the Seine. He had seen an even more brutal beast lurking behind the perfumed manners of the aristocracy than he had ever encountered in the callous faces of the Bedouin. People talked about an era of science and knowledge, but Lefèvre had never seen so many purveyors of excessive vulgarity and dim-witted avarice; people without soul or conscience, formed by the Machine.

In spite of the loss of his faith, he still made regular visits to churches, where he would cross himself in the lofty transept and scream in silence for help. Sometimes he dreamed, as he had as a child after the death of his sister Hélène, of hairless creatures staring at him with evil intentions, and he would wake with a start, gasping for breath.

As the years progressed, and the commissioner survived attack after attack from knife fighters and swordsmen, some with their weapons cunningly concealed in their walking sticks, he gradually adapted himself. He became something of a loner, developed an interest in poetry and Cabbala, and preferred to believe in a secret world behind the dream than in the cabal people called progress.

Lefèvre in the meantime was old and wise enough to be able to place the blame for his penchant for the peculiar on the terrors he had experienced as a young man. The commissioner counted himself lucky that he had not been robbed of his intuition. A sensitivity for hidden intentions, for the allure of happenstance, for the insights of dreams and emotions, for the traces of a clue no matter how vague, had served him extremely well as an enforcer of the law. At the same time, his desire for the tender flesh of the female of the species often drove him into a frenzy. But his best insights came as he tried to fetter his lust. He had convinced himself that there was nothing wrong with the fact that his passions hadn't diminished with age.

But at times like this, as the wind brought commotion to the city, his restlessness opened a door to the past and brought him face to face once again with the Bedouin attacking the outpost near Besbes in the early morning light. He remembered the gaping mouths, the curved swords, the old muzzle-loaders, the women in black from head to toe behind the dunes, night after night, driving the French occupiers insane with their rhythmic wailing.

The commissioner sometimes dreamt about what his regiment had done to celebrate their victory. Then the faces of his old military comrades would appear in his mind, reminding him of a series of photographs Nadar had taken ten months earlier in the Ursuline institute for the mentally deranged. All Paris had lined up to see them.

When he awoke from such dreams, the commissioner always came to the same conclusion: from then on he would use logic and nothing more. Yet deduction, praised by the exuberant Poe's renowned detective Auguste Dupin, remained his weak point. Lefèvre often felt himself more akin to the lacklustre army of plodding policemen Poe described with so much elegant sadism. The commissioner had to make do with half-understood hunches, pieces of a puzzle that took their time to fall into place and shake his intuition from its sleep.

He glanced at the calling card in his hand and then at the house in front of him. 22 Rue Beautreillis. It was an old hotel from the end of the seventeenth century, refurbished, a shop on the ground floor and several splendid apartments on the floors above.

Lefèvre stopped and peered into the shop window.

He could smell money.

And lust.

20

POUPEYE WAS THE KIND OF person who was capable of complete metamorphosis. His diminutive stature was unchanged, but this evening there was something regal about him. His moustache seemed even more metallic, gleaming as if it was made of some strange unnatural material.

Lefèvre put it down to his surroundings. The inventor's workshop was immediately behind a wooden stage that served as a display area and was strewn with mechanical contraptions and female window dummies that did not conform to the conventions of decency. The commissioner had made some trite remarks about them as he sipped at the glass of wine the Belgian had poured for him. Poupeye had responded with dignity, and perhaps a hint of arrogance.

Lefèvre had constructed an alibi, should his visit—inspired as it was by curiosity and gloom—take a wrong turn. Perhaps the eccentric Belgian was planning to blackmail him for one or another reason. A corrupt policeman could be worth a lot of money in times like these. If he tried that, Lefèvre would arrest him immediately. He had given the Belgian's address to the lieutenant on duty when he left the prefecture. He had asked the man to note in the logbook that he suspected Poupeye of international fraud.

The real reason he had decided to visit Poupeye after their chance encounter on the train was sexual curiosity.

Poupeye took the commissioner by the arm. "Your aura, commissioner, tells me that you are a man who enjoys certain pleasures, the type ordinary folk tend to snub. Why? Because they're afraid, of course! *Liberté, égalité, fraternité ou la mort!* Don't you agree? People say that death is the great equalizer. I say they're wrong. Death urges us to distinguish ourselves before our hour has come. Death makes us do the most obscene things. Death makes us kill."

The Belgian's bowler glistened in the light of the oil lamp. The lamplight and the red fabric decorating the walls gave the place the appearance of a dim and shadowy painting. Lefèvre swallowed an impatient response. Café philosophers did nothing for him.

"But I see you are impatient," the Belgian continued. "You are a man of emotions, commissioner, a man with secrets. In your past . . ."

"I don't believe in fortune-tellers, *monsieur*, I've already told you that. And even if they have some kind of knowledge, then it's usually to their advantage that they keep it to themselves."

"Of course. Whatever happens in this room, commissioner, will be treated with the utmost discretion."

Poupeye gestured at a bow in a corner of the room. He walked toward it and picked it up, together with the arrow lying beside it. The commissioner noticed that the tip of the arrow wasn't made of the usual metal, but looked for all the world like an erect penis.

"Such 'love bows' were once used in the Orient during fertility rituals," said the Belgian dwarf. "A naked woman would lie with her legs apart on an ingenious wooden construction, like one of those newfangled delivery tables surgeons use for caesarean sections. The altar was erected in an enormous tent on the night of the full moon. The legs of the female sacrificial victim were pushed upwards towards her shoulders so that her vulva protruded between them. It was smeared with animal fat. The bowman was expected to penetrate her vagina with this artificial penis on the first shot. If he succeeded, an orgy would follow and all the men in the tent would take the woman until death finally claimed her. *Djinns* or evil spirits were thus kept at bay. If the bowman failed, he was handed over to death at the hands of the women who had been herded together in another tent. Legend has it that the mighty warrior Kamal Minoumi shot the penis-arrow into the woman's vagina with such force that it tore through her intestines. He became the symbol of manly vigor, the greatest good in the eyes of the followers of Allah."

Lefèvre came closer. The ivory-colored dildo was highly polished and shiny and had a substantial girth. Its maker had not modelled the contours of his oversized creation on reality but on an artistic repre-sentation thereof, as if the phallus was the head of a snake. There was something menacing about it, but the commissioner didn't believe a word Poupeye had told him. He was expecting the Belgian to suggest he purchase this "unique collector's item" and insist that the accompanying erotic story would raise eyebrows at gatherings of the *nouveau riche*, who were known for having more money than brains.

But why had Poupeye chosen him of all people to display his retail talents? A police officer with a moderate income was hardly the best target for the man's inspired if meaningless sales talk.

"Aren't you impressed by the proportions, commissioner?" asked the Belgian, a hint of malignance in his voice. "The size of the phallus has always been a symbol of male superiority faced with the guile and cunning of the female of the species and her seductive powers."

"I'm not interested in a purchase," said Lefèvre flatly.

A peculiar expression twisted the Belgian's face. "If this does not interest you, what does, commissioner? Why the visit?"

Lefèvre said nothing.

"Because of the words 'erotic secrets from around the world' on my card?" Poupeye continued, sugar-sweet. He took hold of the bow. The frivolous air and tripping step had vanished. "You've had enough eroti-cism in your life. Isn't it time to look for love?"

"A *fata morgana*. I have both my feet planted firmly on the ground."

"Do you think so? When you were a soldier in Algeria fighting for your fatherland, your fiancée left you. Annette married a man of noble birth who had lost his parents when he was still young. There was no one to forbid the marriage. But that's all in the past, commissioner. Annette died five years ago from a disease she contracted from her husband after he had sought to satisfy his desires with women from the Niger region." Poupeye heaved a dramatic sigh. "Now it's *de rigueur* to marry for love, at least among the middle classes. As ever, the aristocracy has closed its ranks and continues to do what it has done for centuries."

The commissioner rested his enormous hand on the back of the Belgian's neck. "How do you know all this?"

Many a suspect had doubled up at the touch of that hand. Some had sought refuge in violence and had not survived to tell their tale. Poupeye by contrast straightened his shoulders. "Look behind you, commissioner."

Had the man given a sign to an invisible accomplice, or were the oil lamps attached to some sort of ingenious timing mechanism? In any event, the light in the room started to fade. Lefèvre turned, ready to counter any form of attack.

One of the window dummies started to move, female and exceptionally beautiful. She was wearing the sort of clothes women wear in the revues: a pale blue smock that stopped under the breasts, and harem breeches made of tulle so fine that the outline of her thighs was clearly visible. Her arms were draped with tiny bells that jingled with each gracious move. The bottom half of her face was concealed behind a veil of gold brocade. The room slowly filled with the captivating rhythms of *Habibi* music. Lefèvre instinctively looked around in search of its source. He was aware that such mechanical instruments were worth a small fortune because they could only reproduce one unique piece of music. He could see nothing in the now subdued light. The room suddenly seemed smaller.

He wanted to grab his hat and bid the pocket-sized charlatan and his conjurer's magic farewell. But in the blink of an eye, the world outside the workshop was wiped away. Lefèvre could feel the heat of the desert sand under his feet and was blinded by the sun bearing down on his forehead.

As the commissioner lost consciousness and slowly collapsed onto the shattered fragments of his wineglass, he realized in a final moment of mental clarity that he had been duped.

21

"YOU ARE AN EXTRAORDINARY WEALTH of information, my dear Bouveroux, especially when there's something vaguely scientific about it," said police physician Lepage with a hint of condescension. He looked at the corpse on his dissection table and sniffed at its fingers with aristocratic aplomb. "This is indeed the smell of silver chloride and mercury vapour. It's hard to miss it these days. Wherever those so-called innovators appear with their newfangled contraptions, photographing the streets of Paris and selling framed copies to the city's moneyed classes to decorate the walls of their homes, it hangs in the air like the stench of the last judgment."

"A photographer, as I thought," said Bouveroux. His expression darkened. He stuffed his hands in his coat pockets and hunched his shoulders.

"If this persists, Bouveroux," the police physician continued, without paying attention to the altered expression on the inspector's face, "then give it a hundred years and people won't have to leave their homes anymore. The entire world will be available on photographic plates."

Lepage was taken aback when Bouveroux cursed out loud and stormed out of the room, his coattails flapping. He sighed. The world was upside down: even the otherwise undemonstrative inspector had acquired the manners of a common laborer.

⋄⟨⟨⟩⟩⋄

In the approaching darkness, the unfinished edifice on the Rue Mouffetard had something malevolent about it. The inspector peered into the attic room, smoking oil lamp in hand, angry with himself for not bringing an escort. Houses without front doors were ideal hideouts for common street scamps and other riffraff, but they could also shelter more dangerous creatures. Bouveroux had made his way through the musty rooms, unable to shake the feeling that he was being followed. Reading about science's latest triumphs in well-lit library reading rooms was one thing, but creeping through a half-finished house in the night in search of a mysterious killer who had adopted the guise of a dead poet was something else altogether.

In addition to the uneasy feeling between his shoulder blades, the inspector had another reason to grit his teeth. Distracted by the airship spectacle earlier in the day and the sense of doom in the streets of Paris, he had treated the body with the Moorish dagger in its back with negligence. A routine matter, he had thought, a banal street fight, an everyday fatality. He had only noticed the smell hanging around the corpse at the very last. But even after he had made the mental link with the deceased's occupation, he had still missed an important detail at the scene of the crime. It hadn't rained that day, but there was little sign of blood near the body. He had only realized later, at the morgue, that the victim had not been killed on the street.

Bouveroux returned to the ground floor. Had he checked every room? The inspector tried to curb his disappointment. He opened the back door and crossed an open courtyard. The owner of the house had followed the modern trend and built a toilet detached from the rest of the house. There was even a heart-shaped hole carved out of the wooden toilet door. Bouveroux opened it and recoiled in horror, not at the smell of feces, but at the sight of congealed blood.

While the blood was still fresh, someone had used it to write a verse of poetry on the left wall of the toilet:

> *I'm fair, O mortals, as a dream of stone;*
> *My breasts whereon, in turn, your wrecks you shatter,*
> *Were made to wake in poets' hearts alone*
> *A love as indestructible as matter.*[6]

Overwhelmed by the stench, the inspector tried nevertheless to understand what lay behind the words, their deeper meaning. He was convinced that this verse too had been penned by Baudelaire. He grimaced. Love could be the cruellest motive, he thought.

And blood the oldest messenger.

22

LEFÈVRE SENSED THE WEIGHT OF meters of earth on his chest. He could smell his own terror and feel the still-twitching bodies of his brothers in arms, buried in the trench they had been forced to dig in the wadi after a surprise Bedouin attack had overpowered them. Shots from the enemy's old muzzle-loaders had sounded tame in the dry desert air, but men had fallen nonetheless to his left and right, gurgling, with a piercing scream, a lingering sigh, or in silence, there in the trench that had become their mass grave. Lefèvre had felt something hit the metal flask hanging from his belt, its force like the kick of a donkey. He had fallen on top of his dead and dying comrades and had remained there, numb, gasping for air, half covered with bodies. When shovelfuls of sand landed on top of him and beside him, he had to use every fibre of his common sense to remain still and not try to struggle to his feet.

After the sand had covered him completely, he took a risk and tied his neckerchief over his nose and mouth. It was almost impossible to breathe. His world narrowed, grew dark and heavy. He forced himself to wait and wait until his lungs were on fire. Only then did he clamber to the surface. His luck was in. The Algerians had finished their work in a hurry. Lefèvre crawled out of the mass grave, gasping for air. The sand singed his throat and his eyelids.

To his left, behind a crop of date palms, he heard camels snorting. Evening had fallen with its customary desert abruptness. The stars glistened in the moonlight like angels from a long-forgotten childhood dream. His thoughts raced in every direction. His body tingled. To his right, close to the oasis, fires had been lit. It was time for evening tea, but first for prayer and Mecca. The paltry remains of his rational mind whispered that it would be better to wait a little longer, until they had rolled out their prayer mats. But Lefèvre didn't listen to reason.

The horizon fanned out in front of him, its golden hue intense in the setting sun. The sentry near the camels didn't have enough time to load his antique rifle when he caught sight of the madman storming in his direction. The French lieutenant's hefty frame crashed into him before he had the chance to draw his curved knife. A pair of hands the size of hams grabbed the sentry's throat and snapped his neck as if it was a matchstick.

Once again the young officer's luck was in. The camels hadn't been tied up for the night because they still had to be watered. Lefèvre leapt onto one of the creatures, grabbed the reins and tugged the beast to its feet. The startled camel gurgled and took off at a gallop. He could hear commotion and screaming behind him. Echoes rolled like thunder, loud and soft, through the dry desert air. Shots were fired, cracking like La Meurthe as its surface covered with ice when he was a boy. Lefèvre didn't look back.

He slowed down a couple of kilometres further, when darkness had fallen completely. He had to spare the animal. On such an uneven surface as this the camel could easily break a leg, and it was his only lifeline. Although the sky was clear and the stars provided plenty of light, its glassy reflection in the sand dunes and the kilometres of shadow they created made it well nigh impossible for him to fix his position.

Lefèvre's throat was raw from the sand he had swallowed. He groped for the flask hanging from his belt and only then realised that it was dented and had a hole in it. He shook it and something inside rattled. He held it upside down.

Instead of water, out came a twisted lump of lead.

23

THE GLOW FROM THE OIL lamp on the table cast purple shadows under Inspector Bouveroux's eyes. The shade was decorated with drawings of oriental dancers. The rest of the room was lit with candles. Bouveroux's lodgings didn't exhibit much evidence of good taste, but there was one item he was proud of: a shabby Louis XV bookcase, filled with special editions and encyclopaedias, propped up against the right wall. The rest of the furniture was simple and drab. With a salary of 211 francs and 72 tin centimes, the inspector wasn't able to indulge himself. But, unlike many in the poorer districts, he wasn't starving. At the 21st district police station, hardened beat officers talked of striking laborers from the Seine-Inférieure eating their dead at secret nocturnal meetings and pledging with mouths full of blood that they would bring down the nobility and the middle classes.

The inspector asked himself if the half-crazed workers were aware of the fact that the standard of living had also drastically declined in recent months for the middle classes. The coke he bought at the market for his fire was of inferior quality and filled the room with acrid smoke. Having to light the fire so early in September was a serious drain on his resources. Nature and the ever more miserable war were keeping pace with one another.

Parisians had insisted almost scornfully that Paris and its military defences were invincible, but now the Prussians were close to the city gates. Bouveroux had the grotesque if only occasional urge to take one of the rifles the *franc-tireurs* were handing out and join the fight. He had received a letter from his brother Henri in Rouen. Henri was a lieutenant in a hastily assembled company charged with defending the city. His faltering sentences predicted nothing less than the downfall of the Latin world and Prussian world domination.

Bouveroux coughed and heard his lungs rattle. At his age and with his constitution it was better to avoid too much excitement, and fighting was completely out of the question. Earlier that evening he had parked himself in front of the fire and rubbed his chest with poplar salve, fancying that it helped relieve the suspicious pain he had felt in his lungs these past few months if only slightly. The words written in blood on the toilet wall still disturbed him.

Bouveroux had a parchment in his hands, a document he had filched from a dying Amazigh years back in Algeria. The text was written from left to right in Tamazight, the ancient language of the Berbers. Bouveroux didn't understand what it said, but a Berber who worked for the French colonizer had once told him that it contained *suryas* that enraged the Arabic elite because of their blasphemous content. The Berber had insisted that the parchment contained a text sacred to the Amazigh, and that it had been written in Numidia in the blood shed every month by the goddess Lil and collected by the moon god Allah, who at set times became *Al-ilah* through the unification of his masculine and feminine aspects. It was only through this unification that the powers of a unique supreme deity emerged. The Arabs were determined come what may to prevent people from finding out that their god had a female counterpart who was just as powerful as himself. Bouveroux had promised to hand over the document to a renowned Berber scribe. The death of the mercenary had released him from his pledge.

The cabbalist he had consulted regarding the document several years later in Belleville had claimed that the Berbers were descendants of the

Amazons and that their women were often literate and wrote poetry. According to an ancient tradition, they wrote their mystical verses in their own menstrual blood when they wanted to put a curse on an enemy.

Bouveroux stared at the parchment's red-brown characters. The document had hardened over the years and its edges were crumbling.

He didn't know why, but when he encountered Baudelaire's verses that night, smeared on a toilet wall at a house on the Rue Mouffetard, this parchment—which was to go to the *Grande Galerie de L'Evolution* of the natural history museum after his death—was the first thing that came into his mind.

The inspector had first suspected that the verses had been written in the blood of the unknown photographer who was now on a slab in Lepage's mortuary.

Now he was no longer sure, and for reasons of intuition that he, as a man of science, was still loath to recognise.

It could be blood of another origin.

He was also no longer sure that the killer was a man.

24

"LEAD IS THE METAL OF Saturn," the voice said, echoing in Lefèvre's head. "It is poisonous to humans, commissioner. The Romans ate from lead plates and they became ill. Their civilization perished. Just like you will."

Poupeye leaned over Lefèvre, who realized he was unable to move. He had the feeling that his head was lower than his feet and it brought back memories of the mass grave and the position he had been forced to hold as the Bedouin covered him with sand. He could still remember the sand in his mouth.

The diminutive Belgian seemed to be standing at an angle and the ceiling above him tilted to one side. An index finger swayed back and forth in front of his eyes. "Lead is your criterion, commissioner. You're poisoning yourself."

Poupeye positioned his face centimetres from that of Lefèvre. It seemed out of proportion, bloated like a balloon, its structure distorted. The eyes became murky hollows, the forehead glimmered like a miniature sun. The commissioner's heartbeat became irregular. His belly protested and he broke into a cold sweat. Nausea flushed his body and left it tingling.

Poupeye's chubby lips came closer. They moved. His voice whispered: "You're poisoning yourself with your craving for physicality."

The commissioner was taken by a vision. He was standing on the Pont Neuf looking down at the waters of the Seine made turbulent by an underground storm. He felt no wind, heard only a thin whistling sound in his head. The turrets of the palaces he could see from the bridge seemed to sway back and forth. The love he cherished for the city had been transformed into fear. His gaze was drawn to the water. It split in two before him as if Moses had struck the Pont Neuf with his staff. The waters rose on either side, and in the gulf between Lefèvre saw the woman in harem attire he had seen just before he fell. Now she was naked, with the exception of her veil. She was in a birthing chair, her legs wide open.

A wooden frame close to the chair housed a mechanical contraption with a long horizontal rod. An artificial penis was attached to the end of the rod, and in the commissioner's clouded mind it seemed larger than life. He blinked a couple of times. The bridge and the Seine disappeared and he found himself in a space that seemed vast and never-ending in spite of a vague presence of walls. Only the woman in the birthing chair and the mechanical contraption remained unaltered. The commissioner realized only then that the machine was driven by a clockwork mechanism.

There was something wrong with his perspective. Poupeye appeared next to the machine and suddenly everything seemed closer, almost within reach. Poupeye smiled at Lefèvre and pulled a lever. The artificial penis started to make jolting movements, driven by the moving cogs. Poupeye rolled the contraption closer to the woman until the penis touched her labia with every jolt. The woman writhed. The muscles on the insides of her thighs tensed. Poupeye pushed the machine even closer. The commissioner heard a stifled shriek, like the muffled cry of a bird behind a veil.

Lefèvre sensed lust take possession of his body, in spite of the circumstances. The poison that held him prisoner gradually focused his eyesight until his vision was almost unnatural. He saw how the woman's external labia had turned red and swollen. The machine pumped relentlessly. The woman pushed her hips forward with each jolt, insofar as the straps holding her would allow. The mechanical phallus stretched open her vulva. It was hard to tell if it brought pleasure or pain; probably both.

Poupeye stood next to Lefèvre. His odor reminded the commissioner of sour milk. He turned to Lefèvre with a bizarre twist of the neck. "The great Leopold Von Sacher-Masoch has to see this, don't you think, commissioner? He would doubtless praise my genius. His *Venus in Furs* would certainly have given even more perfect expression to the magnificence of sexual and moral slavery had he witnessed my invention." The Belgian leaned over Lefèvre. "The flesh of a woman always has something painful about it, don't you agree? When a woman reaches orgasm, the male of the species is inevitably reminded of the sweet pangs of childbirth."

The woman cried out, full of life, fear, pleasure.

The same cry as the murderous child in the *Kasbah*.

25

"Hebrew, Paul! The earliest form of Hebrew in an ancient Berber manuscript. What a surprising conclusion! No wonder the Arabs bore such ill-will toward the Berbers."

The heat was soporific and the air was abuzz with flies, but Bouveroux paid no attention. He looked at his lieutenant, expecting him to speak. Lefèvre cradled a cup of tea in his hands and stared out across the *Kasbah* of Algiers. He drew absently on an old black-wood *chibouque* pipe, which emitted puffs of pungent smoke, tobacco mixed with *hashish*. Since the lieutenant's escape from death in a mass grave and rescue in the nick of time by a French patrol as he wandered in the desert dying of thirst, a barely controllable psychosis had taken hold of him. He had refused the homeopathic phosphor pills Bouveroux carried with him wherever he went and preferred to smoke a local herb that quietened his mood.

In Bouveroux's sedate opinion the twenty-seven-year-old Lefèvre had a nervous character. He was a carthorse with the allure of a thoroughbred. Since the incident in the wadi, his friend and superior officer's behaviour had been curt and eccentric. Bouveroux was aware that such a confrontation with death could be a shock to the nervous system.

Many who had experienced this struggled with bouts of melancholy, interspersed with extreme aggressiveness. Bouveroux had seen enough soldiers undergo a similar transformation.

Lefèvre took the pipe from his mouth. "Centuries-old twaddle about the brothers of Jesus. Don't you have anything better to do with your free time, Bouveroux? Haven't you pinched enough old junk from local palaces?" He sounded grumpy, but Bouveroux knew his friend better than that. Lefèvre may not have shared his thirst for knowledge to the same degree, but he still had the inbuilt curiosity of a man with aspirations. His response had probably been inspired by the heat, their surroundings, the poor wine.

Although Algiers had acquired the air of a European hybrid city in a relatively short period of time, this part of the *Kasbah*, with its alleyways, windowless houses, slender pillars, horseshoe arches, capricious *muquarnas*, arabesques, geometric stripes and stars, was far from Western. The place radiated the kind of sensuality you found in hidden arbors and bathhouses. A couple of turbaned *hadji* passed their table. Their guttural speech, glowering faces, and robust gait were enough to make anyone sit with his back to the wall. The rigid turrets of the Turkish prison and the palace of the pasha who had conquered the city in the previous century towered above the local minarets.

"Would I be better off sweating it out in a hamam, lieutenant, and then submitting to the cooling favors of a belly dancer?" asked Bouveroux with a twinkle in his eye. "If you ask me, they've enough on their hands with you."

Lefèvre looked at his friend. He was sorry he had been so curt. In spite of his tender years, Bouveroux sometimes looked like an old hunting hound, but his sarcasm could be razor sharp at times and he could give as good as he got. Lefèvre laughed and was about to say something kind when a chicken tumbled, cackling and fluttering, from the yellow-tiled roof behind them and landed on top of the lieutenant. The broad-bladed knife that hung from Lefèvre's belt appeared in the blink of an eye. Cackling death rattle, fluttering feathers. The lieutenant peered upwards, brandishing his bloodstained weapon. An explosion of curses, laughter, and hilarity from the children on the roof.

"Don't get so wound up, Paul," said Bouveroux. "The children of *al-Jaza'ir* have always targeted us with their pranks, but they mean us no harm."

Two tiny figures in desert attire, unrecognizable in the swaths of cloth wrapped around their heads as protection against the wind, clattered down the stairs that led up to the roof of the whitewashed house behind them. Dark vivacious eyes glanced fleetingly in Lefèvre's direction. Their shrill voices reverberated against the walls of the narrow street. One of the children pointed a grubby finger at the robust lieutenant, as he slowly returned his knife to his belt.

"What are they saying, Bernard?" said Lefèvre stiffly.

Bouveroux had learned a little Arabic in the two years he had been in the country, in contrast to his friend who loathed the language. "That you're a ghost, or a demon, or something of that nature." He turned toward the children and tried to exchange a few words with them. The smaller of the two jumped forward and laughed. A knife appeared from his burnous, flew upwards in an arc, and landed with a thud in Bouveroux's belly. Lefèvre charged, but the children were too fast for him. They disappeared round the corner, their robes fluttering, then behind an oak door that slammed shut after them and only opened again when Lefèvre fired a couple of shots into it with his *carabine à tige*.

The lieutenant found himself in an abandoned courtyard. He shouted and screamed but no one came forward. He decided to return to his companion, and to his surprise he found a badly wounded man instead of a corpse. With blood frothing on his lips, Bouveroux whispered: "A girl. It was a girl."

26

THE YOUNG *H'ASHASHIN* SALEM AND Khalif, who had been sent by their chief to kill the escaped *kaffir*, knew the desert like the backs of their hands. They also knew how long they could push their well-fed and well-watered camels to the limit. But it took the best part of a day before they caught up with the runaway. He was visible against the red glow of the setting sun, a spot on the horizon engulfed in quivering heat, slowly disappearing behind the ridge of a dune.

The young Bedouins spurred their camels on. It would soon be dark and they would be forced to set up camp. They wanted to get back to their comrades as quickly as possible. The foreigner was alone, unarmed, and was probably without water. Maybe the desert would kill him without their help, but the command they had been given obliged them to cut the enemy's throat with their own *khanjar* and bring back his head as a trophy.

The runaway's camel wasn't far off. They could hear its exhausted rasping. They caught sight of it standing on the top of a dune and hurried toward it. When they reached the top of the hill they saw the Frenchman sitting on the ground, dressed in his coat and kepi, his head between his knees. He seemed to have given up. They jumped from their wooden saddles and treated their enemy to a barrage of insults. The spark from a tinderbox flashed in the night and the Frenchman's coat burst into flame.

Salem and Khalif were dumbstruck. The infidel preferred to die by fire than at the hand of his enemy. They could smell burning skin and they whooped with delight. They ran toward the fire and only then observed that the coat had been draped around a wooden saddle, the kepi on top. The Frenchman's leather belt gave off a smell of burning skin. A sharpened stake suddenly emerged from a pit next to the burning snare and punctured Khalif's genitals.

A half-naked figure, broad as an ape, rose from the sand with a savage roar and attacked Salem with a military dagger. Salem had his *khanjar* at the ready and might have managed to kill the exhausted lieutenant, half-crazed as he was from lack of fluids. But the Bedouin's superstitious fear of desert demons they called *djinns* made him recoil at the sight of his enemy's bulging eyes. The Frenchman's enormous body lunged at him and he lost his dagger. Lefèvre's fevered, encrusted, and brutish face was the last thing he saw.

$\boxed{27}$

THE INTOXICANT AFFECTED LEFÈVRE IN waves. It numbed his body, slowed his breathing, transformed colors and shapes, and jumbled past and present.

He saw things that astounded him: Poupeye had removed his bowler to reveal the hair of a woman. His moustache had disappeared. The Belgian seemed to fall victim to an intense but difficult to decipher emotional outburst.

"The mixture of opium, cocaine, and chloral hydrate inside you is most interesting, commissioner," he said. "It makes the world appear special, don't you think?" The creature gazed at her refined hands and then at her infantile feet. "My real appearance, commissioner, can excite a man. Some men like to dominate, don't they? They picture my childlike form groaning under their aggression. Are you perhaps thinking that my transformation is a result of the *Vin Mariani* I gave you to drink? Would you like to see my naked members? I assure you, I may be small and no longer young, but my body has always been alluring. There's only one detail that might make you lose your nerve. Don't worry, it's still out of sight."

Lefèvre tried to speak. He heard the cackle of birds and then the growl of an animal, dull and gurgling, as if his head was under water.

"Are you in pain?" asked Poupeye. The tiny hand he placed on Lefèvre's left shoulder caused an unpleasant sensation of pressure and warmth. "Your pain is nothing compared to the pain I have lived with all my life. I was given opium as a youth against horrendous *grand mal* convulsions that plagued me at unexpected moments. Then laudanum, and later coca leaf extract—remedies that became my friends and my weapons. I mixed the green fairy with the juices of other plants and added granules of opium. I tracked down people who had visited the Far West and brought back the sap of the cactus the redskins call *peyote*. It opens doors to other worlds. I've seen natives in the Orient kill with powerful poisons, and I improved on their concoctions with my own skills."

The words jarred in Lefèvre's skull.

"People mocked my body when I was young. They called me a bitch, a she-devil, and worse, looked at me with barely concealed revulsion." Poupeye stroked his ash-blond hair. "Can you imagine such an existence, commissioner? My only comfort was to be found in the splendor of books, the wisdom of words birthed by pain and suffering, which resonated with the artistic talent in my blood."

Poupeye's left hand gravitated toward his undershirt and opened it. Lefèvre saw breasts that still exuded the frailty of an immature girl. "Look at me, commissioner. I'm forty-nine years old, but I have the skin of a young woman. See how beautiful I am. Shall I tease you with my nakedness, like the *cocottes* who help you flounder through your sleepless nights?"

The tiny woman pulled open her man's breeches to reveal ladies' underwear, which she routinely pulled to her knees. She stood in front of Lefèvre in a position most women would find humiliating, but her diminutive body radiated a self-conscious pride nonetheless. The commissioner followed the gentle undulations of her belly and was surprised, in spite of his situation, that she seemed so young for her age.

He blinked. Something shimmered between her legs. It seemed to move. It had to be the intoxicant she had given him.

"When I see you walk and sway
"Exquisite your surrender
"I visualise a serpent gay
"A rod and yet so tender."

Poupeye's words were like a charm, as if every letter of the rhyme had been lived to the extreme. Lefèvre only realized that his eyes were closed, hypnotized by the legato rhythm of the verse, when the woman rested her hand on his shoulder. She was completely dressed. She sounded angry. "Have you appreciation for beauty, commissioner? Are you a man with a refined intellect and a taste for the aesthetic? No, you're nothing better than a common pig, intent on possessing beauty in order to destroy it. For that reason alone you deserve to die."

Poupeye's right hand appeared, holding a dagger. Lefèvre tried to close his eyes, but only half succeeded. Shadows rippled back and forth, one of them looming up behind Poupeye. He heard a muffled thud and tried to understand what was going on, but to no avail. It was as if he was in a coffin deep under the ground, which dampened every sound and made it difficult to breathe. He felt something glide over him, so cold it seemed to burn. The muscles in his neck bulged as he tried to scream. All at once he became aware of the tension and exhaustion in his body and feeling returned to his limbs. A spasm of nausea filled his mouth with bile.

When he looked up, dizzy and with a sour taste in his mouth, Poupeye had gone. Lefèvre found an envelope on his own exposed belly.

28

BOUVEROUX SIPPED ABSENTLY AT HIS St. Galmier water, which he had mixed with some manganese preparations on the recommendation of an alternative healer who knew more about human health than the ordinary doctors he had been consulting for years in search of a cure for his obstinate stomach pain. His intestines had never quite recovered from the knife wound to the belly he had sustained in Algiers twenty-five years earlier.

The inspector looked pale and bloated. His sideburns glistened with sweat. His office at the police headquarters of the *Département de la Seine* was cramped and dated. There had been renewed disorder on the streets of Paris that morning after a rumor had spread that Nohant had been stricken by a smallpox epidemic and that the refugees who had reached the capital ahead of the Prussians had brought the deadly disease with them. The police and the National Guard had only managed to disperse the rebellious rabble with the greatest of difficulty. It was time for the French to join forces and defeat the Prussians at the Loire, but instead they were at each other's throats. "Police everywhere, justice nowhere!" *Victor Hugo can say what he likes*, Bouveroux thought, *but he'll be singing a different tune when the swelling horde of malcontents, who have no idea where their next meal is coming from, decides it's time to turn against the folk with the money in their pockets who stubbornly maintain their unassailability.* "Then," Bouveroux muttered to himself, "Mr. Hugo will thank God for the presence of a well-trained police force."

When he caught sight of the commissioner crossing the inner courtyard of the prefecture, he felt the pressure in his stomach intensify. He had known for an age that his stomach was more sensitive to moods than his brain. When the commissioner marched into his subordinate's office, it was immediately clear that he had had a heavy night. His cheeks were red and veined. His checked trousers didn't match his dark overcoat, which he had buttoned carelessly. The cocked hat on his head looked as if it hadn't been dusted for a very long time. The commissioner gasped greedily for air as if he was on the verge of flying into a rage. But one look at his eyes was enough for Bouveroux to know that he wasn't angry.

Lefèvre looked as Bouveroux had found him long ago in the military field hospital in Ouargla, covered in sand bug bites, blistered by the sun, a dehydrated skeleton gulping mouthfuls of air. After a week the beanpole could talk; after three weeks Lefèvre told him his story, his voice still hoarse, how he had survived by drinking the blood of lizards he had outwitted between the cactuses.

"Commissioner," said Bouveroux. "Paul, I have news about . . ."

"Later, Bernard," said Lefèvre absently. He had an old-fashioned logbook with him, the kind sailors sometimes used. He stared at it constantly as if he found it hard to believe he was holding the thing in his hand.

The inspector jumped to his feet behind his desk. "The unidentified victim in the Rue Mouffetard is one of the Baudelaire killings, commissioner. And there's more!"

"Very true," said Lefèvre. His subordinate's words seemed to have difficulty getting through to him. "There's always more. And that, my dear Bouveroux, is because everyone is a liar, including myself. I experienced something extraordinary last night, Bernard. Past and present melted into one. I tasted anew the blood I drank in the desert and I saw my black soul in the guise of a dwarf."

Lefèvre noticed the shocked expression on his colleague's face and smiled. He caught a glimpse of himself in the mirror beside the coat stand. Only part of his face was visible. It reminded him of the fleshy features, stubbly beard, and broad nose of his uncle Jean-Paul Lefèvre, sixty-eight years old and still being nursed by the Sisters of Charity in a mental home near Lunéville. As a twelve-year-old, Lefèvre had been scared to death of the giant of a man, sitting in a chair, his hands dangling between his knees, his hair trimmed short, his eyes like those of a vicious dog that could bite at any moment. His uncle's wrists and ankles had been chained to the chair, which was in turn fastened to the floor. He wore a wooden mask over his mouth to prevent him from biting himself in one of his rage attacks.

Or from biting someone else.

"Paul," said Bouveroux, "I have good reason to believe that the corpse in the Rue Mouffetard is the photographer who took the picture we found on Deputy Pinard. He sold himself as a medium who could make 'ghosts' appear on photographic plates. Our murderous Baudelaire buff clearly wanted to erase his tracks."

He had expected Lefèvre to be surprised, but the commissioner did nothing more than lift his left hand with the logbook and let it fall to his side once again. "A Baudelaire buff, Bernard? Or a rejected mistress? Or more? The key to the puzzle, my dear Bouveroux, is always concealed in the blood. That, too, I remembered last night when the Algerian desert, where I was a murderer, and La Meurthe, the river at which banks my sister was murdered, seemed to melt together before my mind's eye."

29

THE ALGERIAN SUN MADE WAY for La Meurthe in the autumn wind, the surging, eddying waters of his youth that still pursued him. In a corner of his mind, Lefèvre knew that the desert was turning him blind or mad, probably both. He had put on the burnous he had taken from one of the dead Bedouins. At the barracks or the military hospitals you could always take refuge in the shade of the tents or buildings when the light hurt your eyes. But here the desert was flat as a table. Shade was out of the question. The camel he was riding was exhausted. The creature was ready to give up the ghost at any minute. Its humps had shrunk beyond recognition and its head hung low.

The vision of the river that had had such an influence on his childhood faded in and out. Lefèvre shook his head like a badgered bulldog. When his father taught him to wrestle he had insisted that he should never show pain: "You can learn to live with all the horrors life throws at you, boy, except your own cowardice."

The two water flasks on the saddle reminded him of his father's words. He had panicked when he realised that one of his attackers' camels had run away, startled by the flames and the fight. The creature had probably been carrying his pursuers' water supply. The harness of the remaining camel only had a couple of flasks attached to it, and they were two-thirds empty.

He had filled them by mixing the remaining water with the blood of his dead enemies, drained from the arteries in their necks. The first time he took a drink of the concoction he retched, but now he had to stop himself from draining the remaining flask to the last drop. He was obsessed with the idea that the blood would clot because it hadn't been mixed with enough water. He constantly shook the remaining flask to check it, but even then he was afraid that too much shaking would speed up the coagulation process.

His crazy uncle Jean-Paul had been a blood drinker. At least that was what Lefèvre believed, after being plagued incessantly in his youth by the other children in the village who had picked up shreds of gossip about what his uncle had done. They quickly learned to fear his attacks of rage. At a safe distance they would jeer at him, adding that Lefèvre was also a *loup-garou* and that they would lock him up one day in a windowless room with a wooden mask over his face.

Paul Lefèvre took a gulp from his flask. The bloody water triggered an unhappy memory. The clouds of dust on the horizon became the forests of his youth on the banks of La Meurthe. The face he saw was that of his sister Hélène as she looked at her reflection in its waters on a misty October morning.

"I read a fairytale last night, Paul. It was so beautiful, so sad."

"Come with me, sister. I'm going to the timber merchant. I'll show you how I can lift a tree trunk as thick as two men."

"All you think about is being strong, Paul. Girls are different."

"If you're strong, no one can hurt you."

"A strong heart is what you need. Then no one can harm you. That's what the fairytale about the girl with no hands says."

"A girl with no hands? Was she born that way? Like cross-eyed Louis, one of the Martières from behind the mill?"

"No. She's a princess. But her father wanted to marry her."

"Don't talk nonsense, Hélène. A king is supposed to marry a queen, not his daughter."

"The queen died and the king insisted on marrying the princess."

"But that's . . . that's not allowed!"

"The princess refused, and her father was so angry he had both of her hands chopped off. He then tried to drown her in the moat surrounding the palace. The princess begged to be allowed to die a normal death and not be left to drown in the moat. Her father obliged and locked her up in the tower. At night she dreamt that two angelic hands opened the door of her cell, and when she woke the door was open. She slipped out of the palace unnoticed and fled to a neighbouring land where she later married the king. He loved her in spite of her missing hands, but when she bore him a prince, the handsomest child in the entire country, her mother-in-law became jealous and she was forced to flee yet again."

"What a life. Lucky it's only a fairytale."

"She became a beggar, but she never lost her kind heart. People felt sorry for her and gave her food to eat. One day she met a couple of beggars who had nothing and she gave them two loaves."

"Without hands?"

"They were in the knapsack she used to carry her baby. There was a river not far from the place, as wild as the Meurthe. She leaned down to drink, but because she had no hands to scoop up the water she had to bend very deeply. At that her baby fell into the water, but he was rescued by two men."

"The beggars?"

"No. The loaves of bread had come to life."

"That's impossible!"

"But that's what happened. The loaves had souls, and because the princess had given them away to help others they came to life, saved her child, and used their magic powers to restore the princess's hands."

"You made it all up, sis, admit it."

Her face was so open, so clear, so pure, against the background of the Château des Lumières as they passed.

There was a long silence.

"Paul?"

"Yes."

"Will I die a normal death?"

"Why do you ask?"

"I think a normal death is a sweet death."

"I've no idea. I don't even want to think about it. I don't want to die. Not ever!"

Another long silence followed and then: "Brother?"

"Yes."

"Will you marry me one day?"

30

MONSIEUR DUFET POUTED AND ADJUSTED the ridiculously old-fashioned monocle in his right eye. "Commissioner, I'm not accustomed to spying on my tenants."

Bouveroux wanted to urge the man to show more respect for the servants of the law. Aware of what Lefèvre had been through the evening before, the inspector had an inkling that the commissioner wasn't going to beat about the bush.

"Of course not, Monsieur Dufet," said Lefèvre in an affable tone. "But with your exceptional sagacity and judgment of character, I'm sure you can provide a sketch of your tenant to help us trace him. He was Belgian, you said?"

"Indeed, a dwarf-like creature, with a business in exotic attributes," said Dufet. "He paid cash, six months' in advance. With the way things are these days . . ." The landlord raised a single eyebrow. He reminded Bouveroux of a shrew with his pointed nose and his tiny eyes too close together. He looked around. An empty warehouse. But if Lefèvre was to be believed, only the day before it had looked like a scene from *One Thousand and One Nights*.

"An address! Surely you have an address or some kind of identity card," Bouveroux barked. Lefèvre lost interest in the landlord and walked through the room shaking his head. Dufet stretched like a cock about to crow and assured the inspector that he had no reason whatsoever to ask for an address when a gentleman paid six months' rent in advance. Or was the police officer unaware that the country was at war? That people were starving on the streets of Paris?

Lefèvre bent down.

"What were you planning to do when the six months were over?" Bouveroux snapped.

Dufet was taken aback for a moment and muttered something like "word of honor". He quickly recovered. He would have visited the tenant and encouraged him to pay anew. Bouveroux could smell victory. Had Dufet perhaps been given extra money to keep his mouth shut?

Before he could press his point, Lefèvre grabbed his shoulder. "We've no further business here," said the commissioner. There was clarity in his eyes. His lips were pressed shut.

Once outside, Bouveroux found it hard to conceal his irritation. "If he'd given you an address it would have been false, Bernard," said the commissioner. "Someone like Poupeye is a master of illusion and disguise. His performance last night was breathtaking. Today he's the perfect Indian fakir. They say they can make an elephant disappear with a wave of the hand."

Bouveroux was about to speak but the commissioner beat him to it: "Magicians are like that," he said. "They focus on the big picture, but sometimes they forget the details."

He opened his left hand to reveal a piece of broken glass. The red wine that the glass had contained had left a freakish stain.

31

THE COMMISSIONER TOOK A FAMILIAR route through the city that evening. He was armed, his weapon concealed under his coat, but he still looked over his shoulder, first left and then right. A tête-à-tête with Claire de la Lune would relieve his unease. Lefèvre walked down the *Grand Cours*, which people had been calling the *Champs-Elysées* of late after a recently restored palace in which Napoleon III liked to throw festive dinners.

Almost all of Paris was aware that Louis-Napoleon Bonaparte spent most of his nights drunk and rubbing it up with perfumed ladies who had been ordered to mimic his wife Eugénie de Montijo to the best of their ability. They had to have the same flaming red hair as the strong-willed empress, her perfect white skin, the same color of eyes, and the Spanish accent. They also had to share her haughty disposition which, according to Napoleon III, "could dismember a man like a filleting knife". Rumour had it that the emperor deeply humiliated each of the carefully selected *cocottes* as an act of revenge against his consort. He took the greatest pleasure in pissing on them while they listened to a tirade of insults. The commissioner snorted. A country that was proud of the infantile bedroom antics of its emperor didn't deserve to be Europe's leading nation.

He was carrying a cashmere scarf in his right hand, decorated with weird and wonderful motifs from the exotic animal and plant world and cut according to the latest trends. The expensive three-quarter-length coat that went with it had a cape and batwing sleeves. He was sure Claire de la Lune was going to love it. As his feet automatically followed the route he had taken so often in recent months, he thought about Bouveroux, who was now reading the diary entries that had been left behind in the envelope on his belly. Tomorrow the inspector would know more about the capricious killer they had been investigating. Perhaps even be able to identify him.

But would they ever be able to find him? Lefèvre doubted it. When he'd returned to his room, still dizzy from the poison that had crippled his nervous system, and read the words on the envelope—identical at a glance with the verses that had been left behind on the victims—he had the feeling that he was being confronted with an ancient secret: *The artist stems only from himself. His own works are the only promises that he makes to the coming centuries. He stands security only for himself. He dies childless. He has been his own king, his own priest, his own God.*[7]

The words had focused his mind, as if Baudelaire had been standing behind him whispering in his ear that the killer was king, priest, and God all in one.

As he turned the last corner on his way to Claire's lodgings, the hairs on the back of the commissioner's neck suddenly stood to attention. The memory of Bouveroux ranting and raving in his hospital bed in Sidi Abbes as he struggled with desert fever appeared unannounced in his thoughts. His friend's story had settled in fragments, like sharp rocks at the bottom of a dry well. Bouveroux had told him about the latest parchment he had confiscated and that it spoke of lowly spirits that could take hold of human beings. He had told him how to recognise them: shiny metallic eyes darting left and right, a barely perceptible aura of *darkness* surrounding them, a dramatic, overwrought, almost *seething* eloquence. The commissioner was reminded of his uncle Jean-Paul, and all at once he was the boy behind his father's back, peering at the muzzled manacled maniac and listening to the murmurings of the grown-ups around him: *rants, raves, speaks in tongues.*

The shiny eyes, the hunger in his uncle's gaze as it met his own, prompting him to hide his face behind his father's broad shoulders.

The following day, the young Lefèvre had visited the village cemetery and placed a couple of loaves on a grave. He had waited there, long and motionless. When he finally left his eyes were dry, but anyone watching would have been left with the impression that his chubby, awkward frame had an aura of darkness about it.

The memory made Lefèvre shiver. Or was it because Poupeye's shiny metallic eyes had flashed across his mind, forcing him to wonder why he hadn't noticed the *family resemblance* before?

Lefèvre took a deep breath and looked up at the facades and doorways he had passed so many times without paying them the least attention. Tonight they seemed to herald imminent catastrophe.

Moments later, the commissioner stood at the door to Claire de la Lune's lodgings. It was closed. He knocked, but no one answered. His heart skipped a beat. He threw open the door. The room was empty, like Dufet's rented warehouse. Lefèvre could hear the blood pounding in his veins.

He hurried downstairs in a temper and lurched across the courtyard. At that moment a figure appeared behind the murky window of Claire's lodgings. Without looking back Lefèvre made his way through the entrance and onto the street. A strip of light from a streetlamp lit up the window.

A pale face, its eyes encircled with dark stains, watched him depart.

32

Death in my mother tongue is feminine.
She alone in the world has no mother.
Death has no mother, but countless children.
I am her favourite.

—⚬⚬⚬—

I first killed for him in Mauritania, at the hour when the scorpions go
hunting. I had observed him on a journey across a sea as capricious
as the fates. He frequently stood by the rails, deep in thought. He was
twenty-two, but his heart was already old, his hair unkempt. Vertical
wrinkles between his upper lip and his nose suggested sensitivity, and
a sensual character. There was something curious about his eyes: they
reflected their surroundings with a mercurial sheen. I saw the same eyes
when I looked in the mirror. I was afraid he might notice, but he paid
no attention to me. He was dressed as a dandy, but his movements were
stiff and wooden. I saw the child in him, intent on bending the world
to his will, yet cringing at the bark of an unseen dog.

I tried to be as unobtrusive as I could, although I knew that my diminutive figure and my habit would draw questions on board, behind my back. But my story was considered and plausible. In Paris I had had the opportunity to play many a character over the years, but the nun was my favorite. This time I was travelling to my congregation in Senegal where my sisters spread the Sacred Word of Christ and tended the sick natives with their horrendous diseases. During the long, dreary dinners at the captain's table, which tempted everyone present to reveal things they would be less likely to reveal under normal circumstances, I had told the captain that the Ursuline order had been charged by the pope with the task of converting the black Moors, or the Harratin as they called themselves, who lived in the Senegal valley. The captain inquired politely whether we also planned to introduce the nomad Harratin to the rules of etiquette and personal hygiene.

I smiled coyly at my plate. Charles Baudelaire was sitting opposite me, next to the captain. I noticed out of the corner of my eye that he was looking at me with interest, something he had not done before. When the captain inquired about the reason for his journey, he answered with his characteristically insecure impudence that his stepfather had forced him to visit Mauritius the year before. This time he had opted for Mauritania on his own initiative, "because of the magic of the parallel names, which is of such importance for a poet, and to strengthen my nerves."

I had shadowed him in Paris for years before the journey. Now I was sitting opposite him, peering at him from the corner of my eye. The proud melancholy that surrounded him like a cloak cut my heart in two. I wanted to hurt him and watch him glory in it. I wanted to be his beloved, to share his blood, to die with him.

Some loves are inexplicable and cruel and are made from the stuff of dreams.

———⚬⚬⚬———

Oualata was a collection of red clay houses that looked like termite hills, with here and there a couple of dilapidated colonial structures, all of it overshadowed by the French fort. It was said that the harmattan, the blistering north-easterly wind that plagued the region, turned the inhabitants of the former trade crossroads insane at given moments. The water sellers commended their wares all day long and half the night. Water was an expensive commodity and had to be brought in from the south to fill the scarce wells. People in the neighbourhood were known to murmur jealously about the Senegal River bursting its banks at regular intervals. Such an overabundance of water was like a fairytale in Oualata with its gruelling heat, drifting sands, and swarming locusts. The Ursulines ran the fort's military hospital and took care of the French occupying forces, as well as the local population.

After my arrival in the harbour of Nouadhibou I had cast aside my nun's attire. When I bumped into Baudelaire "accidentally" on one of Oualata's narrow streets and started a conversation, I was a man and I introduced myself as the Belgian Poupeye, supplier of provisions to the French forces. He seemed feverish and ascetic. I hoped that my small stature would not remind him of the nun onboard the ship. My talent is such that I can change my face, voice, and movements at will, but there is nothing I can do about my height. He showed no signs of recognition or suspicion.

I preferred not to wait for a more appropriate moment and simply invited him there and then to join me for tea in a nearby teahouse. As was the custom in Oualata, we asked after the owner's wife and children and praised Allah. The tea was powerfully sweet and loosened our tongues. I asked him, half in jest, half serious, if he was a fortune hunter who had come to search for El Dorado under Mauritania's desert sands.

He looked at me, unruffled. "I am a poet, and I'm here to find out what sort of influence places where life is close to unbearable will have on my emotions. I want to know how sensitive I am. A sensitive *disposition is essential for a poet. I believe one must stimulate and challenge such a disposition in order to achieve great things."*

I tried not to appear curious, but he seemed ready to talk about his life. Shortly afterwards, I learned that he had demanded his share of the family fortune from his stepfather and now enjoyed a more than comfortable lifestyle.

"We share the same age, but I fear my family background is much simpler," I said ingratiatingly. "If I had your financial means, I would prefer to stimulate my sensitivities in a different fashion and in another place."

He sipped pensively at his tea. "You don't understand. I experienced the stimulation of which you speak on another journey, with an ebony-skinned woman. But I dreamt about this place and it left me feeling that I should follow my fate, that I had no choice."

"People who follow their fate tend to be romantics."

He shrugged his shoulders. "Two years ago my stepfather insisted I visit the tropics. He thought it would bring me to my senses and rid me of my 'bad manners'."

I laughed. "Something tells me he was amiss."

He didn't smile. "I met a quadroon, three parts negro, one part white, a creature of exquisite chocolate and dangerous panther's blood, with teeth like ivory, and eyes that can steal a man's soul. She was a demon, and that suited me. But the place was too luxuriant, too wild and explosive for my liking. The vegetation on Mauritius clouded my senses, stood in the way of my inspiration, robbed me of my edge."

"May I ask what you're looking for exactly?"

His eyelids were slow and there was something mocking in his gestures, as if the world was beneath him. We were the same age, but he seemed older than me on the outside, and inside he was an angry insecure child.

"I'm looking for the devil, good sir."

The harmattan hissed outside, its clouds of dust crashing against the facades.

I tilted my teacup in salute. "Then you've come to the right place."

33

LEFÈVRE WANDERED AIMLESSLY THROUGH THE streets of the city. He had a vague awareness of where this mental state was likely to lead: first a copious dinner at Restaurant Widermann—the Lorrainer who owned the place could do wonders with a bit of pastry, lard, and marinated game; then a foray into the red light district in search of a fight; and then, if he was still up to it, a street whore.

The commissioner didn't want to be reminded of the unexpected thought that had scurried across his mind when he opened the door to Claire's lodgings and found them empty: *Just like Poupeye's disappearance, as if she was his pupil.*

Back on the street, stiff-jawed, having seen no sign of the concierge of the building Claire lived in, an anxious melancholy suddenly overwhelmed him, followed by astonishment, rage, abandonment, an array of emotions too numerous to name.

His feet had brought him to Saint Germain, past the Pont des Arts. He turned left into the Rue Bonaparte. The fountain in the middle of the square was dimly lit by a lonely gaslight the city authorities had left burning while all the others had been extinguished to save fuel. The water was pale grey, like a fragment of a mildewed mirror. A group of men were gathered around a cart and a couple of horses. The cart was loaded with pot-bellied barrels. The men combined forces to lift them one by one from the cart and empty their contents into the fountain.

The commissioner saw flashes of silver in the water. He had heard that groups of volunteers had been filling the fountains of Paris with fish of late in an effort to combat hunger in the city. One of the men turned toward him as he approached. When he realized it was Lefèvre, he stepped back and looked away, revealing the black forked scar on his left cheek. Lefèvre recognised the young, aristocratic *franc-tireur* with the scar on his face and knew that his fight had been lined up even before supper.

34

THOSE IN SEARCH OF THE devil usually turn first to God, albeit in vain. Those who loudly proclaim that God's moral demands are hard and severe, and parade their own virtues for all to see, tend to be concealing a cesspit deeper than any lover of licentiousness. The first people who taught me this lesson in life were the Ursulines.

As an infant, when the only thing about me that stood out was my tiny frame, I slept in the monastery infirmary on the Boulevard Péreire. Later, when I was about seven, when my weak nervous system started to manifest itself and the nuns were convinced I "spoke in evil tongues," I was confined for a while to a cell underneath the kitchen. That's where I learned to imitate and to hide my true nature. None of the sisters dared breathe a word about the physical deformity that had placed such a heavy toll on my life.

All except Sister Wolf. I called her Sister Wolf because of the constant hunger in her face, her throaty voice, and breath that stank of sulphur. She was obsessed with God and saw evil wherever she looked. Especially in me. I had been in the orphanage for ten years or so by that time and I had begun to realize that I wasn't the same as the other orphan girls.

There's something liberating about looking back at my extraordinary life thirty years later and dividing it into episodes. The moderns, with the *affected Flaubert in front, claim that everything is chaos, contradiction, and transience. But I am in need of clarity and explanation, because my mind is still gripped at given moments by a terrible cramp that wipes everything out and turns my body to stone.*

At such moments I feel as if someone or something has taken possession of me.

For Charles, the devil was the great seducer. I see him as a surreptitious tyrant who settles in your head without permission, comes and goes when he sees fit. Poets portray the devil as something grandiose, but that's not how he really is.

The devil does his work in secret.

When my womanhood started to develop, around my twelfth year, the nuns set me apart when the time came for bathing. The other orphan girls whispered behind my back that I was some kind of animal and not human. I asked Sister Rat, who was small and slight like me, why I was different and why my mother had rejected me. She looked away, told me that God was testing me, and scurried off. Sister Rat also crept into bed of a night with one of the girls. It never took long before her high-pitched gasps and shrieks could be heard throughout the dormitory.

The night was my domain, my classroom, and I quickly learned that Sister Rat's nocturnal naughtiness was pretty normal and hardly worth mentioning. The monastery had declared the human body taboo, but life wasted little time in teaching me that opposites attract. The orphan girls learned from each other and from the cook, who opened her legs with a smile every week for the butcher and the baker, louts with flared nostrils and hairy armpits. Boys and men were the subject of whispered conversations, and then the others would point at me, stare at me sideways, and giggle.

They made my curiosity all the greater. Our shortcomings, after all, breed our most powerful desires. Apart from my body, the uniqueness of which I was slowly beginning to realize, I was fortunate enough to have an inquisitive mind. And fate, in the person of my stepfather, saw to it that I was given an education not usually set aside for girls.

During the day we were taught how to sew and cook. The idea was that the better products of the orphanage might manage to hook themselves a hardworking grocer, or a butcher, or a boilermaker. Napoleon III had declared the tradesfolk the backbone of France. Furious protests from the upper middle class and the aristocracy forced him to swallow his words, but the Ursulines knew from experience that tradesmen were their best "customers."

During the day the nuns would pull their veils over their faces and speak in gentle tones. But the darkness revealed their true personalities. I was charged with helping Sister Wolf in the infirmary, and I got to know her better there during the hours of night. When fever drove the sick to lift their nightshirts and toss back their blankets, Jesus would send her visions. She growled about him penetrating her innards with his light-giving dagger and cutting her to shreds.

I didn't understand what she meant at first. But every human being is an animal with inherited instincts. In spite of my disgust for what Sister Wolf did in her moments of ecstasy—or perhaps because of my disgust—it didn't take long before I started to experience a tension below the navel, a trembling, the glow of a distant fire.

<hr />

One evening I pictured for myself the light-giving dagger of Jesus and imagined what I would do if I were to see Him. A fear both savage and inviting slowly took hold of me. My body convulsed. The dormitory was aglow with a thousand points of light. I arched my back. My fingers gravitated intuitively to the organ I was never allowed to show to others. The crucified Saviour hovered before me in my mind's eye, surrounded by all the naked demons my imagination could muster. A swirling turmoil and commotion possessed me. Then a ripple of warmth ran through my body, beyond description, my muscles tensed and contorted, my breath stopped. I was about to die.

Living on the street among poisoners, thieves, and whores later taught me to accept physical pleasure as one of the things that makes life bearable.

But deep in my heart I will always associate it with the moment at which the insanity I call the Other revealed itself in all its glory. I've shared my bed with many men and women since then, but they've never been able to equal the rod of Christ and how it set me ablaze.

I felt the same when I lay in the arms of Charles Baudelaire in a houri hammam in Oualata and observed in his eyes that he could see the Other crouched beneath my flesh.

⁕⟨◎⟩⁕

My flesh. How can I describe the horror and shame I felt as I gradually came to realize that I was different? I'm left at a loss, even now, when I think back to those days. The memory fills me with an all-consuming desire for revenge.

In spite of my pleasant physical appearance, all I can remember is the other orphan girls calling me "little bitch" and similarly charming names. I belonged to the lowest category of human refuse, all the more because I had been placed with the abandoned children when I was delivered to the monastery. My companions in misfortune liked to say that I had been "found on a pile of manure." Following Ursuline tradition, a dictionary was thrown open at random on my arrival and the first word was taken as my name.

Was it fate's cruelty or sense of humor that gave me the name Simone Bourbier? No wonder the other girls shouted "quagmire" at me.

Simone Bourbier was not allowed to undress. Simone Bourbier was to be washed by the novices, who went about their task with red-faced revulsion. At set times Simone Bourbier felt her entire body shudder, a sign that her tongue was about to twist and her lips foam.

What kept such a miserable creature alive?

Reading and dreaming. Because of my background and the special status I enjoyed in the monastery, I was able to indulge both.

I was unaware that my mother was paying for my education. I only learned about it later when my stepfather started to visit me in secret. He told me why I had been exempted from the household duties the other girls had to perform and why the sisters gave me books and tutored me. That only made my companions even more merciless than before in their abuse, and they would pinch and kick me whenever they got the chance. They had to learn to sew, iron, or make lace, while I was sent to my cell and to my books.

The moments I spent with my books were worth the humiliation. As I read, an invisible hand would ladle me out of my accursed body as if it was a bowl of soup. I was alone with the Word that seemed to have come down from heaven to set me free. I remember the books of Prosper Mérimée with particular relish. They enkindled a longing in me to travel and to study foreign peoples. I devoured his Notes de Voyage and dreamt of travelling to a distant land in search of happiness.

I asked for more books by the same author and I received them. My stepfather was later to explain that my mother would give them to her servant girl when she sent her to pay my monthly account. One of the books was La Guzla, a collection of traditional poetry from the mysterious Herzegovina. The verses opened my eyes to the person I really was: a Lokis, a child born of the union between a bear and a woman.

When I finished the book, I looked around. It was a warm, musty evening. I was all alone, surrounded by the arid smell of books that reminded me of insects.

I lifted my blue orphan-girl skirt and felt around: I was a Lokis in my own way. At that moment Sister Wolf barged into my room. I instantly let go of my skirt, but I could tell from the way she looked at me that she suspected something.

I had learned in the meantime that Sister Rat chose the prettiest and most docile orphan girls to stimulate her bodily ecstasies, while Sister Wolf sought the perverse, the shock of deviation, to help her reach communion with her beloved son of God.

$$\boxed{35}$$

LEFÈVRE LAY ON THE COBBLESTONES close to L'Arche du Diable with his arms around a tree as if he was in love with it. He could still hear the clip-clop of hooves on the street, laughter, shreds of sentences: *An officer of justice in a land without justice . . . Fought like a savage . . . Respect . . .* Then the fleshy thud as they'd tossed him out of the cart.

Lefèvre could smell the Seine, which seemed more and more like an open sewer every day, full of factory filth and the grime discharged by the ships that carried their cargoes to the four corners of the world.

His bones ached. Lefèvre tried to get to his feet, held on to the tree as if it was a lifebuoy, waited until the nausea in his stomach had settled, and then shook his head like a dog trying to shake off an irritating fly.

He felt miserable, but the storm in his head had subsided. Women couldn't be trusted, especially whores. Claire de la Lune was worth ten women. So, he would screw twenty, and he would do it tonight, in spite of the twinges of pain in his chest.

The massive vaulted pillars of the L'Arche du Diable that bridged the Seine seemed to be on the point of keeling over and falling on top of him. He blinked. The beating he had taken from the *franc-tireurs* had had a strange effect on his eyes: the bridges crossing the Seine had turned a pale shade of grey, the gas lamps into blinding stars with halos of light, and the water into an enormous, heaving, gritty mass.

The sound of horses made him turn around. The cart that was coming toward him was full of barrels. Lefèvre hurried to his feet, his legs trembling, straightened his undershirt and picked up his hat. Where was his cane?

He held up his balled fist and stood his ground, stony-faced. But he heaved a sigh of relief nonetheless when he realized that only the young man with the scar and another with wavy hair were still in the cart. Six *franc-tireurs* had been a bit much, but he could handle two, no problem at all.

"So you're up for a fight?" the older man jeered when he caught sight of Lefèvre's hostile stance. "I was just saying to my young comrade in arms here that it made no sense to come back. But he was afraid that the absinthe and the terrible things he had told us about you might have caused us to exaggerate a little when we took you on."

The young man with the aristocratic appearance smiled. "Don't believe a word he says, sir. I bet my friend Ferdinand here that you would be back on your feet and ready for another fight."

"And Henri was right. Frenchmen fighting Frenchmen? Is there anything more idiotic? But try to look at it as a selection procedure, sir: After a good fight we know that a man like you shouldn't be wasting his time in the service of our pathetic government and its puppet emperor. He would be better off with us, because in his heart he shares our ideals." The man with the wavy hair laughed so heartily that Lefèvre's stiff lips slowly curled into a smile.

A high-pitched whistle, followed by a loud rumble.

The Prussians had started to shell the city.

36

I WONDER HOW OTHER PEOPLE look back at their younger years. Mine was filled with half-truths, painful desires, and contradictory illusions. The world around me was shrouded in mystery. A man wasn't a creature of flesh and blood but a symbol to which I would have to subject myself sooner or later. I wasn't really sure what that meant, since I had only witnessed love and hatred between women. Fancy fairytales about kings and princesses made the rounds in the monastery. They often ended in mutilation and trickery.

Those who cut themselves off from the world create their own universe. In hindsight, my universe was more malevolent than the goriest Parisian backstreet, as I was to learn later.

On a restless and miserable winter night, a fourteen-year-old street girl who had come knocking on the monastery door a month earlier and heavily pregnant gave birth in the infirmary. Sister Wolf was the midwife. I still don't know why she insisted I help, but I have my suspicions. For the first time in my life I saw the genitals of another woman and understood more or less what was wrong with me.

When the baby's soiled head appeared, Sister Wolf hissed that this was the work of "the devil's string." As the mother lay exhausted and bleeding on the bed and Sister patted the baby dry, she asked me if it wouldn't be better to offer the child to Jesus. Then its soul would remain untarnished and it would ascend to heaven. She thought my mother should have done the same.

Sister Wolf turned to me. "But no, she let you live, in spite of your satanic tail."

I was holding a pair of scissors in my hand. I'm not sure if Sister Wolf noticed them trembling. She turned her back to me as if to say: Do what you must. I chose another way. I bowed my head and started to cry, gently, as befits a pious young girl.

I heard her habit rustle. Felt her hand. And heard her breath falter.

⚬⚬⚬

I was almost fourteen, but the orphan girls had taught me with their cruel cunning to give the impression I was entirely genuine. Inside I was crafty, and I could tell people's real intentions by reading the subtle physical signs they gave. After that night in the infirmary, Sister Wolf treated me with a mixture of disdain and sympathy, and with a pinch of fear. We were often alone together and I tried patiently to unravel her inner spiritual life. When she talked about the allurements of Satan, her breath would accelerate, her voice deepen, and she would peer into the corners of whatever room we were in.

And, obliquely, at me. From then on I sensed that I had some kind of power over her, but I didn't know to what extent. I inquired as nonchalantly as I could about her life. Her convictions were strong, but a little confusing for the fresh young girl I still was. She believed that the abbess was far too lax with the rules of the congregation, and men clearly horrified her. There were moments when I caught a glimpse of the wounded child within her, or so I thought. She often spoke in monologues about the Evil One. Their intensity always left me on my guard.

I may have been young, but I already knew that cunning and deceit ruled the world. I began to realise that Sister Wolf was deceiving herself and that her true nature was not quite what it seemed.

That set me thinking about the Other in myself.

———⚬☙☙⚬———

In those days it was a question of intuition or necessity, but since reading the books of the Marquis de Sade I've learned that people tend to seek companions in perversity. When we set aside morality, a toxic abyss gapes open in front of us, an abyss we do not want to enter alone. Sacred perversity is the most demanding religion of them all, and purposefulness is God's weapon.

I had a purpose. I wanted to explore the world outside the monastery. I knew that I had to hide the Other if I was to succeed in my plan. During the day I was modest and unassuming. I read and I learned. My stepfather didn't visit me on a regular basis, but when he did he always brought books. He had forbidden me to ask questions about my background. We agreed that we would restrict our conversation to my reading and my future. He was convinced that the best thing I could do was become a novice. But sometimes he talked about himself and his family, because I had learned to hear people out before they realized what was happening.

I developed an obsession for my mother by reading Dostoyevsky. His adulterous, sly, and tearful women convinced me that I was an aristocratic child and that I had been rejected because of my appearance. I had long nocturnal conversations with my mother, which whipped me into a jumble of rage and sadness. I was smart enough to share these emotions with Sister Wolf. My outpourings made her even more sympathetic. One night she undid her hair shirt to reveal an amulet with the letters I.H.S. She looked at me strangely and explained that while the letters were a symbol for Christ they could also be translated in hoc salis. *I asked Sister Wolf what it meant. Her cheeks flushed above the marble-white breasts on which the amulet rested when she answered: "Herein is bliss."*

I then understood with the animal sensitivity of a child that I had her completely in my power.

That night I stripped naked for her in her cell. Until then she had only touched me fully clothed, her eyes closed and her lips pinched. Now her eyes glazed as I removed my undershirt and revealed the lower part of my body. I took her as I alone could. Sister Wolf bit her pillow, whispered my name, and added soothingly but with a hint of fear the name daitya. *I had heard it before. She had screamed it at me in the infirmary that night when she cut the umbilical cord and the child clasped between her fingers turned blue.*

Daitya is the daughter of the devil.

You can recognise her by the tail between her legs.

37

THEY SHARED A MISERABLE CHEESE soufflé, guzzled sour wine from the Alsace, and made each other's acquaintance as men do in dangerous times. There was a lull in the shelling and Paris had returned to its old ways in spite of the ever-present stench of gunpowder. The three men assured each other that Paris could lift her skirts whenever it suited her and that she was capable of shedding her skin like a snake. They were drunk, of course. Any right-minded man would get himself inebriated if his city was being shelled by barbarians.

The quayside on the left bank was one of Lefèvre's favourite parts of Paris. Between the Rue du Bac and the Rue Dauphine, there was a world of second-hand stores, tobacco shops, tiny intimate bordellos, bookshops, and libertines. His table companions had turned out to be a couple of adventurers from wealthy families who loathed the political, military, and social blunders of their operetta emperor and preferred to call themselves anarchists. Lefèvre barked at the top of his voice that they were just bored and had decided to become idealists for want of something better to do.

The older of the two, Ferdinand Castellani, son of a French mother and an Italian count, could see the funny side of Lefèvre's remark.

Castellani, a member of the *franc-tireurs des Ternes*, was in Paris to collect and transport the work of his younger artistic and erratic comrade Henri Toulouse to the provinces to raise some money. He flirted with the ideas of the Russian Bakunin and was convinced that the man's anarchistic principles would change the future of the French working classes. Here in this left bank *table d'hôte*, with its ruddy faces, gravelly voices, and the clatter of plates and careering *garçons*, the duo's lofty ideals, which became more foolhardy the more wine they consumed, seemed farfetched and out of touch.

As a son of the lower middle class, Lefèvre was convinced that he understood the plebs. He didn't expect much good to come from them, in contrast to this pair of snobs who saw the future as a war-game that was going to hand over power to the people, and this time there would be real *liberté, égalité, fraternité.*

The forked scar on Henri's cheek, the hint of a stammer, the wild gestures he used to underline his words, and the remarkable giggle that escaped his lips at given moments seemed to point to a disturbed youth, in part because of the way he looked up to his fellow artist Castellani. Henri Toulouse spoke less about his youth than his older companion, who dished up steamy stories about his attempts to travel to the United States as a stowaway. Henri had briefly mentioned that he was also from an aristocratic family but that he hated his rich father, and his stepmother even more. Lefèvre wanted to ask if the forked scar was the result of a duel, but he kept the question to himself. He was familiar with a Corsican fighting style that often left such pronounced scars. The young poster painter had a fiery temperament and suffered, as soon became apparent, from alcoholism.

Castellani, tastefully dressed in an olive-green tailcoat with a black collar, an ochre waistcoat, and a light grey cravat, constantly praised his young companion's talent and his "judicious" choice of subjects: dancers in vaudeville outfits, whores with green eye-shadow, and drunks on street pavements. He even had a rather pompous sounding name for it: "Post-impressionism, good sir! Raw reality filtered through the singularity of the individual! To the devil with the Salon and its fastidious rules, the accursed Ecole des Beaux Arts with its infantile hierarchy and its praise for stiff paintings of historical subjects. And they call it the highest form of art!"

Lefèvre listened to the two artists and envied them their dreams of the future.

"Paul," said the young Toulouse out of the blue, "I've experienced you as a representative of the law, a very, shall we say, thoroughgoing representative of the law." His cheeks glowed. "So it's only fair that we in turn try to convince you of the unjust path this pathetic empire has decided to follow. You're familiar, no doubt, with the salons of the Count of Rémusat in the Rue de Tivoli. While he and his guests enjoy filet of giraffe, the workers are left to fight over dog paws and rat's claws and worse. The people will revolt against such monstrous injustices. The folly of the aristocracy is beyond belief and history is yet to witness greater. It is the duty of the nobility to channel the workers' aggression and direct it against the Prussians. Instead, they allow the gulf between rich and poor to reach unacceptable proportions. Perhaps it's not too late! We have to become one with the people. Then France will be invincible!"

Lefèvre looked at the dandy sitting in front of him in his ostentatious mauve tailcoat and white trousers and found it hard to conceal a sneer. "Perhaps you're still a little young to win me over," he said. "Come and talk to me again when you've shared the family fortune with the poor."

To his surprise, Henri Toulouse laughed. "*Touché*, commissioner! But the people don't want the nobility's money, not in the first instance. They want better living conditions and inspiring leadership. The young, and I include myself, can see the stupidity of the emperor and his government. A friend of mine, Arthur Rimbaud, is even younger than me, but his poetry is remarkable. At this very moment he's working on a poem piling fire and brimstone on Napoleon III himself. The young aren't afraid to say what their elders think."

Lefèvre smiled. "So you know what I'm thinking, my dear Henri Toulouse?"

Ferdinand Castellani lit a cigar and followed the conversation, apparently amused. Lefèvre had noticed that he was far from condescending toward the young Toulouse, as was the custom in artistic circles when established veterans were confronted with emerging talent. "Nowadays, the young actually do what their elders only dare think about behind closed doors," the stained-glass maker affably contributed. "Rimbaud is an extremely talented young cub, but his morals leave much to be desired. They say his friendship with that boozer Verlaine breaks all the norms of common decency."

"That's my point!" Henri erupted. "Common decency is on its deathbed. Modernity hates hypocrisy. Every individual has the right to follow his most personal emotions."

"Count de Rémusat, your example of the depravity of the governing classes, is throwing a Grand Bal Masqué this evening," said Lefèvre as he got to his feet and looked around, far from sober. "A police functionary like myself always has access to such festivities, not to check whether they uphold appropriate moral standards but to make sure that the waiters and chambermaids don't get tempted by the expensive jewelry of the aristocratic guests. Come with me. Let me show you why the powers that be in this country will never hand over the reins."

"That's one option," said Henri Toulouse as he also got to his feet, evidently just as unstable as Lefèvre. "But before we do that, I have an even better idea."

┌─────┐
│ 38 │
└─────┘

MEMORIES OF MY EARLY YEARS are confused, of course, and mixed with dreams and nightmares, like the memories of anyone's youth. They are also influenced by the person I have now become, so many years later. Who would have thought that I would become worldly-wise, and witness things the average Frenchman only gets to hear about in the stories they tell in fishermen's cafés? I have followed the luminous underground thread that binds my existence. Since the day I was born my life has been polluted by secrets, one of which I have exposed: Our childhood monsters are born of our desire for omnipotence.

I was always a sensitive and thoughtful person for my age. The nuns sensed this and eased their grip on me. Their attitude was also influenced by my stepfather's sporadic visits. After a while they all knew who I was.

By the time I was sixteen I had become the monastery's errant soul. My special status spurred even more gossip about me among the orphan girls. Some claimed I was the bastard daughter of one or another prominent figure, others that my grand mals *were the result of a sinful relationship between a mother and her son. Didn't they bathe me at set times for visits from a man in a stately uniform? When my nervous condition manifested itself I was no longer locked in a cell under the kitchen, as before. They took precautions to* be sure I didn't swallow my tongue, and let me lie until I woke up from what seemed like a normal sleep. My formal education, which consisted of classes in reading, writing, arithmetic, geography, and history, was taken over by Sister Wolf.

The monastery was at odds with the world. I later learned that the world wasn't as wonderful as I had imagined at the time. The monastery building often felt like a fossilized animal brooding over one or another mystery. I remember its corridors better than the faces of those who walked them. It was a square building constructed around an inner courtyard. The ground floor had high vaulted ceilings and housed the dormitories and a long refectory. The upper floors had small windows and the chapel had a turret. The smell in the infirmary reminded me of the rotting cat that someone tossed over the monastery wall one day. The kitchen block had black windows that gave it an aura of malevolence. Its huge smoking chimneys often reminded me of death, which was ever-present in the novels I loved to read. My infant imagination pictured Death as a skeleton in emperor's clothing, with a cloak and a cocked hat.

Whenever I talked about death, Sister Wolf would get excited. I did what she begged me to do, praised Jesus, and took her from behind. One day she whispered afterwards that she had seen my soul: a pretty girl, she said, naked, with slender limbs and frame.

I never told her I could see my own soul whenever the Other paid a visit.

Its eyes red, its jaws dripping, its satanic tail ready to attack.

39

ROTTING HORSE CADAVERS, PILES OF refuse, and three figures swathed in ragged and filthy cloaks around a burning brazier marked the way to the Mosselat, a boarding house on the Rue de L'Echaudé. The rustic four-floored pile, with bars on the windows and dormers on the roof, stood out against the rain-drenched streets. Castellani and Toulouse, who had spent the journey exchanging scathing jokes about Marshal Bazaine, the man who signed the capitulation of Metz and thereby robbed the nation of its regular army, fell silent. The company stepped down from their coach in front of a gate with bas-relief sculptures.

"This used to be a home for melancholics, neurasthenics, maniacs, and lunatics," said Toulouse. A brief sigh. "Now it's a military hospital."

"What happened to the lunatics?" asked the commissioner.

Castellani smiled sourly. "They're wandering around the city, mixing with the ordinary folk. You can't tell the difference anymore."

They crossed the inner courtyard and entered a domed construction with the stench of an abattoir. Oil lamps hung from the lofty ceiling. Only a few were lit. They cast long shadows against the scaling walls, the beds in battle array, and a swarm of obscure figures, some groaning, some screaming, some silent. The senior officers were confined to the left-hand corner, their beds separated from the rest by folding screens. Doctors, nuns, and nurses shuffled back and forth in stained aprons.

Against the wall in front of a row of beds there was a square of shoulder-high screens. Lefèvre could see surgeons performing amputations on a jumble of collapsible stretchers. Painkilling substances were few and far between. Ghastly screams ascended from the dreadful corner. The three men stood in the middle of the room. No one paid them any attention. A young nurse hurried past, clearly exhausted, her eyes downcast, a bucket of slime and blood in each hand.

Toulouse took in the scene, both revulsion and avidity evident in his posture. Castellani felt awkward and self-conscious, moved and confused by what he saw. Lefèvre seemed indifferent. He had seen it all before in his army days.

"Do you understand what I mean, commissioner?" said the young painter. He walked over to one of the beds and leaned over its wounded occupant as if he was planning to examine him.

Castellani took Lefèvre gently by the arm. "Henri was badly treated as a child, very badly," he said with a barely perceptible nod toward the scar on Toulouse's cheek. "A result of the depravity of a highly placed individual who thought that his noble birth set him above the law. It left Henri with a profound aversion to his own class. He has the daring of his years, but underneath he hides the fears and feelings of an old man. His sympathy for the less well off is genuine. That's why he's so defiant."

"We are all the product of our birth and the life we have received," said the commissioner.

"And of our desires," said Castellani, his eyes fixed on the commissioner.

Toulouse joined their company once again. "This is only the vestibule, commissioner," he said. "Come, join me in hell."

40

"WHO WROTE THIS POEM?"

"I did. It's for you."

The general looked at me, his expression peculiar. "Poor child," he said. "Like him, you too have been captured by the Muse."

I told him I didn't understand what he meant. I knew what the Muse was, but I thought she only visited beautiful people.

The general appeared in the meantime to have grown attached to me, more or less. I've never really known why my stepfather visited me. Something fascinated him, but what it was I had no idea. I thought he admired me for my determination to change myself into a human being. How was I to tell him that the presence of other people often exasperated me?

The ennui that I felt was full of disgust and disdain. When I think back, I realize that life seemed a burden even then. It was only when Sister Wolf played my sex slave that I experienced le frisson du nouveau. I've learned since that my exasperation is akin to the taedium vitae, the gloom experienced by the mighty Romans when they had no war to fight.

My sturdy, well-built visitor seemed confused, perhaps a little sad. He read the verses I had written for him a second time and shook his head.

"You shouldn't do it," he said, his words so soft I had to lean forward to understand them. We were in the monastery library. The grey light through the windows fell on his moustache, which itself had turned completely grey in the last year.

"I have to feel the words," I said. "If they light up the dark, then it's good."

"Yet they deal with such ugliness."

"For me, ugliness is beauty."

"So young and already so contrary." He seemed to say it to himself. I let it pass. "Where do all those images come from?" He gestured toward the books surrounding us.

"No. It's all inside me. The world doesn't interest me. I don't need to know it. I am the world."

The general was speechless for a moment. I took a deep breath. "Who is he? That handsome man you spoke about, the man in the grip of the Muse, the man I remind you of?"

"He's not handsome."

"The Muse only visits the beautiful."

The general stared at me for a long time.

He started to pace back and forth.

Then he made a decision.

41

THE OIL LAMP BESIDE THE clock on the mantelpiece started to flicker. The candles on Bouveroux's rolltop desk glimmered in the clock's glass dome. He looked up from what he was reading. A moment away from the garbled notes the commissioner had given him somehow made his room seem all the more pleasant.

Lefèvre had left the prefecture early that day. The absent expression on his face as he reached for his hat and his parting remark about Paris—a refuge for "tinkers and bedbugs"—were enough for Bouveroux. The commissioner was clearly in need of the solace of a woman's arms, and Bouveroux knew exactly where he was heading. Lefèvre had told him some exhilarating stories about a *grisette* he called Claire de la Lune. He had sounded a little sentimental at the time. One evening when they were sharing a coach, Bouveroux had dropped him off at the building where the courtesan kept her boudoir. His older comrade's youthful verve as he stepped out had caught his eye.

Bouveroux asked himself if the street wench was going to see another side of the commissioner that evening, his darker side. He hoped not. Since the incident with the dwarf, Lefèvre had been in a sombre mood and no longer paid any attention to the chaos that had taken hold of the prefecture and the alarming reports of the latest Prussian offensives.

The inspector got to his feet and crossed to his medicine cabinet, which was stocked with arsenic pills, quinine, and coca. He took a preparation for his stomach and washed it down with a good glass of wine. Huge raindrops spattered against the window. Every now and then a deep rumbling could be heard, like the remnants of a clap of thunder. Storm and shell kept each other company.

After work, Bouveroux had made his way to the *table d'hôte* on the Rue de Beurrière, where the food was generally more nourishing, affordable, and rich in fibre than elsewhere, the latter feature being of particular importance given his poor health. The proprietor, Monsieur Villepier, had offered him rat stew without daring to look him in the eye. Only six months earlier the man's cheeks had been veined and ruddy from the cheerful local wines he served in his restaurant. Now his skin was translucent and pale.

The inspector had picked at the dish without relish. His thoughts turned to Lefèvre and their years of friendship. There was little point in trying to disentangle the past. Fate was capricious and at once unavoidable. Only one thing was certain: Something had happened to Lefèvre early on in life and he had never quite recovered from the shock.

Bouveroux sighed. He knew what it meant to live with a broken heart. Years back, in the arms of Marthe, a woman with a tragic capacity for love, Bouveroux had listened night after night to her erratic heartbeat. Marthe suffered from an infirmity that brought a blush to her cheeks and sent shudders through her body like electric shocks. The doctors she could afford diagnosed the strangest maladies. Bouveroux had loved Marthe more than his own self. She didn't mind him burying his nose in books for hours on end. She would busy herself with sewing, and when he glanced up at her neck every now and then he sensed an inner warmth that bound them together like an unseen umbilical cord. Marthe had suffered terrible convulsions when she died. The inspector had locked himself up for three days with the curtains drawn. For three nights in a row he had stared at death crouched in the corner of the room.

On the fourth day, the inspector opened Marx's *Communist Manifesto*: "A spectre is haunting Europe . . ." He slapped the book shut and turned instead to Burnouf's *Introduction à L'Histoire du Buddhisme Indien*, throwing it open and reading the first words his eyes fell upon: "Detachment is the true Mahayana—the great vehicle." Bouveroux chose a third book at random from his bookcase, Flaubert's *Madame Bovary*. He read: "The priest stood up and took the crucifix; she stretched her neck as if she was thirsty, pressed her lips against the body of the God-man and with all the strength that remained to her she kissed it as passionately as she had ever kissed it before. He then recited the Misereatur and the Indulgentiam, dipped his right thumb in the oil and started to anoint her: first the eyes, so covetous of every earthly splendour; then the nostrils, so indulgent of sultry breezes and sweet scents; then the mouth, so ready with lies, which had groaned in pride and lust; then the hands, that had welcomed such gentle caresses; and finally the soles of her feet, which had once carried her with such haste to the satisfaction of her desires, and which now would carry her no more." Then he had understood: Marthe was speaking to him through his books. A completely insane idea, absolutely unscientific, but it had brought him consolation. He went outside. The sky above Paris was so clear it had brought tears to his eyes.

Now Bouveroux turned around and looked at the pages on his desk. If it was true that Marthe's soul could speak to him through books, what message was this erratic story, evidently written under enormous emotional duress, trying to get across to him?

Of one thing he was convinced: The person who wrote these words had never experienced consolation.

42

THE OLD, FADED CLOAKS TOULOUSE had picked up en route reeked of decay. But the young painter insisted they disguise themselves. "It's dangerous for well-dressed gentlemen where we're heading." The rain was torrential, aggravating the stench of the cloaks.

Baron Hausmann had had many of the city's slum districts demolished in recent years in response to Napoleon III's renewal frenzy. Broad boulevards with guttering had taken their place. But the "Polish Field," one of the highest districts in the city, had remained unchanged for centuries. The slum had been cleared in the eighteenth century after a cholera epidemic. Its ruined houses stood out against the pale night sky. The broken streetlamps attached to the facades with iron stakes had no light to offer. In the midst of this wasteland—rumour had it that the Catholics planned to build an enormous basilica in the place and call it *Sacre Coeur*—there was only one source of light. As they approached, Lefèvre realized it was an oil lamp attached to the front of an old *cantine municipale*. He managed to decipher the words *Au Rendez-Vous des* . . .

Men with rucksacks and berets queued in disorder at the doorless entrance. He could see a couple of oil lamps burning inside. The newcomers were surveyed with suspicion. The atmosphere was hostile, enough to make the hairs on the back of Lefèvre's neck stand to attention.

Toulouse's eyes appeared yellow in the lamplight. "Look without the preconceptions of your office, commissioner," said the young *franc-tireur*. "Look with the eyes of a human being."

Castellani hushed his young companion. "The poorest of the poor come here for provisions. They and their families have no other choice. They survive on this atrocious food." He spotted the misgivings in Lefèvre's eyes and gestured toward a man with a narrow face, an angular nose, and the slowly blinking eyes of an owl. The man took a painfully slow step to one side and let them in.

The stench of a slaughterhouse filled Lefèvre's nostrils. The man behind the improvised counter looked up at Castellani. His left eye was a mass of fibrous tissue, a barely open slit. "Oh là là, the defenders of the fatherland, or what's left of it at least! In the mood for some of my delicacies? Make sure our friend Admiral Bazaine gets a double portion. He needs all his strength to give those Prussians a good hiding! Or have you come to paint my portrait and sell it to one of those rich bastards with their fancy dinners and well-stocked fireplaces?"

"We've come to buy," said Toulouse with a hint of pride, as if he was about to purchase something precious. A darkness had crept into him that irritated the commissioner.

The butcher raised his thick bushy eyebrows. "Take your pick, *messieurs*," he said, his neck darting back and forth like a rooster. "It's not from the best Normandy stock, but it's fresh, you can be sure of it."

Toulouse and the butcher exchanged a knowing glance and the young artist nodded almost imperceptibly in Lefèvre's direction. The butcher's head turned like a cat honing in on its prey.

"The choice is yours, good sir," he said, his lips parsimoniously pursed. "A *connoisseur* of fine meats, by all appearances."

Lefèvre took pleasure in the undiluted malevolence of the human animal standing in front of him. He glanced at his two companions. Castellani seemed a little concerned, as if he had gone out of his way to be there and was slowly losing his patience. The young Toulouse glared at him maliciously. He probably identified himself with this wretched horde and the ideals of the rickety republic the workers had been championing of late.

"Make up your mind!" someone shouted from behind. "And don't be expecting baby thighs that look like tender suckling pig. The carcasses they use are tough as old boots." An abrupt yelp followed, like the yowl of an African hyena.

Lefèvre turned and stared at the long narrow face of the man in the doorway who had spoken. His lips were thin and blue, his tartan scarf tattered, his beret shiny with fat. Toulouse rested an appeasing hand on Lefèvre's shoulder, but the commissioner shrugged it off. He flipped his walking stick and poked the man in the stomach with its lion's head handle. He fell to the ground with a surprised grunt and before he had the chance to get back to his feet, Lefèvre pressed the handle against his Adam's apple. The man flailed and gasped for breath. A woman behind him with a massive goiter in her neck hissed and cursed.

"Where did you get this meat?" said Lefèvre. A searing heat, as in the desert at noon, scrambled his brains.

The man coughed. Saliva appeared in the corners of his mouth. Lefèvre pressed harder.

"Good friend," Castellani whispered cautiously in his ear. "You've seen enough. I think it's time to withdraw to safety. Look around you."

Lefèvre raised his head. The crowd had started to force its way inside. There were no threats, just tight lips and glaring eyes. Some were carrying knives, others cudgels. The moon made their eyes red.

"They eat the meat of their dead," said Castellani, "but our blood would be a welcome extra."

43

*W*HEN *I* FINALLY LEARNED THE *identity of my twin brother, I realized at the same time that it was time to leave the monastery. An undercurrent had found its way into my life that furnished me with an unshakable conviction, just as a swan knows when the time has come to migrate. I knew that escape would be simple, but I was still without a plan. I knew my twin's name and was aware that he had grown up in a different world and didn't even know that I existed. Yet in my dreams I encountered him in distant lands, he brooding over dark thoughts, me as pretty as a nightingale, masked in gold-embroidered veils. I pictured him do to me what I did to Sister Wolf. I never allowed him to uncover my face, not even when he gasped my name in the heat of passion. In my dreams we both had the same eyes—the same color, iris, expression.*

Escaping from the monastery was a trifle. Now that I knew my real name and had discovered my hidden talents, I felt strong. Sister Wolf called me her divine scorpion when I made her thighs tremble and she rolled her eyes upwards until only the whites could be seen.

My deformity had been transformed from a curse into a blessing. The general had told me why I had been placed in the orphanage: Shortly after my birth, a few minutes after the birth of Charles Baudelaire, my father summoned the family doctor to a meeting in his study. The doctor was an old friend and very religious. He refused to operate on me and advised my father to dump me in the gutter. "Let the devil take care of his own creations." After a long battle of conscience, my father decided to follow his God-fearing friend's advice. He saw me as a curse God had called down upon him because he had abandoned his priestly calling. But my mother stole a march on him and chose to have me adopted by the Ursulines.

Knowledge is power, a medieval philosopher once wrote, and I can only agree. When I knew who I was, I also accepted my deformity and became proud of it. I became aware that I had the power to manipulate people and threaten them, and I was determined to develop my skills.

The monastery could no longer contain me.

In short, I hid myself under cover of darkness in the cart that brought the weekly wash to a nearby laundry. The doors opened, the wheels rumbled over the cobblestones, no one saw me under the piles of linen that smelt of congealed blood.

I inhaled the stale female odor deep into my lungs. It gave me an energy that wriggled through me like a serpent.

My tail grew warm, as if it was filling with blood.

"I love you," I said.

44

THE LATEST ROUND OF PRUSSIAN shells scattered mushrooms of yellow smoke across the city. Bouveroux stood at his window and asked himself who would ensure law and order from then on.

And how?

He turned back to the notebook the commissioner had given him. The dagger he had found in the back of the unfortunate photographer lay beside it on his desk. Bouveroux decided to take the weapon to the prefecture the following day, something he should already have done the day before. Procedures were important, especially in the present climate. The Paris police had to do its work with the utmost care and attention, and continue to function.

He ran his finger over the pages he still had to read. What was he to make of this report, its text interspersed with signs that resembled Egyptian hieroglyphics and scribbles that appeared to represent peculiar costumes and masks? The inspector tried to line up the facts: It appeared that Charles Baudelaire had a twin sister who came into the world with a bodily defect shortly after his birth and, according to an old French tradition, was whisked away to a convent. Her first and most obvious physical shortcoming was her height, which squared with the commissioner's description of the diminutive Poupeye. The inspector found the second deformity more difficult to grasp. A "demonic tail"?

Bouveroux imagined that the young woman's life had been marked by life in the monastery and a distorted love of God. He stood in front of his cherished bookcases. Somewhere in the chaos there was a book testifying to the Satanism that had taken root in a number of French monasteries in the eighteenth century. He particularly recalled the misdeeds of a certain priest, Xavier Forneret, who had not only practiced necromancy but had also "transformed" the nuns in the monastery of La Trappe "into pigs." Forneret held the young novices prisoner in a pigsty and took pleasure in copulating with them in the mud "in honour of the Saviour who had been betrayed by a woman." The study also spoke of mental and physical torture practiced by priests and nuns, which no one in his right mind could imagine. From the vague but sinister reflections of Baudelaire's twin sister concerning "Sister Wolf," an observant reader could determine that she suffered from religious delusions with a sadistic hue.

Since his soldier days in Algeria, Bouveroux had treated religion as more dangerous than opium. But the established religions were not alone in clouding the mind and vexing the senses. The papers were full of rumours, some describing black masses using hosts filled with the blood of menstruant virgins mixed with the seed of the priest. Zola's naturalism, which dictated that the close observation and detailed description of reality deserved pride of place, had already encountered a reaction that was best described as hysterical mysticism.

Bouveroux finally found his *Encyclopaedia of Medical Anomalies*. Much research had been conducted in the 17th century into people with "tails" after explorers discovered that the coccyx of primitive peoples often continued to grow. Some "tails" were little more than fleshy appendages of horny tissue; others were clearly an extension of the spinal column. Bouveroux read that the Greeks had also been familiar with the condition, referring to its sufferers as *lamiai*. The Ancients ascribed enormous magical powers to people with such malformations.

Bouveroux turned toward the window, distracted by the explosion of a Prussian shell on the opposite bank of the Seine. An arrow-shaped flame, white as phosphor, shot into the sky and disintegrated in a shower of red embers. He returned to his book. Would he have hated his body if he had been born with such an affliction? Would a tail have driven him insane? He perused the images in the Encyclopaedia: people with four eyes, people with horns, people with three testicles. As if a person with a normal physique wasn't unfortunate enough in this world.

Well, look here: In 1820, a certain Dr. Broussa recorded a detailed description of the tail of a Kurd. The appendage of the twenty-four-year-old contained four vertebrae. Its tip looked like the tail of a pig. The inspector tried to picture Simone Bourbier naked. A small woman with the tail of a pig? Reason enough to lose one's mind.

Lefèvre had told him he was convinced that Poupeye intended to kill him while he lay paralyzed and anaesthetized on the stretcher. Why hadn't Poupeye done so?

Bouveroux had always been a man of ideals. He had learned a lesson in Algeria as he watched Lefèvre try to stop the bleeding in his belly. The message was clear: In the Medina in Algiers, a young girl, a child he did not know, had stabbed him with a knife out of pure hatred. What did his enlightened ideals have to say to that?

Bouveroux later concluded that the young Muslim girl's hatred only remained obscure to someone like himself, but not to the likes of Paul Lefèvre.

Perhaps the mysterious woman with the tail had seen something of herself in Lefèvre.

Look . . . there it is again . . . page 324 . . . the chapter by Ragozin on the Chaldeo–Babylonians. When such a *lamia* was born, the Greeks were convinced that blood would flow in the family. Murky allusions to forbidden love and challenging the gods filled the chapter.

Bouveroux concluded that the instincts and desires of normal individuals did not apply to Simone Bourbier.

That meant she would be difficult to find. It would be easy for her to merge into the general chaos of violence and destruction.

Nevertheless, Bouveroux reasoned, it was more than possible that she still had a score to settle with the commissioner.

There was no need to look for Simone Bourbier. She would come looking for them.

You see, Bouveroux? Books have the answer to everything.

45

SOME MOMENTS IN LIFE ACQUIRE extraordinary significance and anchor themselves in one's memory. Others merge with dreams and deceit and become distorted, like reflections in a carnival mirror.

When I saw my twin brother for the first time, I was immediately struck by his eyes. He had just walked out of number 6 Rue de la Femme-sans-tête, where he shared cramped quarters with a black dancer by the name of Jeanne Duval. We were both twenty-one; he appeared twice as old. But his eyes were the same as mine. I recognised boundless ennui, unfathomable rancor, heart-wrenching sadness. His austere lips had an air of dissatisfaction about them, a feature I also recognized in myself when I was alone and had no need for a mask. We also shared a tiny, almost invisible cleft, a mere shadow in the middle of his chin.

The similarities one would expect of twins ended there. Men often described me as "charming" because I was small and slender. What they meant was that it flattered their vanity when they lay in bed next to my childlike body because it gave them the illusion that they were big and strong.

And capable of hurting me.

My infantile frame and my tail gave me an authority when I was naked that I did not possess clothed. Thanks to my sexual powers, I was convinced that jealousy was a stranger to me. But when I saw him leave the apartment of his mistress, a vulgar bohémienne, *it hit me like a battering ram.*

Why do we do what we do and think what we think?

No one knows, but once in a while a truth manifests itself that cuts through our every doubt. I immediately sensed a desire for my twin brother that out-matched every other. I fantasized about us together as naked animals in a steaming jungle, ready to tear each other to pieces.

I soon became aware that my desire to mount him was growing stronger by the day.

A longing that eliminates common sense is like a war that defines its own laws. It pays no attention to limitations or practical difficulties. I took pleasure in my perverse craving, honed it with the wildest of dreams, let it engulf me. I gloried in the pain I suffered at the thought of what he would do to me once I had him in my possession.

And I to him.

46

ONE OR ANOTHER PEACOCK IN this company of aristocrats said: "Count Favier wants to sign an armistice." Someone else replied: "Where is the France we were once so proud of?"

Lefèvre nodded to a nearby butler and grabbed a new glass from his tray.

Castellani and the commissioner had left Henri Toulouse behind, as he unrolled a canvas and set about painting the cruelty of the ravenous crowd in colors that seemed metallic, lacking the pure transparent light that used to be so typical of Paris. The mob calmed considerably when the young aristocrat produced his painting materials from behind the butcher's counter. Lefèvre had wanted to ask Toulouse how often he had visited the place, but decided not to when he saw how the people posed for him without complaint. They stuck out their chests; some tidied their hair; they tried to restore a little pride to their hungry eyes. They understood that Toulouse was like them and granted them a dignity no one else could, in spite of his fancy clothes and tousled curly hair.

"He paints cannibals," Lefèvre had muttered under his breath to Castellani, who had opted to accompany him to the *Bal Masqué*, "but he's a cannibal himself."

"No," the stained-glass maker had responded. "You're wrong, commissioner. The boy is devouring himself."

Lefèvre stared at his empty glass and winked at a servant dressed as a rooster. The man's red comb wobbled back and forth as he filled the commissioner's glass.

Rue de Tivoli. Rive Gauche. The Seine, normally so charming, had been sullied by the war. On their way to the party—organised by Count de Rémusat, the owner of a number of foundries that specialized in the production of cannons for the French army—he and Castellani had avoided talking about what they had witnessed. Instead they had talked about the socialism that had been plaguing Paris and other major European cities. The socialists had pushed France to the edge of civil war, Lefèvre had concluded.

Castellani had shaken his head and glared at him ironically. He changed the subject: What did Lefèvre think of the faith of the Hindus that had been increasing in popularity among the nobility? Did he believe that he would come back after he died to live another life? Perhaps as an ant or a dog?

"Spare me such misery!" Lefèvre had snapped. "One wretched life is more than enough for me."

"What do you want then in *this* life, commissioner?"

"To come to grief in the arms of a certain woman, one who knows how to bewitch a man," said Lefèvre without the least sarcasm. "A noble death, if you ask me. Especially at my age."

Castellani smiled. "Such women are to be found on every street corner in Paris."

"*Her* witchery is of a different order, dear friend. She has a poisonous sting, sharp enough to penetrate the hardest skin, and when she goes she leaves it behind. Let me assure you, *comrade*, the effects of its venom are efficient and irreversible." The commissioner had shaken his head as they entered the mock Greek vestibule. "It makes you rot, slowly, from the inside out." He caught sight of himself reflected in a thousand fragments in the crystal chandelier above their heads.

"Surely her sting is life itself," said Castellani. "Sooner or later it makes all of us bitter and slow."

Butlers bowed and scraped at the doors to the grand salon. Neither gentleman had an invitation; instead, Lefèvre held out his police identity card. Civilization may have been crumbling, but it still ensured that a police officer of Lefèvre's rank would not be refused in such circles. He was expected to reinforce the aura of inviolability in which the obstinate nobility continued to believe, in spite of the tattered, ever-growing mob that filled the streets and the threatening glares that followed every coach. Both gentlemen were accompanied by a valet to a separate vestibule where they left their hats and coats.

Lefèvre glanced at his companion's profile, his face adorned with a thin tattoo of wrinkles, lean, serious, a little wilted. Castellani's expressionless gaze was somehow reassuring. His long, pallid fingers were handsome and alert. The light cast murky patches of yellow on his slender neck. Lefèvre sensed a tightness in his chest, the need to breathe deeper.

"I had a sister I loved very much," he said unexpectedly. For a moment he had the strange illusion that he could feel his uncle Jean-Paul's wooden mask fastened tight over his mouth. "She was eleven when she died," was all he could say.

Castellani stopped in his tracks. His reaction took the commissioner aback. No words of sympathy, no wide-eyed surprise. The light caught a tear as it rolled from the corner of the man's left eye.

"Les papillons aiment mourir, commissaire."

With those words, Lefèvre sensed the odor of dead roses that filled the vestibule. *Butterflies like to die.* It was a statement that held all his remorse. The two men shook hands without a word, turned, and made their way into the grand salon.

The enormous open hearth was ablaze with burning logs. Marble statues of Greek athletes and shepherdesses adorned the niches between the velvet-curtained windows. Venetian lamps cast a bluish light that shrouded the guests in shifting shadows. The merrymakers were dressed in extravagant costumes and were in the highest of spirits, like a bunch of street urchins in a park. The Red Death danced with a matronly Indian, cocked hats wore sinister Chinese masks, a chubby clown dressed in a crude monk's habit carried a bell in his left hand and jingled it to his heart's content without disturbing anyone in the drunken rabble. A cowboy with wide leather breeches cracked his whip and a sultan perched on a sedan chair supported by four black slaves waltzed around the room.

The women formed the focal point of this animated throng. Lefèvre recognised the voluptuous curves of Madame Tardivat, dressed as Juno. Her archrival, Mademoiselle Berquet, was dressed as Aphrodite in a scanty negligee that mimicked sea foam. Countess de Turcotte had done the unthinkable and dressed as a nobleman, complete with old-fashioned rapier, musketeer gloves, and riding boots. Her tight-fitting jacket was unbuttoned to the navel.

"Look around, commissioner," said Castellani. "Which scene scares you the most? A bunch of wretches braving the rain in search of fresh meat, or this noble lunacy?"

47

A CENTURY AGO, THE FRAUD *Wolfgang von Kempelen presented his chess-playing Turk, an automaton capable of beating the most experienced chess masters. Le Maçon, my mentor, told me that the Austrian empress Marie Thérèse had been over the moon with the machine. He alone managed to uncover the secret of the robot's chess-playing intelligence. Le Maçon is prone to boasting. He was convinced that Von Kempelen had hidden a dwarf with incredible chess skills in his contraption.*

I repeated his story to a whole series of wealthy ladies and gentlemen, adding that the dwarf was my cousin who had lived more than a hundred years, and that at the end of his life he had confessed everything to me. They laughed heartily, of course, but no one believed me, in spite of my own considerable talent for deception. But their refusal to believe was not because the story was too peculiar. I once managed to convince more than a few rich upstarts to buy shares in El Dorado with stories of the Indian tribes I had escaped in South America. But then I had a tiny gold ingot with me as "evidence." When an otherwise incredible story is combined with something tangible, people are inclined to believe it.

When it came to Von Kempelen's deceit, I had nothing to show my audience. The automaton had been destroyed long ago and Von Kempelen himself was dead. For a while I played with the idea of digging up the corpse of a child, cutting off a hand, aging it in a jar of acid, and telling everyone it belonged to my dwarf cousin. I never carried out my plan because there were other ways of encouraging the rich to part with their money. The increasing popularity of spiritism and Satanism made it easier to make a living as a fortune teller or a medium. But I continued to tell people about Von Kempelen's contraption because I liked the moral of the story: The dwarf demanded more and more money to keep his secret and, driven to despair, Von Kempelen set the machine on fire moments before a performance. He explained the screams that emerged from the machine as his own, brought on by the anguish of having to watch his invention go up in flames.

My audience grinned with delight at my story's cruel conclusion. Deep inside they sensed that it carried a warning. The reason I continued to tell it was personal: All my life I have felt like a screaming dwarf inside a burning machine. The purity of the artistic soul that idolizes beauty is alive in me, but because of my exterior form everything I touch turns to filth. I cannot describe the cruelty of that transformation process. It has made a killer of me, but the worst murder I ever committed was of myself.

Nor was I believed when I told people I had a tail. But in contrast to my story about Von Kempelen's automaton, I had evidence to support my claim. I asked enormous amounts of money to prove it and was given what I asked. As a result, I established something of a reputation for myself, and men of noble birth insisted on sharing my bed. It excited them when I took my turn and mounted them as they had mounted me. They clawed at their pillows and sobbed tears of lust that restored their youthfulness. Three years after I escaped from the monastery and learned to live on the street, I was mixing with the frivolous and unpredictable company of fortune tellers, mediums, transvestites, Orientals, Freemasons, and frauds. We buzzed like bees 'round a honeycomb. We dazzled the rich with our trickery and defied them with our deformities. We sucked them dry, offering amusement, entertainment, and disgust in return.

I devoured the stories of vagabonds from far-off lands with greed: the voodoo enchanters, the American spiritists, the insane who believed they could do magic. It wasn't long before Paris started to stifle me. I wanted to travel, see the world. I had put aside enough money in the meantime, but something held me back. I had established a habit of following my twin brother at set times in one of my many disguises, one of my second skins. I felt chosen in one way or another when I saw him in heated café discussions with famous names from a world that was closed to me. I looked on as he flirted with Mme Sabatier to gain access to the circles that dined in the Rue Frochot.

He distributed his poems, wrote pieces for journals, published ecstatic reviews in the newspapers of books I considered worthless, empty, trivial. When Ernest Feydeau published his infantile and scurrilous novel Fanny, *my brother, with a talent I both idolized and envied, published a letter to the author praising and applauding him. He grovelled at the feet of Sainte-Beuve in the hope of acquiring recognition in the man's newspaper column "Lundi," but to no avail. I only had to look at him to know what he was feeling. We were one single soul forced by fate to exist in two bodies.*

Foraging through the city in my brother's wake took me to the places where the members of his ridiculous hashish club got together. He wrote rolling sentences in his essay "Wine and Hashish Compared as a Means to Achieve a Multiplication of the Individual's Potential" about the "extraordinary poetic engagement" the herb released in him. In those days I was already taking opium on a more or less daily basis and I discerned in the dreams he described the same tendency to ecstasy and melancholy I myself experienced.

His first poems, published in obscure rags, I read aloud while Le Maçon crouched beside his water pipe, his face expressionless. When I had finished reading he told me, dazed and drained, that he wasn't surprised that my brother had chosen evil as his poetic leitmotif. According to Le Maçon, Baudelaire had no other choice, since all the other domains were already occupied: Victor Hugo's ravings represented the earth, Musset's the hysteria of love, and Flaubert's cynical licentiousness modernity.

I was often angry at my brother for crawling through the mud in an effort to be accepted by the Masters of Literature. But it didn't last long. I knew that he would be recognized one day as a disturbing poet, a greater compliment than the bourgeois writers he flattered and rivalled would ever receive.

169

His verse, replete with subtle references and allusions, had a more powerful effect on me than opium. I was in love with that part of him that belonged to me. He hungered for intoxication and ecstasy. I had both at my disposal, in abundance!

I had everything he lacked and more.

Except that one thing, talent, the soul's magnifying glass.

The exquisite pain of creation.

My stepfather had admired my poems, but after reading Charles Baudelaire's first sonnets I stopped writing forever.

48

TUTÚN SI RÁBDARE.

Smoke and wait.

Those were the words of the Romanian gypsy king Lapuseanu as he and Bouveroux had, years ago, lain in wait for hours on end in a Paris suburb for the killer the newspapers had styled "the gypsy devil" because he targeted adolescent gypsy girls. Bouveroux was convinced that the killer wasn't going to put in an appearance and had asked Lapuseanu what to do. The gypsy king's advice proved right. Bouveroux had learned a lesson that day, a lesson that wasn't to be found in books.

But the inspector was plagued by the feeling that he was about to lose his self-control and that it could happen at any moment. The Turkish tobacco that usually calmed him only made him worse. Self-control was a matter of will. When did you know that your capacity to command your own thoughts was at its best? When you could bring your desires and imagination back into line after giving them free rein for a while, or when you could bridle them from the outset?

Bouveroux tried to concentrate on the manuscript. Perhaps he should thumb through the pages he had passed over in the hope of discovering some kind of conclusion or even a confession. Although the situation was now a great deal clearer, he still did not understand why the commissioner had been so upset when he finished reading the entire document. Its truth content continued to preoccupy him. Bouveroux was no lover of literature and knew little about it, but he suspected at times that these outlandish stories were the invention of a second-rate writer in search of attention, someone who had exploited the recent killings to launch his own disturbed fabrications.

On second thought, however, it seemed a roundabout way of attracting attention. In their desire to entertain the masses, newspapers and journals avidly serialized the most bizarre stories imaginable. Bouveroux had little doubt that they would have published texts such as this, if presented to them. Simone Bourbier hadn't.

The possibility that the text was not an insane story but represented the truth thus remained undiminished. According to Bouveroux, the female writer was mentally disturbed to say the least. The garbled chronology and implausibility of some of the events certainly pointed in that direction. It was all very different from the simple family histories Victor Hugo tended to pen. Or was she a modernist innovator à la Flaubert, who saw nothing but chaos and confusion in the world and was convinced that dreams had more influence on life than reality?

What about the document's style? When it came to literature, the inspector felt like a carthorse with blinkers. A carthorse couldn't possibly discern the truth, let alone aesthetic quality.

An explosion close-by shook the apartment building. Bouveroux noticed that his hands were trembling. In his young days he had owned a dog, Graziella, a fearless English pointer that had indulged its hunting instincts in the parks of Paris. But the sound of thunder made Graziella quiver, so much so that Bouveroux often feared the creature would waste away under the sideboard, where it always sought refuge in a storm. He never forgot the unfathomably sad, almost reproachful eyes that stared back at him as he lay on his belly in front of the sideboard and gently repeated her name.

Bouveroux suspected that every artistic soul felt the same way as Graziella when it thundered outside. Such tortured natures often sought refuge in absinthe, laudanum, or opium, as the author of this logbook had readily admitted. Bouveroux imagined that all these factors combined to induce a creative intoxication that turned the entire world into a dream factory.

The fact remained that his friend had believed every word of the manuscript and had left the prefecture in a state of distress. He remembered the commissioner saying something strange as he put on his hat: "If the mother wanted to kill me, did the daughter hold her back?"

49

"WHY NOW, HÉLÈNE, OF ALL times?" the commissioner muttered to himself. "Why choose now to turn everything upside down?"

Everything has its time, said the dead Hélène before she disappeared into a cultivated swirl of money and might.

The salon smelled of perfume, liqueur, and sweat. Outside, the rain had returned. The wind carried the sound of exploding grenades across the city, as if God had a barking cough. Count de Rémusat was wearing his third costume of the evening. He looked hideous in his French Polynesian islander outfit, complete with penis gourd, and his bloodshot eyes, which betrayed an excessive consumption of wine and cognac, only added to his ugliness. The count was doing his best to persuade Juno to present her derrière to his gourd. He had wrapped the pointed end in a three-colored scarf for the occasion, but Madame Tardivat deftly avoided his advances as she mingled with the boisterous dancing horde.

The orchestra struck up a tune for a popular oriental dance, lustily praised by Flaubert in his *Voyage en Orient*. A number of women, all of them under thirty, imitated Salome's dance of the seven veils. One of them was a *coufieh*, an effeminate Negro with a tiny head, bluish lips, dazzling eyes. The man wiggled his hips with enviable bestial perfection. The Bedouin orchestra—fanned by fashionable giant ferns—had been joined by a group of *darbuka* players. Their drone rumbled through the room like an incantation.

Someone tapped Lefèvre's shoulder. "For the Greeks, Thanatos was masculine," said Castellani. "But we've learned in the meantime that death is feminine, haven't we, commissioner?" He pointed his patrician nose in the direction of the dancers; the women had formed a circle around the Negro to the accompaniment of piercing shrieks of laughter. Lefèvre noticed how the Italian ambassador stroked his short beard as if it gave him enormous pleasure. The man exchanged a couple of words with his companion, a woman dressed in a remarkable medieval costume reminiscent of fairy tales with red apples. "*Qui non si muore mai,*" said Castellani, so quietly that Lefèvre leaned forward to listen. "Here one never dies."

"Not here, perhaps," said the commissioner.

"People are dying all over Paris and the entire country," Castellani concurred. A shadow covered his face. "War may be a horrendous thing, but in essence it's a banality, the consequence of common greed and cruelty. But what we fear the most is death brought about by someone driven by passionate love or insatiable hatred."

The commissioner looked his conversation partner up and down. "Tell me, Monsieur Castellani, why didn't you stay back with your friend Toulouse, then?"

Castellani smiled. "When I realized who you were I decided I would be safer with you, although you appear to be a little flustered this evening if you don't mind my saying. Aren't you in charge of the investigation into the Baudelaire killings?"

"You read the papers," said Lefèvre. "In spite of the war, or perhaps because of it, they love to publish ghost stories."

Castellani shrugged his shoulders. "People have no shame these days, commissioner. But there are thinkers nevertheless who have been trying to make connections. Did you read Edmond de Goncourt's musings in last week's *Le Rabelais?*"

The commissioner shook his head.

The painter seemed worried. "Edmond claims that the killer is an admirer of Baudelaire and is intent on getting rid of anyone who treated the man unjustly or spoke ill of him."

"A bold suggestion, Monsieur Castellani, and tempting in its simplicity. But this theory seems closer to Zola with his dockworker's imagination than the ethereal Edmond de Goncourt. Everyone knows that Zola is obsessed with mental disturbance. His characters are thus free to do the strangest things and he has no need to explain why."

The commissioner gulped greedily at his wine. Castellani studied his companion's face. Lefèvre's plump cheeks were accentuated by two broad vertical folds. His nose was squat but ample, not unlike a hamster's. He may have been on the wrong side of fifty, but the commissioner's barrel-shaped chest and heavy-limbed almost antediluvian build exuded a stiff sense of purpose.

"I have to admit that naturalism has sucked existence dry of its poetry," said Castellani. "Your critical approach cheers me, commissioner. I thought you were only interested in facts."

"I believe in the supernatural because I've experienced it," was the commissioner's curt response.

Castellani moved closer. There was fear in his eyes, the glistening fear of a deserter in a world of soldiers. "Baudelaire has featured in my dreams this last couple of nights, as a butterfly in stained glass. I gave him the piece one evening more than ten years ago at La Closerie des Lilas, when a bunch of painters, dancing girls, and revue artists had gathered at the café to celebrate spring. Baudelaire was completely out of place. He just sat there pallid and sombre in the midst of the chaos and tomfoolery, grinning dejectedly on one side of his face. I was young, prone to impulse, a lover of life without restraints. The Master sat in the middle of the hubbub nervously correcting the latest edition of *Les Fleurs du Mal* with a huge blue pencil. I asked him why.

"He glared at me, but his response was genuine. He was unhappy with the result of his work. Certain metaphors had become unbearable.

His images were too explicit, his rhetoric too classical. The cadence was fine, he admitted, and there was a sense of incantation in the verses, but in his opinion the *ambivalence* that characterized true masterpieces was insufficient. What courage! Surrounded by a voracious assembly of *reputations*, youthful artists who worshipped him and were thus capable of tearing him to shreds at any moment, he dared to criticize his own work out loud.

"I spontaneously handed him the results of that day's work, a stained-glass window. He was surprised, a little taken aback, not unpleasantly. We looked together at the window and it was then that he noticed it: A butterfly had melted unnoticed into the glass, and in spite of the heat it had kept its shape. Even its blue feelers had survived. Impetuous as I was in those days, I read meaning into the butterfly's presence. I told Baudelaire that he was a rare butterfly petrified in a world of heat and color and that I felt sorry for him. Struck by my own imagery, I was overwhelmed by boundless feelings of love for this tormented gentleman, whose poems I knew by heart.

"His reaction was alarming, to say the least. A blush of rage filled his cheeks. He grabbed my work and smashed it to pieces on the floor. I lost control of myself, grabbed him by the collar and punched him several times in the face. The onlookers pulled me away and I returned, sobbing, to my lodgings."

Lefèvre's response to his companion's outpouring was unexpectedly condescending: "I imagine you now see yourself as a petrified butterfly."

Castellani's face darkened, but he did not avoid the commissioner's eyes. "Ready to be smashed to pieces, commissioner," he said.

Lefèvre sensed an enormous vulnerability in his voice.

50

WHO WOULD EVER HAVE THOUGHT that Simone Bourbier could transform her pathetic life into such a masterpiece of lies and deceit? When I was twenty I discovered opium's red hues and the violet and green of laudanum. I enlisted as Le Maçon's apprentice, determined to become Satan's scorpion of love as Sister Wolf had predicted.

In short, I was a thief, a fraud, and a medium, and I knew all the tricks in the book.

But like an artist paid to write a eulogy for one or another dead author or painter, who knows in his heart of hearts that he is worth so much more than his so-called betters, I knew that my real talents went far beyond what I had learned. I sometimes sensed the pure flame of a power inside me that I was as yet unable to tame. Sacrifices were expected of me. Self-denial, no doubt. Outrageous barbarities.

I waited for a sign.

When I heard in 1841 that General Aupick had forced my twin brother to make a trip to India because of his rebellious behaviour, an unbearable anxiety took hold of me. A curious feeling of loneliness made my entire body quake, as if a spinning top had lodged itself in my chest. My first idea was to embark with Baudelaire and introduce myself during the journey as a lover of poetry. I fantasized about reading him Banville and Gautier and watching him quench his thirst on the poetry of such masters. The low, almost angry horizon and the restlessness of the sea would give my presence a mysterious character. I saw the light in the cabin where he would kiss me, compressed into dazzling beams like in the monastery chapel of my youth, conferring the faces they touched with the quality and timelessness of marble. But as my dreams reached their climax, despair crept in. How could he ever love me? My body may have been attractive at first sight, but only perverts could bear the appendage between my legs.

Le Maçon was a pervert. In essence he was a man of unrefined instincts, which made him long all the more for the supernatural. He had a feverish temperament, a constitution sensitive to molds and mildews, and prone to problems of the lungs. From time to time his feverish nature ignited a fire in his brain, making him rave and talk gibberish. He indulged the coarsest masculine desires, under the illusion that this would lead him to the transcendental, to what he called the noumena. *His supernatural talents were few and far between, his ability to pleasure a woman in bed virtually nonexistent. But he had a bizarre power of persuasion that made people believe in their own dreams. Le Maçon convinced me that I had genuine supernatural gifts. In his eyes they were a result of the abnormal in me. All I had to do was believe in them.*

When Charles embarked for India, Le Maçon and I were busy with a complicated extortion racket involving a close relative of Napoleon III. I forced myself to indulge my greed and suppress my love. I was intent on leaving the poverty of years on the street behind me, the years that followed my escape from the monastery. I used Charles's travels to embrace the obsession that fate bound us inseparably no matter what. I didn't dare speak to him in Paris, restrained as I was by superstitious fear, but there would be other opportunities, other travels.

Then no one and nothing would restrain me.

51

"THE DOCTOR, A DECENT, LOUSE-RIDDEN fellow with a lopsided moustache and prominent Adam's apple, had clearly been plucked from the
belly of a northern province. He prescribed liquorice tea whatever the
ailment, even for soldiers with serious gunshot wounds whose days were
numbered. Three times a day, warm if possible."

A few ladies giggled at the impudent young poet as he read aloud
from what he called his story-in-the-making. Others stared at him over
their fans with angry or affected eyes. He was wearing a shabby soldier's
uniform, had a roguishly fluffy beard and shifty eyes. He had just been
discharged from the front for, in his words, "gross cowardice." Zola himself had introduced him and apparently had high expectations of the man.
Lefèvre listened in amusement to the young Joris-Karl Huysmans, who
claimed that his story-in-the-making—*Sac au dos*—was set to evolve into
a literary pearl. When all was said and done, immortality in the world of
letters was such a foolish notion, enough to make a person raise his eyebrows in surprise at so much empty vanity and shrug his shoulders. But
Lefèvre remained fascinated nonetheless by people with artistic talent.

He had another reason to listen with interest to Huysmans. The war,
a mistress he both loved and loathed, thundered like a train through the

young man's words. Lefèvre pictured lines of young soldiers dressed in blue-black jackets, blue linen trousers with distinctive red stripe, and tall kepis, singing as they departed for the front. He knew their fate. There was no meaner butcher than the war. Girls wept, parents mourned, dogs hung their heads, but it was the young men themselves who faced death or mutilation.

To his credit, Huysmans—a mere slip of a lad—managed to communicate the war with the Prussians in the east of France with such a sense of doom that no one in his audience was left unmoved. Silence filled the grand salon. Count de Rémusat stood at the front with his head hung, lost in thought. His penis gourd looked like some ridiculous signpost pointing toward the battlefield. Hugo, still an imposing figure with his grey-bearded lionesque jowls, his prominent nose, and the conspicuous bags under his eyes, seemed to be pleased with the invisible fear that slithered through the salon. He popped his thumbs in his waistcoat pockets. His eyes met Lefèvre's and he inclined his head as if to welcome an unspoken compliment.

The young Huysmans concluded with an enigmatic smile: "The soldier's rucksack, ladies and gentlemen, is our future! It is filled with mouldy cheese and diluted, sour wine. It's lying in the mud, surrounded by hungry rats. Pick it up, hold it, cherish it. It's all we have left."

The applause was hesitant and was drowned out by a slightly grating voice: "Those who speak of the future must possess the third eye and consult the serpent of Tenebe!" The intervention was immediately followed by asthmatic gasping and wheezing.

52

IT HAPPENED PRECISELY AS *I had hoped: Baudelaire put a premature end to his forced Indian adventures. He returned to France via Mauritius and became a hashish user in Paris. I saw him occasionally in the company of the woman who had birthed us both. I wished her the loneliness and humiliation I had experienced since the day she rejected me. I pictured her throwing me out of the nest like a young cuckoo. And Baudelaire? Maybe one day he would be so unhappy as to hang himself from a streetlamp like De Nerval. He would call out with his last breath: "Le rêve est une seconde vie." I had already learned that dreams made people the willing victims of their own delusions.*

In the meantime, an increasing number of dullards had taken up the practice of Satanism as a fashionable diversion of choice, replete with circus-like affectations. But experience taught me that demons had the power to mirror realistic situations in the material world, that they could frustrate people's plans, tempt them to extremes in thought and deed. The Bible, which few read as it ought to be read, describes them more or less as they are: older than humanity, endowed with a longing for lawlessness, living on cruelty and pain.

Satanists are born, not made by sham mediums. Omnis determinatio est negatio, *God must first be denied, then the journey toward the more-than-human can begin.*

I often nourished such thoughts as I stood in a doorway opposite Hotel Pimodan, where I would wait for hours because I wanted to see Baudelaire's eyes when he returned from a meeting of his hashish club. An unforgettable place, the Pimodan. Mythical Egyptian animals on the stairs, a baroque doorway, and inside an apartment with gloomy vine- and vine-leaf-patterned wallpaper, prints of what they called les contemporains, *the indispensable cigar stand, and a buffet full of excellent wines and the infamous "green fairy."*

Baudelaire would spend his time there dreaming about the masterpieces he was going to write. I read the after-effects of his phantasms on his face when he emerged onto the street: superlative conceit, a new opinion about the world, a slogan that would be welcomed with applause by the young artists in Café Dinochau or the Moulin de Montsouris. If "the prince of Paris"—as the youth were inclined to style him—headed out one day without a hat, then the day after, dozens of young men could be seen strutting hatless along the city's boulevards, and the day after that, hundreds.

A well-dressed dandy full of inner vitriol, the Other in me would murmur when I followed Baudelaire like a faithful hound. One day . . . soon . . . mine.

For a moment, perhaps.

But a moment can be an eternity.

53

A SMILE OF SELF-PITY CROSSED Bouveroux's face as an erotically charged image of the mysterious woman with the tail crept across his mind. It had been a long time. Perhaps it was true that a man's desires needed more stimulation as he advanced in years, opening the way for the likes of de Sade, or Gilles de Rais, who offered young girls to a demon he called *Barron*.

He had noticed as he read that the author's behaviour had changed: She now treated Baudelaire like a character in a book, looked into his head and knew what he was thinking, much like a child who is convinced that the world is his own creation.

Bouveroux had seen fewer and fewer children playing on the streets in the last couple of months, but he remembered the sense of endearment he felt when he watched their agile, carefree bodies. Perhaps the author had had the same effect on men when she was young.

She must be close to fifty now, he thought. Was it possible that Satanism had taught her the secret of preserving her youth? Bouveroux shook his head at the thought. He realized that he wanted to see what her tail looked like.

He slapped his thighs in amazement. The story was beginning to get to him! The inspector had read a couple of tales by the renowned

Edgar Allan Poe, but he hadn't experienced the same *frisson* so many had reported, nothing more than a vague sense of admiration for the author's hysterical tempo.

But this document was of a different calibre. The desire and mysterious alienation it oozed were almost stifling. It was as if it had been written by a bodiless ghost stealing through the streets in the wake of a loved one.

Where did the enormous sense of compassion come from, the tenderness, or what passed for it? Confused, he thumbed through the copy of *The Flowers of Evil* he had procured after the murders. Now that the Prussians had tempered their shelling and Paris's still-surviving dogs had finally stopped howling, he was left with the feeling that a sort of tired resignation had descended upon the city. It made him long for his bed. *Either everyone is important or no one is important*, Lefèvre had once said to his men—apparently unrehearsed—when they had found themselves surrounded in the fort of Touggourt and had decided to break out that night. When he was finished speaking, the soldiers under his command thrust their rifles into the air as one, their bayonets flickering like tiny forks of lightning in the sun.

Against the background of the Franco-Prussian war, the Baudelaire killings were of little importance.

But: *Either everyone is important or no one is important.*

What happens when a young undeveloped child is labelled garbage and treated as such?

If it can't communicate with humans, it begins to believe it can communicate with demons. If it's reduced due to a deformity, it will do whatever it takes to attract the attention of the world.

Bouveroux's analysis suggested a possible explanation for the murder of de Cassagnac: The killer's brutal mutilations had transformed de Cassagnac into a parody of a woman. Was that perhaps a reference to the way she saw herself?

The inspector shook his head. How could a man like him imagine himself in the shoes of such a person? For years he had cherished the veiled hope that the brutality of the world concealed a fragile tissue of worth. He was born to follow the rational thread between one pure thought and another, but his work as a crime fighter had introduced him to a world of intense passions, a world that had made him focus on his emotions. And what had it achieved? A poorly camouflaged addiction to drink.

But, he realized, he had only downed a half bottle of wine that evening.

And at least he had grasped a philosophical truth, if only one: Everything, from the most vulgar lechery to the most selfless altruism, has its roots in pain.

54

YOU HAVE TO CREATE YOUR own eternity.

When Charles Baudelaire confided in a teahouse in Oualata that he was in search of the devil, it wasn't difficult to entice him. I played the role of a Frenchman who had been to Oualata more than once, and I played it with verve. I told him that I had gained the acquaintance of the inhabitants and their red clay houses on which the women painted magical dholi with a mixture of mud and camel shit.

Le Maçon had taught me their meaning before I left for Oualata, although he was extremely angry that I was "abandoning him."

As a pair we were "invincible," the best swindlers in Paris. But when he realized I was deadly serious about leaving for Africa, his behavior changed. He became sly and opportunistic, and so he remained. He taught me how to carry myself as a man, how to put the right kind of pressure on my vocal cords in conversation, how to create the illusion of stubble, how to bind my breasts. It's remarkable that men also prefer to deal with a smaller person of the same gender when they're doing business. It gives them a sense of superiority.

The African gold mines were Le Maçon's idea, as were the exceptional diamonds found on giant statues on islands in the Pacific Ocean. He had a gift for "producing evidence" of these sensational discoveries, but didn't

have the talent to tell a believable story. I worked out the details and suc-
ceeded—in masculine guise—at fooling the unsuspecting rich into parting
with their money. Unfortunately, Le Maçon wasn't able to turn our earnings
into profit. He not only threw away his money, he also wasted his wealth of
esoteric knowledge on whoever wanted to listen. As a result, he was always
short of cash.

Before I left for Mauritania, I learned from him that there was a mdrasa
in Oualata where students from various African countries came to study the
Moorish religion. But if God is in the neighbourhood, the devil is never far
off. The young students were pious to the extreme during the day, but at
night they were unable to resist the primitive urges of their race. Everyone
knows that Negroes are particularly keen on the act of reproduction. On
top of that, Oualata happened to be a religious centre and a garrison town
all in one, a combination that resulted in extremes. At night, the French
soldiers and the pious young bucks would meet in certain houses guarded
by bloated eunuchs.

I first fired Baudelaire's imagination with allusions to ancient Moorish
customs in the teahouse near the camel gate. We relaxed on cushions and
puffed at a water pipe. Then I told him the uncensored version of a magic
ritual involving a hartani, a black woman who had mastered old spells in
Hassaniya Arabic and was an expert in sexual magic. I insisted on being
present during the ritual, explaining that magic involving blood and sex only
worked when three were present.

He peered at me feverishly over the mouthpiece of his water pipe. Oualata's
hot season was too much for his neurasthenia, that was clear. He was perched
on the edge of insanity. The urges and tensions inside him wafted toward me
like the malignant wind that crept over the desert at night. I told him that the
hartani was beautiful but dangerous. That excited him, and when Charles
Baudelaire was aroused the rapport he sensed with death made him talkative.

He started to lament in short staccato sentences: "I don't understand why
I'm alive. I never wanted it. What cruel divinity has forced this existence upon
me? Who am I? As we speak, someone else is looking at you through these
eyes of mine. As I inhale this bitter smoke, I'm back in Paris with my black

mare Jeanne, melting into one, without fear, without thought of the past or the future, only the glorious now. I came here because the worshippers of Allah forsake wine. I wanted to order my mind, but the hashish is worse than the wine! The further I run away from death, the more malicious its grimace. Have you ever pictured the fires of hell? I do every day. A dreadful angst takes me by the throat. But the fear of being dependent in my old age is even worse. My father was a giant of a man, and as a boy I loathed and detested him. But at the end he lost control of his bodily functions and would lie in his own feces, curled up in shame like a shrivelled monkey. I was only six at the time, but even then I couldn't keep my eyes off the spectacle. All you could see were his eyes peering over the clean white sheets the nurses provided for him three times a day. Every day he muttered, 'I'm on the mend, absolutely! Next summer I'll take a walk through Paris!' Those eyes, good sir, still follow me, because they're my own eyes, pure unadulterated terror."

"You can only overcome your fear of death by becoming its instrument," I said. "Do you seek immortality, sir? Then your poetry, about which you speak with such enthusiasm, should not be so apprehensive. Your sonnets should elicit shame and rage in the hearts of those who read them, now and in every generation to come."

The glimpse of bemused fervor I saw in his eyes made my tail hum like a tuning fork.

I'm a greater artist than my brother. I possess the art of beauty, born in the hideous and evolved into perfection. I have developed the capacity to delude far beyond its other practitioners, adding intoxicants to sharpen its effect. Just as a poet gets drunk on words and thinks he can see what isn't there, I have used my herbs and chemicals to create new worlds for those I deceive, rob, and murder. Just as art has the power to slaughter reality, if only for a moment, I have taken the lives of lesser creatures who thought they were better than me.

But I did not want to take the life of Charles Baudelaire. I wanted his soul.

---·◦◦◦·---

After the customary greeting, I gave the ruffiano money. "Messu comb'ah crer'h," *the eunuch murmured.* "Welcome to paradise."

Paradise? Language can be the greatest liar. In places like Oualata, it was normal for several people at once to engage in the act of procreation in the huge mud-built chamber of the combakrer: men with women, men with men, men with children. They mounted each other like animals in a pen, far from the silk and damask of the Parisian bordellos. The Arab men shrink at nothing in such matters, and take particular pleasure in a woman's anus, thus preserving her virginity. But their orgies are confined to dark and dingy places like this, because they must conceal their deeds from Allah's wrathful gaze.

The ruffiano had clearly seen everything human bodies had to offer. But I knew he would think I was a djinn if he saw me naked, so I took the necessary precautions. The amount of money I gave him allowed me to demand exclusive use of the place for an hour. I told him we needed to be alone for the "divine ritual" we were about to perform. Such excuses always worked in that part of the world.

In addition, I had mixed cantharidin with the juice of the poppy and some local herbs. My twin wanted to ride Neptune like a horse and wield his trident and I was determined to make his dream a reality. But it was vitally important that he did not recoil at the last moment. The cantharidin would take care of that.

The hartani was a mixture of Muslim and Nubian. She had dotted her black eyelids with silver antimony and concealed the lower part of her face with a band of velvet. She smelled of butter. Her loins bore a tattoo, branded onto the skin like an animal. She had long legs, curvaceous and slender, lively buttocks, a feisty young filly.

The French legionnaires have a name for such black creatures: gazelles, a term adopted by their Arab masters. The white of her eyes was coffee-brown.

I noticed that my brother was taken aback by this, but he behaved manfully, determined to incarnate the dandy he believed himself to be. Her master, she told me in broken French, had named her Hara. Baudelaire, to the core un homme de lettres, *told me rather smugly that it was the Persian name for Eve and then muttered something about the serpent in paradise.*

"The serpent in the garden of Eden wanted to share in the bliss Adam and Eve enjoyed," I answered. "Was that such a terrible sin? Was that reason to call it Satan?"

The cantharidin silvered his eyes as he bared his teeth.

55

PEOPLE TURNED AND STARED AT the old man who had invoked the serpent of Tenebe. He stuck out his chest and righted his Jewish magician's hat with his left hand. Having caught the attention of the audience, he introduced himself as Eliphas Levi, a senior member of *La Fraternité de la Société de la Mort*, and announced that in a few moments he would predict the future with the help of a medium. Lefèvre and Castellani exchanged a knowing glance: The good count was prepared to use every theatrical trick in the book to amuse his audience. His guests in the meantime had downed so much exquisite wine that the spirit of death, at whom they had only just been scoffing, started to manifest itself between the folds of the curtains. Lefèvre despised spiritists, secret societies, and the rest of the circus. *That's how it goes with Death*, he thought. *You can challenge him, spit in his face, run away from him, try to forget him, but Death will never change. Death is the future.*

Levi, a pompous elderly gentleman with a tubercular wheeze, took to the stage and did his best to amuse his audience. A political joke, a splash of sexual innuendo, a little palmistry—de Rémusat did the honors and agreed indifferently with the fortune teller's every prediction. It wasn't difficult: a long life, a string of mistresses, and a handful of castles in the seventh *département*.

Lefèvre noted that the despair he had been trying to avoid the entire evening was creeping closer by the minute. What did he have to do to give his life a little renewed flavor? The commissioner sensed an inexplicable rage take hold of him, as if he wanted to escape his own body. He knew that it was in reality a question of fear and shame. He always felt the same when he sensed the presence of the ghost of Hélène.

"You are surely aware, esteemed friends, that French generals are experts at continuing to fight old wars in which they suffered defeat, when they're already in the middle of a new one," said Levi, who had a sonorous and penetrating voice in spite of the nasty cough. "How are they likely to fare this time against the tyrannies of Bismarck? During our military campaigns in Mexico, our esteemed generals were too cautious. Do you think they're now likely to be overconfident?"

Count de Rémusat bleated like a drunken goat and slapped his thighs. His penis-gourd got stuck in Madame de Massignac's shepherdess costume. "Napoleon's planning to captain the troops himself!" the nobleman sputtered. "He's suffering unbearable pain from a stone in his bladder, is in constant need of a chamber pot, and can't manage more than a couple of minutes on his horse!"

The assembly laughed and gloated ostentatiously. "Our emperor's been blown once too often by those whores at the Place Pigalle who spend their nights chewing opium balls," one of the guests roared. "Their saliva is worse than that of Cerberus . . . enough to give anyone a stone in the bladder."

The response was less rowdy on this occasion and the laughter thin. Levi took advantage of the change in mood. He gave a sign to the servants to lower the lights. A table was carried onto the stage, at which Levi took his place. "Ladies and gentlemen," he said. This time his voice sounded measured and authoritative. "You're thinking what an affable charlatan this old man is! A wonderful way to pass the time . . . fill our glasses! You smile condescendingly when you hear me call myself a

Satanist! For you they're all the same: spiritists, Rosicrucians, fakirs, mediums, you name it. They're all doing excellent business, and why? Prussian shells may bring destruction and the fear of death, but we're more afraid of what happens *after* we die. The same charlatans spirit you away from reality with their séances and their necromancy. You love it. It's easy, as I've just demonstrated. And let me assure you: It's a money maker. But a true Satanist? That's a different story. If he practices the ancient arts correctly, he becomes an authentic oracle. Who has courage enough to hear the *true* future?"

Castellani tugged the commissioner's sleeve and wanted to say something. Lefèvre waved him aside. He was aware that the wine had gone to his head, but his thoughts were still clear. His senses started to play tricks with him as in an opium dream. The air in the ballroom seemed heavy, creating an aura that shut out the rest of the world. The commissioner had the feeling that the room had detached itself from Paris and transported itself to the portals of hell. He sensed the demon from his youth standing to his left, its yellow eyes flickering. And she was there too, Hélène, on his right. He heard her speak in a gentle tone, as if the intervening years had been a mere fantasy:

> The demon twists and turns forever at my side;
> Surrounds me like the air, intangible but real;
> I breathe it in with greed, its fire I feel
> It fills me to the core. I am its bride.

Be silent, thought Lefèvre, *be silent, please.*

As if it were a sign, an explosion of jeers and taunts from the spectators interrupted his reverie. Did the old beggar doubt their courage? The future was in their hands! Puffed up and insulted, they demanded an apology.

"Handsomely done!" said Castellani patronizingly. "Cheap revues like this are enough to make people forget we're at war."

A woman ascended behind the old man as if from the ground. She was dressed in the garb of an Egyptian goddess and she gracefully swayed her hips. The hubbub subsided. Oohs and aahs surged back and forth. Flute music, its source impossible to determine. Lefèvre frowned and exchanged a glance with Castellani. The stained-glass maker shrugged his shoulders and winked toward the exit.

But the commissioner was glued to the spot when the voluptuous woman with almond-shaped eyes opened her mouth and started to speak. The timbre of her voice took him by surprise: seductive, insistent, slightly mocking.

> *Like a constellation of death*
> *The heavens sparkle*
> *With a spirited bal masqué;*
> *Cannons sputter victory rounds*
> *Prussian Pickelhauben spit blood*
> *And force the French to their knees.*
> *Their emperor crucifies his guilt;*
> *Anointed by fortune, a hero in his mind*
> *He forgets the victory of the grave.*

A wailing sound made way for a thin whistle. The shell's explosion was an anticlimax, a muffled rumble that sent a collective sigh through the assembled merrymakers.

"Even Victor Hugo could write better poetry," Castellani mumbled in Lefèvre's ear. "Martial law commands more respect than civil law, commissioner. You should have this place cleared to 'protect the safety of the guests.' Then we can spend the rest of the night in gentler arms."

Lefèvre nodded absently. He suddenly became aware of a desire to take someone into his confidence. He was fifty-three. Soon it would be too late and the people in his world would never have the chance to be real people, people of flesh and blood, and even the tiniest sparkle of love would be lost to him forever. The woman on the stage swayed with elegance, as if she was about to utter a new oracle.

"You are insulting France, good woman!" Count de Rémusat bellowed, penetrating the general din. Exaggerated emotion brought on by excesses of alcohol made his voice shrill.

Castellani sighed. Lefèvre understood a barely audible "I rue the day I was born."

"Are you also tired of life?" he said impulsively.

The stained-glass maker's whiskers moved as he gritted his teeth.

"Let me tell you something," said Lefèvre. "It's important to me and now is the moment. Tonight or never. I don't know you and you don't know me, but I have a sense nonetheless that we are kindred spirits."

Castellani raised his eyebrows, but didn't appear surprised. "And your duty?" he said calmly. "What will the prefect say if you abandon this esteemed company?"

Lefèvre looked around. The crowd jeered, drowned the oracle out, surged toward the stage. Eliphas Levi raised his arms in a gesture of calm, winking at his companion that it was time for her to take her leave.

"If anything happens here, my report will put it down to the Prussian shells," he said. "These days, who knows *precisely* what's going on in Paris?"

56

MURDERERS, ROGUES, AND RASCALS HAVE *called me "inhuman."*

Why?

Because I have placed love above all things.

I'm too human.

What do we know about dreams?

Dreaming is the only human talent that matters. In our dreams we can be God, build palaces without equal and send them soaring through the air at a snap of the fingers, and we can make the world bow down at our feet.

What do we know about truth?

Truth is a figment of the material world's imagination, held out to us as a reward, as if we were dogs.

My immense and merciless love made it possible for me to dream reality in this life.

When I was awake I had to walk a dangerous path strewn with inner torment.

But when I dreamed, assisted by my ever-increasing expertise in African plants used for centuries by féticheurs, I was the flower of evil, the bride of Satan, pulling aside the bogus curtain to expose the filth inside the temple of the world.

People say that true love is self-denying. People say that true love seeks nothing more than the happiness of the beloved.

Such are the words of troubadours and their cheap sentiment.

True love is mystical and cruel.

It is reserved for gods and demons.

Humans have to make do with a diluted version, a mixture of true love and the infantile desire to be cradled.

The curse I bear between my legs has given me the temperament of a primitive animal. But being human nonetheless, I am forced to endure a longing to be cherished.

This contradiction has left me noxious and impetuous, and often takes me out of myself.

When my brother lay in the arms of the hartani, his limbs limp, his gaze absent, the time came for me to undress. My heart sank. I would just as happily have taken a knife and murdered them both. But I had no time to lose: There was clearly no heat being generated between my brother and Hara. The waves of animal lust I had expected to engulf them were supposed to give me the courage to effectuate my plan.

Now I had to seek power from within.

On that decisive night in my life I was nothing more than a woman in need. Shame and desire, hatred and affection raged side by side. I was inconsolable and longed for compassion.

I leaned over Charles. His eyes were closed, his breathing light and shallow, his cheek hot and dry.

"Jeanne Duval is lying at your side, with her ebony curves, her high waist and endless legs, her regal attitude and her untamed loins, goddess and animal in one, and all you can do, Charles, is fall asleep?"

He didn't react. I pulled his arms, beat his chest. Hara withdrew into a corner like a terrified animal. His member was cold and sickly pale. I rubbed it with rhinoceros fat mixed with powdered Yohimbe bark. I placed my hand on his chest. Moments later his heart started to race, one of the early effects of the Yohimbe. His body moved, his eyes rolled in their sockets. The foam of passionate intoxication brought about by the Yohimbe appeared on his lips.

Hara stared in astonishment at his penis as it turned red and straightened itself. I whispered anew in his ear that his "glorified whore" was ready to mount him. The cantharidin did the rest: His eyes opened, and I could see through the lust in his eyes that I had taken the form of Jeanne Duval. He threw himself at me, and while he took me with all the power his frail body could muster, I buried my head in Hara's lap as she watched and gasped.

When his seed exploded inside me, the tail between my legs became hot, dry, and invincible.

Hara was never able to speak about what she then saw. She completely lost her head.

57

SOMETHING HAD ATTRACTED HIS ATTENTION.

A thought that had shaved past his consciousness like a razor.

Bouveroux set the notes to one side.

The bombardment had subsided. Bouveroux had read in *Le Moniteur* a couple of days earlier that Krupp's steel cannons, which were breech loaded with armour-piercing shells, were inferior to de la Hitte's front-loadable bronze cannons, which could be fired at greater speed. The patriotic article had saddened and angered him. The French couldn't see the forest for the trees. This war was going to cost France rivers of blood and enormous amounts of money, not to mention the irreparable shame of defeat. The journalist had concluded his piece with the bombastic words: "The dagger of French bravery shall pierce the cold Prussian heart."

The dagger.

He picked the weapon up from his desk.

Bouveroux realized he too had been unable to see the forest for the trees.

He could hardly believe his own eyes.

He had *refused* to recognize the dagger because of the memories the Arab weapon brought back to him.

The pressure in his stomach became unbearable, as if some terrified prickly animal was twisting and turning in his guts.

The inspector remembered word for word what Lefèvre had told him a couple of months earlier in a café: "She's drawn to exotic things. I gave her that dagger as a gift, the one that carved a hole in your belly in the souk in Algiers."

Bouveroux pictured the half-apologetic, half-mocking grin on his friend's face when he said, "You never know with a blade like that. And if it's cursed, then a witch like Claire de la Lune will know what to do about it."

58

"IF YOU HAD SEEN LA Meurthe through the eyes of my youth, Castellani, you would understand why I listen to dreams in spite of my rough exterior. When winter arrived, and the *oualous* stopped sending their tree trains down the river to supply Baccarat's crystal factory with firewood, the water took on a purple hue. Between Lunéville and Nancy lie the vast forests of Lorraine, where dark stone bridges have been built across the water. Where La Vezouze and La Meurthe merge, there are dozens of little waterfalls. When we were small, Hélène and I thought that veiled water spirits were hiding under the white-crested waves, waiting to pull us to the bottom. We had a place where we pretended I was a daring knight who saved her from a dragon. It was on the riverbank, surrounded by twisted willows. In the summer there were thousands of catkins and I used to tease Hélène with them.

"One autumn day I was lying there in our place, asleep, daydreaming, who knows? It's such a long time ago. For some unexplained reason I raised my head, although I hadn't heard a noise. Ten yards ahead of me I saw my uncle Jean-Paul and my sister Hélène crossing the bridge. Was it the way Hélène followed her uncle with her head hung and her arms limp? My uncle's huge angular head and glassy eyes had always filled me with awe. There was something awkward in his step. He marched ahead of my sister like one of the ancient Roman generals my father had told me about. I don't know why, but I got to my feet, climbed the hill, and followed them. They then took the turn for Curey sur Vezouze. They were only a couple of hundred meters away.

"I hid myself behind trees, in gulleys, crouched like a hunting dog at the side of the road. Neither of them looked back, not once. Their outlines stood out in sharp relief against the steely autumn sky, reminiscent of an old etching. What was I thinking? I can't remember. My uncle's brawny yet tranquil frame tugged my sister along, without a word of protest. Fifteen minutes passed, perhaps more. Then my uncle suddenly turned and Hélène stopped in her tracks. I was in the middle of a row of trees close to the river and didn't dare move. Hélène bowed her head even further, as if offering her neck to an executioner.

"He grabbed her in his chubby arms, which always smelled of pork jelly, and tossed her over his shoulder like a ragdoll. Without looking back he clambered to the left, up the incline where La Meurthe is supplied by one of the streams that spring up in the Vosges. The narrow channel was littered with rocks and pebbles and its banks were thickly wooded with elm, making it easy for me to follow. In later years I couldn't get rid of the idea that I already knew then what my uncle was planning. If that's true then I'm as much a monster as he and the insanity in his blood is hereditary. What can I say? I was almost thirteen, hardly a child, but not yet a man. Do you know what a shock to the nerves feels like, a serious shock? It's like a bolt of lightning cutting you in two.

"I remember it as if it was yesterday. My uncle, the pig butcher, the village idiot who made our family the laughingstock, stripped the clothes from Hélène's body. What surprised me most was the intensity with which he raped her, knowing that he was usually easily distracted, like a child. He uttered a high-pitched, resounding roar, and slowly got to his feet. I lay in the grass, pressed into the hill. I could smell autumn in the fresh grass beneath me and could feel my heart pounding against the ground. My uncle lifted both arms in the air and did a sort of dance. A scream escaped my lips. Jean-Paul turned and held up a warning finger in my direction. He laughed. All the while, Hélène lay on the ground with her legs apart.

"My uncle laughed again, but then he stiffened as if he'd just had a thought. I hared down the hill. Jean-Paul called after me with his throaty voice. I heard his bleating reverberate along the river, halfway between a plea and a curse. I raced home. I had to stop two or three times from the stitch in my side. My breath peeped in my ears, as if my uncle was running after me on his huge, squeaking sandals. I looked back. There was no one in sight, but I still kept running as fast as I could. When I got home I needed time to calm down and report what I had seen.

"My father's face turned deathly pale. I think I fainted at that point. All I remember was our housekeeper putting me to bed and saying 'poor boy' time and time again. The gendarmes took hours to find Hélène. My uncle had hacked off her arms with his butcher's axe. He had also amputated her legs. Perhaps he had been afraid that his doll would run away as I had done. My uncle was arrested the same day. He was rambling along the riverbank, rasping at everyone he passed. He was locked up in an asylum. I locked myself up inside of me. I've never been able to escape.

"I remember the unspoken accusation in my father's eyes: *Why didn't you stop him?* In spite of his strength, Jean-Paul would follow like a cart-horse if you tugged on his braces. He was colossal, much stronger than a normal man, but he was so docile that the village butcher let him help in his shop. People laughed at him. Most of the time he didn't understand, or he would just grin stupidly. When the police showed him my sister's body with his dried-out seed on her belly, he was emotionless, as if he was looking at a slaughtered pig.

"I didn't stop him, Castellani. That knowledge has haunted me all my life and prevented me from loving any other person than my sister."

59

"I'm informed that a woman of easy virtue keeps her boudoir here, good sir. Open the door."

"There's no one here but me. The occupants—all of them respectable citizens—have left the building for fear of the Prussians."

"I still insist that you open up." Bouveroux showed the tall, slightly stooped, hollow-eyed concierge his police badge. He gestured to the coachman to ride on and watched the glow of the coach's lamp flicker against the house fronts on the Rue de Lappe as it departed.

"Don't the police have anything better to do?" the concierge sneered.

"The Prussians are bandits, it's true, but they're outside the city. Our job is to settle scores with the bandits inside the city."

The concierge lit an oil lamp and crossed the inner courtyard. Bouveroux was surprised at how tall he was and at the freakish shadows cast by his crooked form. A bitter wind engulfed them both with the smell of saltpetre. Bouveroux pressed his hat firmly onto his head.

"Bandits? The Prussians aren't bandits, they're savage barbarians."

"They have some of the best scientists."

The concierge looked over his shoulder. The reflection of the light made his right eye appear like a black stain. "And even better philosophers and mystics. There's something frightening in the Prussian soul, officer. War for them is something mystical. The bond between soldiers, blood brothers, sucking up the energy of the dead after battle, that sort of idea. All very mysterious and barbarian, while on the surface they seem so orderly."

The man opened the door to the building at the rear that had been divided floor by floor into apartments. Bouveroux looked up. There was no light to be seen in any of the windows. "They say that Generals Trochu and Ducrot are set to clip their wings, in spite of their renowned Prussian savagery," he said absently.

The concierge spat on the ground and stared slyly at the inspector. "The rich eat fried elephant trunk. The poor eat each other. Let me warn you: Paris is facing the bitterest winter it has known for centuries. *Homo homini lupus*."

Bouveroux disliked the man. He had a reflective mind, but there was something dank and dreary about him. "You're a man of clear convictions," he said with as much neutrality as he could muster.

The smell in the stairwell was unfamiliar to the inspector. It wasn't exactly pleasant, but nor was it bitter or sour. There was something animal and musky about it.

"The apartment I'm looking for is on the second floor," he said to the man's back. The concierge lumbered up the stairs in front of him without a word of response. A surprising picture filled the inspector's mind. He had the feeling that he saw the face of the man climbing the stairs in front of him changing into another one. He fumbled instinctively for his pistol.

But when the concierge turned at the top of the stairs he seemed spritely and animated, a little roguish. "It's Pascal's law, good sir: In times like these, the literate are forced to work as concierges while well-dressed monkeys run the empire."

"Open the door immediately," said Bouveroux, intentionally brusque. "I don't have much time." He saw no point in getting into a discussion with this strange fellow.

The concierge bowed derisively and produced a bunch of keys from his trousers pocket. He looked like a hawker who had hawked his last item. The door flew open. The smell in the apartment was more intense.

The living room was empty.

"Satisfied, Monsieur l'Inspecteur?"

"Where does that door lead?" asked Bouveroux, pointing to a door in the right wall.

"The kitchen and the sanitary facilities," the man curtly replied.

The hairs on the back of the inspector's neck stood to attention. "Open it."

The concierge glared, walked ahead of the inspector and opened the door.

That smell again, even stronger.

There were signs of recent use in the kitchen: a couple of plates and a tray in the sink. But the shelves were empty. The inspector sighed and was about to turn and leave when a shiver ran up his spine as he passed a large built-in cupboard. His right hand reached automatically for the cupboard door. He opened it and recoiled. A shrivelled head with empty eye sockets peered back at him.

The mummified head had black skin.

Hara was never able to speak about what she then saw. She completely lost her head.

Bouveroux turned to the concierge, a sliver of darkness skulked in the corner of his eye, a blinding flash, then nothing.

60

THE DARKNESS WAS COMPLETE, COLD and indifferent. It kept the pain at bay. Someone struck a match and lit an oil lamp. Bouveroux gasped for air; his head throbbed. He tugged at his chains, but soon gave up.

The concierge leaned against the wall by the window, his face in the shadow cast by the lamplight.

"I'm given to understand, Monsieur Bouveroux, that you are a lover of science, logic, and deduction." The man's voice was hoarse, a little smug, like the voice of an actor.

"Don't tell me you're clairvoyant," said Bouveroux. "I advise you to let me go, and . . ." To his surprise, a slight gesture of the man's hand was enough to silence him. The dizziness in his head, the sense of being out of contact with himself—where did these sensations come from? Bouveroux had been in fights before and had taken enough blows. They usually fired his obstinate fighting spirit, which was hidden deeper within him than Commissioner Lefèvre's rage.

"No," said the concierge. "Sadly, I'm not. But your friend has talked a lot about you, you know . . . to a certain woman."

"He's not my friend. He's my superior."

"Oh? Have the years since Algeria put distance between you?"

"You seem to know a lot about us." Bouveroux tried to think. What did the man want? He didn't seem particularly dangerous. Why then did he feel such fright?

"You'd be surprised how much a man will confess to a whore. Especially if he's sweet on her but won't admit it."

"What do you want?"

The concierge was conspicuously silent. Bouveroux looked him up and down. Tall, thin, wavy hair, not the youngest, a little moth-eaten, the type you would walk past on the street without a second glance. But if you looked a little closer, you could see that the man had an intensity in him that electrified the room.

"Like everyone else, I want wealth and power." But his voice sounded indifferent, as if his thoughts were elsewhere. Bouveroux jumped when the concierge peeled himself from the wall, lurched toward him a couple of steps, and peered down at him. His breath smelled of copper. "How much do you know?"

Bouveroux looked his attacker in the eye. "About what?"

"Do you know Simone Bourbier?"

"Is she real?"

"Answer me."

"Only from her memoirs. And I didn't read everything."

"So you never met Claire de la Lune?"

"No. The commissioner talked about her, but we never met."

"Does your friend know you're here?"

His first instinct was to lie, but he was convinced the man would notice and that it would only make things worse.

"No."

The concierge appeared to relax a little. "Tell me where Lefèvre is at this moment."

"I don't know. I was looking for him and had hoped to find him here. They're expecting me back at the prefecture any minute . . ."

The concierge smiled. "That was a lie."

"Believe what you like. I—"

The knife appeared in an instant, hacking to the left of his head. Bouveroux felt a searing pain and stared aghast at the bloody ear as it landed on the floor.

"I might not look it, inspector," said the concierge, "but I am a desperate and furious man whose life is in danger. That puts *your* life in danger too, understand?"

In spite of the blood throbbing in his cranium, Bouveroux had a flash of intuition. He was about to die. His fate had been settled. Would it be quick and merciful or slow and painful?

The dripping blade appeared beneath his chin and pushed his head upwards. The man stared at him with the same intensity as before. He nodded gently. "I see you understand, inspector. The choice is yours."

61

THE COMMISSIONER AND CASTELLANI SAT head to head at a *table d'hôte* in the Rue l'Egout deep in conversation. The wine smelled of ink. The remains of a meal, for which an old dog had offered its life, were scattered across the musty tablecloth. Tender puppy meat was impossible to come by. The mongrel's stringy flesh stuck between their teeth.

But they paid no attention to the messy table, or the sea of dour faces, or the noise, or the smoke. People spoke loudly and gesticulated wildly to drown out their fear of the shells. As a result of what they had witnessed that night, Lefèvre and Castellani had set aside formality and exchanged intimate experiences.

"I love death and fear it all at once," said Lefèvre. "People used to know how to die. They had a God who had promised them final victory. They spat in the face of death. Now we're left with the philosophers and their Nothingness. What makes us want to live forever? Why can't we accept that our time has come when it presents itself? Pride is to blame, the pride of our accursed souls. And my soul is prouder than any other. Since my youth I've seen Hélène appear as a ghostly garment, an empty shell, bouncing like a kite in a strong coastal wind: *Why are you still alive?* I've sought danger, challenged death, engaged in duels I would normally have been unable to win. I've insulted death as often as I could, stared it in the face, cursed it. But my fear, respect, and love for death have remained the same."

"My mother was a wise woman," said Castellani. "She drummed it into me from an early age that the Bible speaks of three different heavens. The third heaven is paradise itself, but the majority of us aren't pure enough to get in. When you die, commissioner, ask the angel you call Hélène to take you by the hand. If you find yourself in the first heaven, you'll have to put up with the wiles and allurements of minor demons. If you find yourself in the second, you'll have to look at yourself in the mirror of your soul and judge yourself . . . not exactly the easiest task. If you arrive in the third heaven, then Hélène's love must be outstanding and you will be set free of the contradictions that plague you."

A figure appeared behind Castellani, his arms flailing in the air. The commissioner automatically reached for his weapon, but recognized the figure in the nick of time. "No . . . but . . . what a surprise!" the young Henri Toulouse roared, with a blush on his cheeks and a ferocious glint in his eye. He patted Castellani on the shoulder with gusto. "I was hoping I might find you in this excellent establishment. Haven't we spent many a pleasant hour here, philosophizing about art? Gone are the days! Those wonderful meals? Gone forever! And you, my dear commissioner! Is that a blush? War or no war, the wine they serve here in the Café Robespierre loosens the tongue and dulls the brain. Don't you agree?"

Lefèvre surmised that the young *franc-tireur* was under the influence of one or another intoxicant. The fellow nearly collapsed, recovered just in time, and grabbed the back of a chair. "The night is still young, gentlemen! By the way, please excuse my behaviour . . . The Muse is a soldierly mistress, merciless with the whip, forcing an artist like myself to follow his instincts from time to time. But such impertinence has its advantages. The sketches I made this evening of those wolves in human form have left me elated."

Toulouse grabbed Castellani's glass uninvited and emptied it in a single gulp. Lefèvre cast an amused glance at the stained-glass maker who smiled paternally at his young pupil.

"What a night," the young artist continued eagerly, "magic everywhere. Perhaps death is out there waiting, guiding a Prussian shell in our direction? But if that happens, they'll say we lived a glorious life! Listen, you have to hear this . . . something really strange happened to me."

62

"YOU'VE COME TO TERMS WITH death, Bouveroux. I can see it in your eyes. I'll give you a potion with fast-acting poison when this alcove is almost bricked up. I'm a sentimental man. My tears are mixing with the mortar. Do you see them? They are the proof that I'm not lying. I don't want to do this, but I have to. Let me tell you a farewell story, to help you understand what a dismal state this country of ours is in. You'll probably think it extreme, perhaps even incredible. You are, after all, a member of the middle class.

"What do you know about the things that are going on in the belly of the monster we call France? Hunger and scarcity change people into animals. Animals, Bouveroux, have unheard-of capabilities some might describe as magical. Don't look at me like that. If you prefer not to be blindfolded, you should look away. I can't stand it when people look me in the eye. It has nothing to do with your impending death. That's a *business matter.* Circumstances have forced me to kill you. Your curiosity is to blame. And yet it pleases me to be able to exchange ideas with you before we say our last goodbyes.

"I presume you think I'm crazy. But the strangest thing is, and forgive me for turning the tables, I think the same of you. I simply cannot

214

understand why people resign themselves to a God and a morality that are completely arbitrary. Somebody made them up, good sir! All my life I've been plagued by this lack of comprehension. It caused terrible problems when I was young. I had an inquisitive soul. I wanted to belong, but no matter what I did I failed. So I concluded, after much reflection, that beings exist, like me, that have a human form but are not part of the human race. Don't you think that's a frightening idea? I did at the start, until I realized it's what made me who I am: *different*.

"Be that as it may, I promised to satisfy your curiosity before you die. That's the least I can do. You see, you should never trust other people in this life. And let me assure you I've lived long enough. I've amassed fortunes with ease and lost them just as quickly. At this moment I'm poor. I was planning to do something about it with the help of Simone Bourbier. Her origins, like mine, are questionable. People living with a family secret often wish they were someone else.

"But I digress, and our time is short. In the eighteenth century, a certain philosophical alchemist and Freemason by the name of Cagliostro lived at the court of Louis XVI. The man was a pupil—some say, a son—of the renowned Count de Saint-Germain, the greatest magician of all time. Cagliostro made a name for himself at the court by predicting the killing of a senior clergyman, a friend of Cardinal de Rohan, and a lady-in-waiting, both down to the last detail. Cagliostro was a wise man: He didn't go so far as to say the deaths of the two beautiful individuals he had predicted were murder, but he described exactly what their bodies would look like when found.

"A few days later, his prediction proved to be exact. Everyone in the capital was gossiping about the ghastly details of the killings. The genitals of each victim had been cut off and sewn into place on the other's body. Cagliostro's name as a clairvoyant magician was established forever. Some courtiers were heard to whisper that he had committed the murders himself under orders from Cardinal de Rohan, and for reasons that spoke for themselves: The father confessor of the lady-in-waiting, who happened to be one of de Rohan's mistresses, had extended his pastoral services to include the body of his confessant in addition to her soul. No one could prove the theory. No one dared put the slightest obstacle in the path of the cardinal or Cagliostro, who had worked his way into Louis's favor with his predictions.

"But the rumors persisted. As Cagliostro walked through the corridors of the palace, a voice hissed 'vicious murderer' from behind one or another brocade curtain, followed by the sound of running footsteps. Cagliostro was constantly looking over his shoulder. The only way he could survive this courtly hornet's nest was to maintain the king's favor. When revolution threatened, Louis wanted to know what the future held. Cagliostro predicted he would live to a ripe old age, reign long and victorious, and enjoy the love of his people to the last. The magician had no choice, but he knew exactly what was going to happen. Less than three years later the French Revolution broke loose. But by that time Cagliostro was already safe in Rome where he was advising the pope in the utmost secrecy.

"Crowned heads and their like often have a penchant for clairvoyants, especially in times of disorder and war when a little supernatural advice can come in handy. Who is planning to stab them in the back, smuggle gunpowder into their bedchamber, poison their wine? Are there spies at their court? They're prepared to pay good money for such information. A couple of years ago, before I fell into discredit, I was a welcome medium at the court of Napoleon III. When I was in good spirits, I would conjure accordions in the air playing the prettiest of melodies, and fill salons with the sweet smell of roses. I made ghosts appear in the palace fountains and even produced ectoplasm from my nose. And for all these tricks I was generously rewarded.

"But after my fall I experienced bitter poverty. I needed a kill-or-cure remedy to get back on my feet. My old friend Simone reminded me of the Cagliostro affair. I hadn't seen Bourbier in a long time. Loners like us only connect when we have to, then we each go our separate ways. Simone is a madam who supplies Napoleon III and his special needs. You'll have heard stories about Napoleon III and that zizi of his.

Not exactly the most reliable part of his anatomy. It's certainly not the fault of our sparkling empress, that's for sure. Rumors are making the rounds that Napoleon isn't averse to a tender little pecker every now and then. That's where Simone comes in. She supplies the peckers and other specialities that would send your sense of decency into a serious spin.

"Simone is unique. She claims in certain circles that she's the rejected twin sister of Charles Baudelaire. And Baudelaire, what a character! Intense! Died of the Spanish pox, they say. I can believe it, a whoremonger like him perished by the Morbus Gallicus, otherwise known as 'syph.' And what a death! But don't get me started. Never speak ill of the dead, eh?

"Anyway, I was talking about Simone. I noticed she only told a trusted few that she was the poet's sister and that she'd been locked up in a monastery at an early age. If I had been her I would have shouted it from the rooftops, especially after her brother started to make a name for himself. And after he died there would have been no shutting me up! If you ask me there's something not right about that story of hers, although it's an excellent sales pitch. Paris is bursting at the seams with stories that are much harder to believe than my Simone's. Some claim they're descendents of the sun god Ra, or that they share the same blood as Madame de Pompadour. Others are convinced they're children of Cardinal Richelieu's bastard son. Tasty fables, all of them. A veritable feast! But who would want to fantasize about being related to some obscure poet? Hardly a reason to publish your memoirs, don't you think?

"By the way, that document you were on about, the one Simone wrote. I'm keen to take a look at it, very keen. I'll pay a visit to your rooms later and will carefully read it. I had no idea our Simone had literary talent, although it was obvious that she was the eccentric type. You mentioned she dressed as a man. She had good reason to deceive people, take it from me. That vague odor of liniments and zinc ointment that hangs around her, for example. A sign of wanton depravity! Nothing to write home about, those physical signs of the depraved sickness she's carrying in her loins. But her mind, that's another matter. Darker and darker, more and more confused: events, people, her personal history, all whisked together in her inner chaos. Surely you're curious to know why? How could you possibly embrace death without an answer to this question of the century?

"Let me satisfy your curiosity, inspector. Not only is she being eaten from the inside out by the 'tropical bubo,' but she also became acquainted with the opium pipe. What bliss! She took to it like a duck to water, but it made a monumental mess of her mind. By the way, your brains will dry up and be used later for science. With a little luck, of course, since they'll have to find you first in this alcove. Be that as it may . . . and forgive my long-windedness, I'm a little bit excited. Where was I?

"Ah yes, while enjoying the pleasures of a water pipe, Simone told me about her plan to recreate the Cagliostro affair for that superstitious idiot of a Napoleon III. I was fascinated! A highly original idea! And artistically justified. I figured in the first instance that she would snuff a random couple of useless candles at the emperor's court. 'Do you know what, Le Maçon,' said Simone with her little-girl's voice that could be so smooth yet so slippery, 'when there's a war on, one more death doesn't make much of a difference, not even when it's someone from the emperor's entourage. But what if there's something supernatural about it? What if it looks as if the ghost of Baudelaire is wreaking revenge on every small-minded pest who made a fool of him when he was still alive? The papers will be full of it. Our poetry-loving emperor will be convinced of your skills as a medium and ask you to predict the outcome of the war. You'll far surpass Cagliostro, Le Maçon. Napoleon III can be lavish with money when he wants to.'

"As you can see, our Simone can be convincing when she puts her mind to it. At the start I wasn't too keen on the symbolism she wanted to incorporate into the murders. Avoid the frills, I thought to myself. A couple of simple murders would be more than enough. But Simone gradually convinced me that Napoleon III would be like putty in my hands if I accepted her proposal. I can hear her now: 'Charles-Louis Napoléon is just crazy about poetry and the supernatural!'

"On top of that she had a condition that suited me down to the ground: She insisted on doing the murders herself. *Murder as art* was what she called it. I accepted. I wasn't born yesterday. Her suggestion left me out of it, should an inventive policeman like yourself ever get involved in the investigation. Simone was the killer. I was just an innocent clairvoyant! I didn't know then, of course, what I know now.

"Oh, my poor back. At my age, laying bricks can be hard on the spine. Have you shut your eyes, inspector? Am I boring you? I'll keep it short. Simone kept her side of the bargain. The killings she arranged, details of which she shared with me weeks in advance, had exceptional flair. Excellent material for my dramatic predictions!

"Does it surprise you that a series of murders can be devised in such a fashion? It shouldn't. Simone and I are members of a fraternity much older than the soggy divinities people worship these days. Bourgeois morality and pathetic Christianity aren't our style, inspector. But our time has come, Monsieur Bouveroux. You won't live to see it, but there are dark clouds forming on the horizon of history. This miserable war between the French and the Prussians is destined to nourish a much grander conflict, a great war that will change the face of humanity and our continent forever. I foresee terrible weapons destined to take the lives of hundreds of thousands of young men as they hide in rat-infested trenches. Flying machines will sow destruction. Vehicles like giant steel tortoises will crush bodies and spew fire. Can you picture it? A slaughter of unheard-of proportions! And you had written me off as a satanic scoundrel, hadn't you? Come now, Monsieur Bouveroux, a little perspective wouldn't go amiss!

"But even visionaries like myself have to live, Bouveroux, and money is not unimportant. Everything is possible in the Second Empire if you know the right people, you're in the right place, and you do the right things. But every plan has its weaknesses, even if you think you've covered every contingency. You have to minimize them, and you can only do that by being careful. That's why I didn't communicate directly with Simone about the speed with which I had gained the trust of Napoleon III. Rather, I used a whore by the name of Claire. Simone treated Claire—a tasty creature—as if she was her own daughter. And why didn't I communicate directly, you ask? At that stage in the process it would have been extremely annoying if any of the courtiers caught sight of Simone and me together. Suspicion and intrigue in the Champs-Elysées are simply grotesque, I can tell you. In the last analysis, the circles *that matter* are small and everyone spies on everyone. So we were extremely discrete.

"It didn't take long before I had convinced the emperor that I was an exceptionally talented medium. When the hubbub of war grew louder, Charles-Louis asked me to predict its outcome. I gathered my courage and asked for fifteen thousand gold francs. Not for myself, I added immediately. I convinced the emperor that the money would be used to establish an academy for clairvoyants, which would train talented young men and women to advise and assist the French dynasty. Fifteen thousand gold francs! Simone and I had agreed in advance that I wouldn't collect the money myself. Money was beneath a man of my status, and we didn't want the emperor to smell a rat. As Napoleon's trusted confidant in matters sexual, Simone was perfectly placed to collect the money.

"Well, my dear inspector, four days before the emperor was taken prisoner in Sedan by the Prussians, I predicted that he would win a great victory: 'Your army will cross the Rhine and French flags will flutter from here to Berlin. Victory is inevitable!' Napoleon III was in the clouds. He showed me caskets full of medals he planned to dole out to his generals after the battle. He wanted to pay me right away. I proudly refused, observing that accepting money might taint my talents. He found my response magnificent! Simone was to collect the money that same day and begin the necessary preparations for the 'paranormal academy.'

"That was three days ago. And what did you see upstairs in Claire's apartment? An empty boudoir. And, believe it or not, the whorehouse where Simone once ruled the roost blew up the night before last! A Prussian shell, they're saying on the street. I have my own opinion! She's a fine one, that Simone. She's been in every corner of darkest Africa. The stories she tells are enough to make your hair stand on end. She was initiated into the African magical arts. It's no laughing matter.

"Take the mummified head of that Negress Hara, for example. Now that you've seen it I have to kill you. I have no other option. But I was just as shocked as you when I opened the casket. A powerful amulet! The blacks call it an *ouanga*. I had to act immediately and without preparation. Killing a person tends to revitalize chosen ones like myself, deep in the darkest recesses of the mind. But one has to be careful. Terrible things can happen when gifts bundled in such a manner get out of hand. *Ouangas* are demons in material form and they can go wild!

"Anyway, the bird has flown and so has the money. I'm deeply disappointed in my fellow man, and especially in Simone. I'm also very angry. My only hope is the commissioner, who is tenacious, apparently, and familiar with Claire. And you've made me very curious about Simone's memoirs, which you received from the commissioner. I'm hoping the puzzle will lead me to Simone, who has gone into hiding. I also hope she's still in the country.

"To be honest, I don't understand why Simone passed on her memoirs to Lefèvre. There are too many obscurities in this affair. Her notes simply have to contain the key to solving this unsavory business. That's why it's high time I said goodbye. But look, I changed my mind. I didn't prepare a poisonous potion to shorten your suffering as I said I would. I've always been a liar. I take pleasure in the more refined forms of torture. It's the way I am. I wish it were different, but I'm a child of the devil. There's nothing I can do about it. People only interest me when they fall prey to dreadful anxiety. The energy it gives me!

"The Count of Saint-Germain's renowned elixir, which he claimed made him immortal, didn't exist. What made him young were the murders he committed in secret. People like us prey and live on the extreme emotions of others in their death throes. It's hard work, Bouveroux, let me assure you. Look, one more brick and your tomb is complete. Your neck muscles tense. Your eyes bulge in their sockets. Your gagged mouth prepares itself for one last scream. Who would think of looking for you in a bricked-up alcove in the cellar of an abandoned apartment building?

"Take comfort in this, Bouveroux: At certain times, determined by Masonic ritual, I shall return to this spot. Then you won't be alone in death. I will place both hands on this wall and a *shock* will penetrate me to the core and make me young again."

63

WHY DID HE HAVE A sense that something wasn't quite right? Lefèvre walked in silence next to Castellani and Toulouse, listening to the young painter's description of the bordello they were about to visit: "a picture of paradise." But the fellow had never set foot inside the place. He was just following the directions of a "girl with a high Russian forehead I would have called Olga had I brought her into the world."

Toulouse included an animated description of what had happened earlier that night. As he was sketching the row of poor people standing in line for "cheap meat," a young woman approached him. She told him she "had been watching the three of us and had quickly understood that we were out of place."

"It's not easy to hide the manners of a gentleman under a grimy mantle," Henri had bragged. The woman, "well-dressed and with a cheeky glint in her eye," had told him about the "recently opened" brothel where she worked. "There's a smoker's room where the girls display their wares in every imaginable form, but always with class and sophistication. The interior is English style, with oak woodwork, spittoons, and the most aromatic cigars." But in spite of every effort on the part of the madame to bring in clients for her "fresh young fillies, children almost," the war had left the place empty for a couple of days. But three gentlemen with the courage to mix with the plebs "at feeding time" obviously had enough "package between their legs" to brave the shells.

Lefèvre interrupted at that point. "Well-dressed with a cheeky glint in her eye? What was *she* doing there at 'feeding time'?"

The young painter was caught off guard by the question and snorted indifferently. "A destitute mother? Brothers with walking sticks as arms and legs? Bawling sisters rubbing their hungry tummies? A father bent double and crooked, desperate for a chunk of meat to bite on with the few teeth he has left? Even the whores are underfed these days, commissioner. In any case, this charming creature seemed well-fed to me, and I'm determined to prove my eyes weren't deceiving me. To me she was a classic beauty, with an ambiguous aloofness in her demeanor that roused me like a young dog. Let me make a suggestion, commissioner: This evening you leave your suspicious policeman's mind behind you. We've fought each other, drank wine together, spied on cannibals. You and Castellani have amused yourselves at the antics of the aristocracy, and I have made a magnificent sketch. And as grand finale we get to visit a brothel! Can you imagine a more perfect evening?"

"At my age?" said Castellani good-naturedly. "Some mulled wine and the breasts of a lover as cushions to sleep on."

"Ferdinand, such romantic images are hopelessly *démodés!*" said Henri, feigning despair. "Love is a whore. She spreads her legs for you while she's thinking about someone else."

"A roasted pheasant in red wine sauce spreading her legs just for me isn't thinking of someone else," said Lefèvre. "And she won't give you syphilis."

"What do I care," said Toulouse pigheadedly. "The whole world is infected with the clap but won't admit it. There's always been syphilis and there always will be syphilis. We're all going to rot in the grave one day, with or without it. When I melt inside a woman and soothe

the pain in my soul, why should I be thinking about syphilis, for God's sake?"

"It drives some people insane," said Castellani gently.

"If I don't live life to the full, I'll go insane," said the young painter. "Rue Chabanais. Well, look at that, we're here already. Come on, gentlemen, time to be butterflies!"

64

How can this be? Why this sudden clarity, this tranquillity, this grace?

My hands are chafed from tugging at my shackles. The gag in my mouth is like sandpaper. But the feeling that my body is being torn to shreds from mortal terror has gone.

In the darkness around me I gradually discern a familiar form. A sense of bliss overcomes me as it did when I was small and saw the pigeons in the gutter preening each other's feathers. I, Bernard Bouveroux, am buried alive in a bricked-up alcove. My time has come. What then is this bliss that is surging through my veins?

My life has been a sad spectacle, with myself as its reluctant audience. Melancholy has run through my fingers like water. Because I didn't understand the meaning of life, I forced myself to believe in progress. I imagined a time when Humanity would be elevated to the divine by the Machine, liberated from the devil inside. Now that I have stared the devil in the face and witnessed Evil, I no longer need to believe. All I need is the courage to accept and submit.

Heaven and hell are but nothing in the presence of such great love. She bows toward me.

Marthe, my dearest wife, I've missed you so much. All my life I was greedy to know more and more. But I never knew that you loved me so . . .

65

"A GLASS OF ABSINTHE, COMMISSIONER?" Her voice was coaxing, with a teasing undertone. Lefèvre watched her bend to the wheeled tray by the four-poster bed. Her body's gracious lines formed an erotic challenge, but also accentuated her vulnerability. With a woman like this, a man's thoughts irrevocably turned wild.

"No."

"But you deserve it. You were very sanguineous."

"A man's passion can be brutish at times."

"A glass of wine, then?"

"A *houri* once offered me a glass of wine in Algiers. She had led me on a spicy journey of discovery to every part of her body. I should never have accepted her offer."

"Why not?"

The commissioner pointed to a raw scar close to his heart. During earlier encounters Claire de la Lune had fondled it gently with her finger. This time she leaned over and kissed it.

"That's not all. When the female creature that was dressed up like the Belgian Poupeye offered me a glass of wine I woke up in tethers and almost paid for it with my life. And just a few minutes ago, you told me she's your mother. That's enough to make a man very cautious, don't you think so?"

Claire de la Lune turned her porcelain face toward him. "True, but who saved your life in those precarious circumstances?"

"The man in me would like to think it was you. But the policeman in me isn't satisfied with your explanation."

When the three gentlemen had arrived in the vestibule of the brothel and handed over their hats and coats, they were told that Madame was away and that a dowager would receive them in her stead. The substitute had all the qualities of a reliable bourgeois widow. She shepherded them to the reception room where the girls were on display. Lefèvre noticed her glance at him vigilantly and it set him thinking. Perhaps they had met in another establishment?

The girls were plentiful and the decors in which they presented their wares were inspired. Toulouse muttered something about his "dream girl" and how disappointed he was not to see her among them. He asked about her. The dowager responded with gestures of apology and tried to tempt him with a black-haired girl from Indochina, barely of age, charmingly attired as an Indian squaw. Castellani was taken by a burly creature dressed as a Greek temple dancer. Both men were easy victims. The dowager took Lefèvre by the wrist and whispered in his ear: "She wants to speak to you. Through that door, commissioner."

"Who?"

"You'll see, commissioner."

The reference to his office went hand in hand with another meaningful glance. Lefèvre had opened the door without looking right or left and walked into the room. Claire de la Lune was lying on an oriental four-poster surrounded by pillows and veils, wearing nothing but a see-through chalwar, her eyes crystal clear and inviting. Lefèvre was about to say something when she spread her legs for him. She then turned and offered her derrière to him on her hands and knees, like a cat desperate to mate. She didn't say a word. The commissioner had resigned himself to the inevitable.

"Next thing you know I'll be agreeing with what the moderns have to say," the commissioner now continued when Claire remained silent. "Life as an impenetrable chaos. Not that I find anything attractive in such a worldview."

"What is there about my explanation that's not to your liking?" While Claire de la Lune appeared to be calm, tiny signals betrayed her unease. The hand that raised the wine to her lips was so tightly wrapped around her glass it made her fingers turn white.

"Who was the young lady who advised Toulouse to visit this establishment? I would like to meet her."

Claire de la Lune smiled. "*Touché*, commissioner. I confess. It was me, and not Emmanuelle as I told you earlier. Don't you understand that a woman, even a woman like me, has her pride? It's best for a man not to know how much a woman yearns for him."

"Women say such things when they're intent on distracting a man. How did you know where we were?"

She offered him the glass from which she herself had sipped. This time he accepted. "You may be a police commissioner, Lefèvre, but you know little about what's going on in your city. In spite of his aristocratic background, Henri Toulouse belongs to an underground revolutionary organization, the *Société des Amis du Peuple*. My mother, a crook and a swindler her entire life, happens to be an important member of this motley network and they support the workers' revolution. I found out where you were via contacts in society's underbelly, and that Toulouse and Castellani were with you. I managed to find a coachman willing to brave the Prussian bombs and hurried to get here. But I thought it better not to present myself openly and . . ."

The glass of wine stopped at Lefèvre's lips. "So you decided to tease our young rooster with descriptions of this *maison d'amour* and take advantage of the situation to wait for me here?"

Claire smiled. "What would you have done if I had spoken to you when you were surrounded by cannibals? You would have slapped me in the face because I had disappeared, and marched off in the opposite direction, too proud to listen to what I had to say. Women are weak, commissioner. The violence in men obliges us to be cunning."

Lefèvre thought for a moment. *"Les Amis du Peuple* . . . Aren't they the old Carbonari? I thought they—"

"Were executed with the other strikers in Lyon during the weavers' riots? Such organizations never die. They cocoon, take a different name, continue to fight."

"To what end? To give power to the workers? What would happen then to our civilized world? If the workers revolt, they'll plunder Paris and paralyze the country. Is that the future you're after?"

Claire de la Lune pursed her lips. The commissioner noticed that she looked different, less childlike. "This isn't the moment for ideologies, but for confessions. I was an accessory to the so-called Baudelaire murders. I was the liaison between a man I knew only as Le Maçon and my mother. My mother committed the murders. She is insane, and I would have met with the same fate had I tried to resist her.

"I'm putting my life at risk by telling you this. I would rather be arrested than face my mother, now that she knows I've betrayed her.

"But before you lock me up, I have a story to tell, and a proposal to make."

66

"I WAS TWELVE AND IN the clouds when my mother finally told me about my father. She claimed he was a great poet. Was I to believe her? My mother was a born liar who took pleasure in tormenting me. She knew how much I loved poetry. But after listening to her bizarre story, which she told with malevolent satisfaction, I was determined to meet my father. I wanted to show him I could write and that my handwriting was beautiful. But my mother assured me that I would lose the power of my legs at the sight of his metallic gaze. I would be even worse off than the little girl with the matches in Hans Christian Andersen's story.

"What should a child think when her mother tells her that her father sold his soul to the devil? He became a dark shadow in my life, something that made me shiver when I touched it. When I got older she gave me a couple of his poems to read, sonnets that left me with a picture of an unkempt and dishevelled man, racing through the streets of Paris, his open coat flapping in the air, being chased by crows, muttering to himself that he had to find the black coach that had taken away his tears. The image of an angry-looking man with pointed ears gradually made way for an influence that was more subtle, but equally terrifying.

"The rhythm of his language and the allure of his words excited me. I became giddy when I read them. I rubbed my legs together. I imagined reading my own poems to him when we finally met for the first time. It was set to take place in a park, surrounded by statues looking down on us from above. He would listen in silence and then nod appreciatively. The statues would heave marble sighs of admiration.

"My mother refused to tell me more. She was busy with other things in those days, although she always insisted that my father was the love of her life: 'a scorpion that penetrated my heart.' Around the same time, I noticed that she continuously talked about money. The brothel in which she had raised me had made her rich, but it didn't seem enough for her. My vision of life was frivolous, superficial. I didn't care about money. I dreamed of fame and pleasure. Money could bring me those things, my mother assured me. I later discovered that my father once wrote a poem about a woman's hair being a powerful fetish. But a fetish is ultimately a symbol of doom and destruction.

"My mother's fetish is money. She never had enough. She blamed her greed on her youth. She had regular epileptic fits, but I knew what I had to do. When she was recovering in bed I would bring her soup, and she would sometimes linger in the past and talk aloud with her eyes closed. I heard fragments I didn't understand at first. But I understood the emotions: anxiety, rage, confusion, desire . . . I even felt them myself! I started to form a terrifying picture of my mother. She had always been strict, and subject to fits of anger. But her ramblings slowly made me aware that she was capable of a great deal more.

"Even the man who visited her from time to time, with whom she withdrew into her private quarters, scared me. I was told to address him as Le Maçon. The dark fire in his eyes, the ashen complexion, the enormous hands, the bluish hue in his skin. I asked my mother with the impudence of a thirteen-year-old who spent her days surrounded by whores if she slept with him. She beat me with her cane and laughed. 'Le Maçon only uses a woman's flesh as an altar when he's sleeping with the devil.' Every time I saw that man I was reminded of those words.

"Time oozed past like honey from a spoon. We moved to a larger building. Silk and damask appeared, oak panelling, the most expensive clothes. She started using prettier girls. Mulattas. My mother treated them with contempt. When I asked why, she barked 'those unshaven cunts stink like the sewers.' They reminded her of a black woman my father had been seeing. That was the way she spoke, the language of the street molded by hardness of character. But her clothes were refined, and her manners too. She could converse about art and politics with the aristocrats who were finding their way to her *maison d'amour* in ever greater numbers. A fine bunch! Bowing and scraping and pomaded moustaches. Handmade hats and walking sticks with inlaid gems. But the girls told me about their demands behind my mother's back, their disgusting habits, and their personal delusions.

"I felt protected when I was surrounded by the ladies of pleasure, but when my mother appeared I would make myself scarce. The *cocottes* knew how much she scared me and they helped me. I started to lead a secret life. I fantasized about the power I would one day exercise over men. The girls told me I was beautiful, delicate as a Chinese vase, graceful as a doe. Their words were smooth and sweet to my ears. But every time my dreams puffed me up, my mother was there to deflate me, and push me back 'into the shit where I belonged.' *Il faut être toujours ivre*, my father wrote. Nothing could be closer to the truth! I wanted to be drunk from dust till dawn to wipe out my life. Existence is nothing but gloom, poisoned by unattainable dreams, enough to empty the most optimistic soul.

"So what do you think, commissioner? Let me guess: I'm not the only child that has been beaten, who isn't quite sure who her father was. But my mother and Le Maçon were more than simply vulgar and violent. They had an aura about them that cut to the quick. Did you ever read Dr. Roussignol's account of Victor, the wild boy of Aveyron? His story is full of the most amazing things. But should someone ever write the story of my life they'll find many more and much stranger things to relate. I grew up surrounded by wolves in human guise, big talkers to the last of them.

"And the nonsense they spoke! The First International, world revolution on our doorstep. The worship of evil in all its forms through the centuries. African sorcery. Egyptian rituals. French politics . . . A pell-mell of claptrap. I had also discovered that Le Maçon and my mother were addicted to opium. When my mother had been smoking, she sometimes drawled on about a nun from her youth called Sister Wolf. According to her, Sister Wolf had strangled a bastard child born in the monastery hospice as a sacrifice to Christ. Such twisted stories made me even more afraid than I already was. I dreamt of escape. But I knew nothing of the world. Every time I broke the rules I was punished with an iron hand. The conversations between Le Maçon and my mother almost drove me insane with fear. The future, if they were to be believed, was going to be worse than ever before. They gloated at the idea and concocted plans.

"How can I describe the pain and anxiety of such a youth, commissioner? The truth is I can't. Nor can I explain what made my mother let go of the reins all of a sudden. Everything changed in the space of three weeks, just before my fourteenth birthday. In those days I wasn't *exactly* sure what was going on. It was only much later, after I stole my mother's memoirs, that I realized the full extent of the ordeal she had put me through. Don't ask me for details, please. Even a confession has its limits.

"She started treating me differently after what happened, looking at me with different eyes. As the years passed I came close to feeling human in her presence. She taught me how to pleasure a man and how to lie. I became a talented liar, so talented she never realised how much I hated her. After reading the truth about what she had done to me in her notes, I dreamed every day of revenge. But her power over me continued. I had to wait a long time for the opportunity to present itself. Her fetish provided it. In spite of her steadily increasing wealth, and the fact that her clients belonged to the highest echelons of society, she never stopped trying to devise ways to bring in more money. I had long suspected that she was bribing well-placed individuals and planning murders, but I only confirmed my suspicions a couple of months ago.

"She came to visit me at my apartment, which was under Le Maçon's supervision. She was very excited. She told me about a plan Le Maçon had concocted. Its 'modernity' appealed to her. Her behaviour had grown stranger of late. She took arsenic preparations to stem *le mal anglais* that plagued her. She complained about her eyes, claiming that some invisible sprite had been poking them with pins. Le Maçon, she informed me, was intent on convincing the emperor that he was an excellent clairvoyant. What a triumph it was going to be! Le Maçon would describe a couple of sensational murders down to the last detail before they took place. My mother had jumped on his ludicrous suggestion without thinking and insisted on playing her part. She wanted to use the opportunity to murder a couple of people who had humiliated my father while he was alive. The murders were to be an 'amoral work of art', a symbol of the times.

"You've seen her notes, commissioner, and read them I presume. Do you believe that my father was really her twin brother? I do! I saw them together years ago, and I'll never forget what I then witnessed in my mother's eyes. Please don't ask me to explain. No, let me return to my confession. My mother told me that I had to help her. She had contrived 'artistic' murder scenes and was playing with the insane idea of immortalising them on photographic film. I realized that she had completely lost her mind, but an entire life under her influence had left me powerless and unable to defy her. I dream of resisting her when I'm alone, but when I look in her eyes a strange paralysis takes hold of me, as if an invisible hand is squeezing my throat.

"I had no choice but to obey. Before long she was talking about her crazy plan as her life's work, the ultimate demonstration of her love for my father. As a result of her horrifying behaviour I started to see her as the reincarnation of Medea. Don't laugh. You should have heard her rant about the love of her life and the revenge she was about to wreak. It had become an obsession. Your work has taught you that people can have many different faces. They pop up their pretty umbrellas and smile at you benignly in public, but behind every façade lurks a vampire or a werewolf. In some instances, the creatures that control them show through their skin. I call them shadow people.

"I have always lived in a world of shadows. Reality for me is intangible. If I take hold of a chair I'm never sure if it's real. And if it feels real, my brain wants to know what makes it so. That is why I didn't doubt for a single second that my mother had a tail the moment I read about it in her memoirs. Well, of course! Obviously! Not an ounce of doubt, although I had never seen her completely naked.

"All my life I have feared for my sanity because I was surrounded by shadow people. I often heard Le Maçon proclaim that human beings were in the control of non-human presences that manifested themselves in what he called *ahrimanic doppelgangers*. So many big words just to say that people do things they don't understand. 'Naive and out of touch' is how scholars nowadays protest such theories as *doppelgangers*. But their rambling descriptions of syndromes they call *phrenopathy* and *débauche crapuleuse* often refer to the *unconscious*, a collection of passions, desires, and dreams that can rise to the surface and make us surprise even ourselves. Their explanation doesn't seem less foolish than that of Le Maçon. Hasn't science only recently discovered that electrical currents run through our nervous system? Le Maçon sneers at such 'discoveries' and insists that the electrical energy is caused by demonic creatures known even to the Babylonians.

"I sometimes believed him. But more often than not I was convinced they were both insane. What kind of person would commit murder just to acquire a reputation as a medium? People with the lowest moral consciousness? Or people who are *possessed?* And what about their accomplices?

"I might call myself an 'accomplice,' but in reality I was only privy to their plans, which they discussed with me openly. They laughed and toasted to a radiant future. I bit my lip, waited, and prayed for an ally. That ally was you. When my mother selected you as her next victim and organized the scene intended to lure you into her trap, fate granted me an opportunity.

"Anyway, you know how close you came to dying. But just as 'Poupeye' was about to carve your heart from your chest she had a seizure, a *grand mal*. I had stolen her memoirs a couple of days earlier. Up to that point I had only read fragments and had always returned them to avoid suspicion. But I wanted firm evidence to back up my claims. I first intended to get them to you anonymously, but I had to change my plans when my mother announced that you were to be her final victim. I thought for a moment that she had read my mind and that she wanted to hurt me. A shiver ran down my spine, cold as ice. Then she continued to talk and I realized it was just a coincidence.

"Or perhaps not entirely. Months earlier I had told her that you had put Baudelaire in jail years ago. I confess I also told her about the photographic image you discovered on Deputy Pinard's body. And yes, I managed to convince Dacaret to pose for the photo like 'a moonlit corpse' when he visited me in my boudoir. He was happy with the picture, found it original, funny. My mother had figured that it would be found by Prefect Banlieu and then be published in the papers. The uproar would have been enormous. But you upset her plans by keeping the portrait secret. Because of your atypical behaviour, Le Maçon's predictions turned out to be less accurate, although they covered every other detail.

"I was at a complete loss when I heard you were to be her next victim, but I had to cooperate with her plans. When she suffered a *grand mal* at the ultimate moment, I realized that the powers of light were also at work beside the powers of darkness. I leapt from the perverse machine she had devised, caught her as she fell, and left her notes lying on your chest. I then sped her away. I couldn't wait until you regained consciousness. Le Maçon had been charged with 'cleaning up the mess' and I expected him at any minute. I bumped into him with my mother in my arms.

"He recoiled when I told him that your assistant Bouveroux had burst in in the middle of the ritual. When my mother finally came around later that evening I told her the same story. She believed me because I was able to describe Bouveroux in detail based on stories about him I had heard from you. She was so convinced that she cleared out my boudoir that same night to erase as many traces as possible. I had to return to work in my mother's brothel, the place where I had lived the fate of Antigone thirteen years earlier.

"Thirteen years of disgust! That's why I was no longer afraid. I wanted to contact you and tell you everything. Luck would have it that one of the girls who works here—a confidant and also a member of *Les Amis du Peuple*—saw you arrive in the company of her good friend Henri Toulouse. I wasted no time in devising a way to get you to my chamber.

"Now I'm keeping my promise. With the fifteen thousand gold francs Le Maçon had wheedled out of Napoleon III, my mother devised a daring plan that would bring in a great deal more. I'll tell you about it and it will amaze you. But first you have to promise me one thing . . ."

67

"WHAT ARE YOU TALKING ABOUT, commissioner?" said Prefect Banlieu as he stroked his moustache. The prefect stared out of the window as if some incident or other on the boulevard was a source of virulent irritation.

The new day seemed to mock the bombing of the previous night. Sulphur-colored daylight, the sun high in the sky, nothing out of the ordinary. Lefèvre noticed that there was a bottle of anisette on the prefect's desk. Banlieu's cheeks were aglow.

"Communards supplied with money by a woman—a bordello owner, no less—to buy weapons and smuggle them into Paris via the catacombs in readiness for an imminent popular uprising?" Banlieu took a deep breath. "One of the weapons is a Gatling machine gun stolen in Sedan by mutinying soldiers? Has everyone gone mad, or is it just you?"

Banlieu had a weak receding forehead. Lefèvre was thankful he had managed to keep the satanic elements and Baudelaire out of Claire de la Lune's story.

"There's strong evidence that the conspiracy is not a fabrication, sir," he said. "The Gatling was smuggled into the city in parts, together with thousands of rifles. It's now being assembled in *Le Passage des Druides*, a catacomb beneath the *Place d'Italie*."

"A Gatling," said the prefect pensively. "A smart choice, I must admit, for a bunch of apes. Such newfangled machine guns are much better suited to urban warfare than cannons. I'd never have thought that—"

Lefèvre cleared his throat. "The operation was executed by *Les Amis du Peuple*, sir. We've dealt with them before and we know what they're capable of. An organized communard revolt seems inevitable. We'll have to act quickly."

"My dear commissioner," said the prefect with a frown. "You were charged with the investigation into those insane murders. And now this!"

"I have good evidence that the Baudelaire murders and this present matter are related," said the commissioner cautiously. "But we first have to interrogate the members of *Les Amis*."

"The times we live in!" said the prefect. "Are you sure . . ."

"If the prefect can spare ten of his men, we could go down into the catacomb and—"

"Whatever you want, Lefèvre. An uprising against the Second Empire, controlled from a bordello!" The prefect heaved a theatrical sigh.

"History has witnessed stranger things, sir," said the commissioner.

"When do you need the men?"

"I was planning to go down tonight." The commissioner felt dizzy and leaned unobtrusively against the prefect's desk for support.

Banlieu looked at him with suspicion. "You've been acting strangely of late, commissioner," he said. "I hope you're not sick?"

The commissioner smiled. Tiny beads of sweat formed on his face.

"I didn't get much sleep last night, sir," he said.

Banlieu stuck out his chin. "If you're wrong about this, sleep will be the last thing on your mind."

68

"Bernard?"

Outside, the wind rattled against the old windows. The door to Bouveroux's apartment was open. The inspector was a cautious man and would never leave his door open. The commissioner rummaged in his jacket for his Richards–Mason, pushed the door gently, and poked the barrel inside. A quick glance to the left and right. The living room was empty. The bedroom door was also open.

Lefèvre walked toward it, slowly, but it too was empty. The ash in the fireplace was cold. There were books open on the desk. A hefty tome, the *Encyclopaedia of Medical Anomalies*, caught Lefèvre's eye. Its pages contained images of people with a tail, mostly natives from distant islands. A copy of *The Flowers of Evil* lay open beside it, with the silver medallion Lefèvre had given to Bernard and Marthe sixteen years ago to mark their wedding adorning the left hand page.

The commissioner reluctantly leaned over the right hand page and read:

> *A heart that hates oblivion, ruthless censor,*
> *The whole of the bright past resuscitates.*

The sun in its own blood coagulates . . .
And, monstrance-like, your memory flames intenser![8]

A reflection on the setting sun in autumn, but for an instant Lefèvre felt he was not alone in the room. A shiver ran down his spine; his weapon waved back and forth.

"Bernard?" The timid voice of a thirteen-year-old waking in the dark, sensing his uncle by the bed, his enormous hand ready to strike.

Lefèvre was already at the door when it dawned on him what wasn't right about the inspector's apartment. A thorough search confirmed his intuition.

The memoirs of Simone Bourbier were missing.

69

THEY DESCENDED SIXTEEN METERS BELOW street level and saw the lanterns. The trapezium-shaped corridors of *Le Passage des Druides* reminded Lefèvre of a description of the inner core of an Egyptian pyramid, given him by a soldier back in Algeria. The soft sand muffled their footsteps. The officers under Lefèvre's charge were nervous. The rear passageway was dark, the two at the front were illuminated with lanterns. There was a clanging sound, not far off, and the vague sound of voices. The officers spread out.

A man in a workman's beret appeared from the first gallery. He was unarmed and carrying a lantern. He was startled at the sight of Lefèvre, but he quickly recovered, smiled, and opened his mouth to greet the commissioner. Lefèvre pointed his Lefauchaux and shot Henri Toulouse in the chest. The young social reformer fell to the ground with a scream that reverberated against the limestone walls.

Voices resounded in the third gallery. Lefèvre lunged forward, emptied his rifle, and pulled out a pair of revolvers. His men followed at his heels, yelping anxiously. Figures scuttling in the darkness, the bitter smell of gunpowder, deafening gun blasts. In the chaos Lefèvre saw what looked like a young girl fleeing toward the rear catacomb. He ran after her, pistols blazing.

For her there was no escape.

For him there was no way back.

70

THE PRUSSIANS SEEMED TO HAVE limited their shelling of the city to the hours of night, at least for the time being. Seeking regular cover from incoming grenades, the officers filled two carts with dead bodies and Lefèvre gave them careful instructions. The little woman was to be taken to the morgue, the others were to be counted, identified, and reported to Banlieu's administrative services. They were then to be buried in a mass grave in the paupers' cemetery.

When the men were gone Lefèvre looked up at the sky. He remembered how Toulouse's face had lit up, how he had smiled when he recognized the commissioner, then tumbled to the ground. A good death, wasn't it? Oh well, yet another restless night with gusting winds and a cloudless ferrous firmament.

A building on the opposite side of the Place d'Italie had taken a hit; three chimneys and a craggy wall were all that was left standing. Faint ribbons of smoke coiled upwards from the ruins. Lefèvre thought of Bouveroux, who only the other day had mockingly quoted from de Maistre's *Collected Works*, words from the beginning of the century: "Nothing can restore the power of Prussia. This renowned edifice, built of blood, filth, false money, and pamphlets, has collapsed; the country is gone forever."

Bernard would not have approved of what he had just done. It was better that he had disappeared. Prey to a Prussian shell, like so many other Parisians in recent months? Lefèvre shook his head, grabbed a lantern, and descended once again into *Le Passage des Druides*.

His men had seized the smuggled weapons. It was an impressive pile, but closer inspection had revealed that most of them were old, written-off army rifles. The Gatling was nowhere to be found. Hardly surprising. The commissioner had made up the story about the machine gun to help convince the prefect. In a world full of lies, a mixture of truth and half-truth could be useful at times.

The catacombs still smelled of gunpowder and blood. The arched niche at the back was filled with skulls, centuries old, piled up in disordered stacks. A wrought-iron wheelbarrow was parked in the corner, left over from an earlier plan to empty the place. The threat of war had put the plan on the back burner.

The rear wall was made of protruding stone blocks. Lefèvre counted three blocks to the right beginning with the middle row. He used a crowbar to make a hole. A dark niche with some scattered bones became visible. The commissioner put down the crowbar, grabbed the lantern and placed it in the niche. He carefully inspected the narrow musty space and nodded to himself a few moments later as if responding to an inner voice. He then smashed the remaining blocks with the crowbar.

According to Claire de la Lune's instructions, the first niche should have contained what was left of Napoleon III's fifteen thousand gold francs. She had insisted that at least ten thousand francs remained.

All the niches were empty, apart from the crumbled remnants of a bone or two.

71

THE DOWAGER ONLY DARED LOOK at the sweating dust-covered man in front of her out of the corner of her eye. She raised her hands. "Monsieur, I swear it! All the girls left in the night! I advise you to do the same and seek a place of refuge. The Prussians are coming and the establishment is closed."

The brute pushed her unceremoniously out of the way and headed for the room she had shown him the night before. A lengthy silence ensued. The dowager wrung her hands, but stood where she was as if she had been turned into a pillar of salt.

She heard the sound of breaking wood and smashing glass, and the stifled snorting of an angry bull.

72

THE WINDOWS OF THE MORGUE were shattered and its corridors abandoned. The lamps in the main dissection room were broken or out of oil. Coffins marked with chalk lay crisscross on the floor. Some of the dead, half-naked or in night clothes, had been caught in their sleep by the shelling. The only light in the room was from the lamp in the commissioner's hand. He held it out to every coffin until he finally found her.

She had been placed with the children because of her diminutive stature. She was wearing the gold-speckled shawl, the blue skirt, and the boots she had been wearing when he killed her. He leaned forward and looked long and hard at her smooth face, which had suffered little from the passing of the years. Her silver-blond hair was tied back with a clasp beneath her shawl. Lefèvre placed the lamp on the floor, crouched, and lifted her skirts. He took a knife from his jacket and cut open her undershirt and her drenched underpants. He paid no attention to the stench and examined her genitals. The *caroncule* was inordinately large and looked like a penis. The commissioner estimated the clitoris to be ten or eleven centimetres in length. The labia appeared at first sight to be a tiny scrotum.

The commissioner leaned closer to get a better look and noticed that they were swollen and stuck together. This quirk of nature had seen to it that Simone Bourbier was an outcast from the day she was born and lived her entire life bent on revenge. This deformity had led her to claim, or believe, that she had a tail. Lefèvre opened the labia with thumb and forefinger and pressed his middle finger inside. Simone Bourbier had a normal vagina. He ran his hands upwards under the dress. Small breasts, firm for her age, well-formed. In spite of her hermaphrodite appearance and her small stature, this woman could have borne a child.

"The things we have to do to earn a living, Paul," said Lepage behind his back. The commissioner didn't turn. He slowly rearranged the corpse's clothing and then looked up at the police physician.

"Indeed, Lepage, indeed." Lefèvre got to his feet and dusted himself off. "We all face demons from time to time, confront the evil in their eyes, and we pretend it's a mere bagatelle. Just like the best of accountants, we enjoy a little game meat in the evening, a glass of wine, a welcoming bosom. But sometimes we wake up with a start in the middle of the night and we bite our lips until they bleed."

"Did you bite you lips until they bled, commissioner?" The doctor's face seemed waxy and pale in the light of the lamp, his chin up, his eyes dull and narrow.

"More than that," said Lefèvre. "My entire body was bitten to bleeding last night. But that's nothing new to you, eh, Lepage? Tomorrow is another day, another opportunity for disgust and horror, nothing new, you get used to it after a while." He gestured toward the corpses around them and then to the tiny coffin at their feet. "I unmasked the Baudelaire killer. But who cares? Paris has other things on its mind. On the chessboard of life we no longer count. A month ago we were servants of the law. Now there is no law, only the law of war. People have their breaking point, Lepage, and so do eras."

The doctor nodded. The commissioner noticed the bags under his eyes, the left eye slightly squinting from exhaustion. "The civil war everyone is whispering about, commissioner, is it . . ."

"Inevitable."

"And who is likely to win?"

"Capital."

"The capital we serve."

Lefèvre smiled.

Lepage sized him up and came to a conclusion. He pointed to the body of Simone Bourbier. "Did you have a proper look, commissioner?"

"What do you mean?"

The police physician got to his knees and spread the corpse's legs. He winked at the commissioner to come closer. "Take a good look between her thighs . . . More to the left. There, camouflaged with salve."

The commissioner followed Lepage's finger and saw an ugly brown patch on her inner left thigh largely concealed by a pinkish cream.

"Is this what you were looking for, commissioner?" the police physician inquired as he peered sidelong at Lefèvre. "If this was the killer who managed to mimic Baudelaire's handwriting with such skill, it's ironic, don't you think, that she would have died of the same curse as the poet, had you not despatched her first."

73

THE RED COMMUNE FLAG HUNG wet and wilted above the steps of the Pantheon. The communards and deserters from the regular army had captured the Hôtel de Ville, and the revolutionaries now had weapons and other supplies at their disposal, in addition to guts and pride. Paris had become a city of barricades, a chaos of opinions, and a hodgepodge of social classes. They all wanted the ideal republic: down with the aristocracy, the clergy, militarism, monopoly, and privilege.

The nobility and the bourgeoisie were holed up in the wealthier districts of the city. Some had been hunted down and slaughtered. Those who were able stayed calm and lay low, waiting for better times. The government in Versailles sent warships steaming up the Seine to the bridges of the Monnaie. Adolphe Thiers, the provisional head of state, had acquired permission from the Prussians to conscript French prisoners from the war that had been raging only a couple of months earlier into a revamped army under the command of Marshal Patrice de Mac-Mahon. The marshal hated the communards and made plain his intentions to root them out completely.

The revolutionaries even mobilized women and children. In a packed church of Saint-Germain-L'Auxerrois, Louise Michel, daughter of a chaplain and a servant girl, and chair of *Le Comité du Vigilance Républicain*, addressed the assembled women. Michel sneered at the indecisiveness of so many men and decided that equality between men and women also meant that the women should get involved in the struggle. The ladies present almost demolished the place in their enthusiasm. They were more radical than the men, some of whom were still hoping to reach a compromise with Thiers, in spite of the fact that units under General Gallifet had already chased *les fédérés* from the left bank of the Seine.

Paris was bombed anew, this time by its own countrymen. Spies stalked the city, making the people suspicious of one another. The old police force fought with the new, which had been established by the communards. Long lines of citizens followed the railway lines out of the city to avoid the bloodbath. The Commune forced up weapon production in the cartridge factory on Avenue Rapp. More often than not, the National Guard had to face advancing Versailles forces with one rifle per three or four men. The Porte de Versailles, the Porte d'Auteuil: they managed to hold their ground, but for how long?

Night fell and the pouring spring rains drenched the barricades.

74

THE YOUNG WOMAN SENSED THAT something was wrong when she entered her apartment. It was already too late. The door slammed shut behind her. Most of Belleville's streets were dark and unlit at night, but lamps on the Rue de L'Orillon, with its stately mansions and walled gardens, were lit sporadically. The outline of a figure by the window, broad and menacing against the light from outside, made her spirits sink. She straightened her back nevertheless and asked with apparent calm: "How did you find me, Paul?"

Paul Lefèvre lit a lamp. Its pale light illuminated his angular face. He was poorly shaven, had grown an unkempt moustache in the months that had passed, and was shabbily dressed. "It's my job to find people, even in the chaos of Paris."

Claire de la Lune was radiant. She wore a pretty brown skirt and a grey-blue jacket over a silk blouse with elegant bows. Her long, shiny hair was tied up in a bun. Her fingers glistened with precious stones and she had golden earrings in her ears.

"I hoped you would find me."

"Shut up." His voice was calm, but it was still enough to make her step backwards and press her hand to her chest. "No more lies, Claire."

"I didn't—"

"Our last night, in your mother's brothel, I already knew in my mind that you tricked me once again, but my heart convinced me I should give you one more chance. Isn't that the fate of the Moderns, Claire? We believe in nothing so we just gamble, gamble on love, gamble on happiness, *gamble* on honesty. And that's what we call feelings."

"Paul, I—"

"My feelings have died in the meantime. Now pure reason is in command. We had an agreement, Claire. In exchange for half the money, I would see to it that your mother didn't survive the police raid. No survivors, no witnesses. That was the deal, and I kept my side of it. I even shot Toulouse as he helped prepare the communard uprising. An unpleasant surprise, let me tell you. I quite liked the young brat and regretted doing what I did. But the end always justifies the means, doesn't it? Where is the money?"

"It's not here," she blurted. "I'll have to . . ."

Lefèvre sat down on a couch and gestured to the chair opposite. Claire obeyed. He placed his walking stick on his knees. She stared at the heavy lion's head.

"Your mother," said Lefèvre. He seemed pensive and there was even the hint of a smile. "A demon from hell, that's for sure. When I examined her in the mortuary I felt I understood her. So much drive and ambition in such a tiny body. That deformity down below that filled her with both shame and—deep in her heart—pride! And then her grotesque plan . . . A success, all told, if not exactly as she wanted and with some unexpected delays: the plebs ransacking Paris, the communards insisting, raucous and loud, on a new world. But the powers at work behind the scenes, the powers that control them, ran off with the money just the same. That's exactly what your reckless and insane mother wanted to do. That was all she wanted in life. You told me yourself. What do you want, Claire? What kind of future do you have in mind?"

"I don't need money, Paul, I need . . ."

"Don't say it, I know already. A woman like you needs *love*."

"Is that so strange? After what I've been through?"

"A woman like you needs lies, more and more lies. Take that confession of yours: your entire life in a nutshell, you said, your eyes downcast, self-critical. A fabulous performance, Claire. Bravo! Applause!"

"It wasn't a—"

"You mean you mixed a tiny droplet of truth with a bucket full of lies? I can believe that. Don't worry. I don't want to know what was true and what wasn't. You'd probably choke on a fresh batch of lies."

"So what do you want, Paul, apart from the money?"

"I want you to admit that you are the murderer and not your mother."

"My mother was the one who . . ."

"Of course, perhaps you planned this together. But you were responsible for at least a couple of the killings. When I left your mother's surprisingly empty brothel after that shameful episode in *Le Passage des Druides*, I was suddenly reminded of the first killing, Albert Dacaret. The concierge told me about a suspicious nun who had appeared just before the murder took place. She was a vigilant woman, used to keeping an eye on people. If the nun had been particularly small of stature she would have mentioned it. I decided to pay another visit to the establishment on the Chaussée d'Antin. That brothel wasn't unexpectedly empty, Claire. On the contrary, it was packed and busy. I had another chat with Natalie, the young whore who witnessed Dacaret's death."

The commissioner smiled. "This time I was a lot more thorough. And what do you think she told me, Claire, after a little encouragement? The nun who had come into her room hadn't invited her to pray for her own salvation, as she had told me on my first visit. She had threatened the girl with a knife that was 'jagged, like a bolt of lightning.' A *kris* from India, like the one hanging in your boudoir. One moment that pretty nun was gentle and radiant and the next she was a fury, with eyes, according to Natalie, 'worse than the devil's.' She was terrified and did what she was told. Dacaret had fallen out of the bed during copulation, foaming at the mouth. Natalie ran outside in a panic. When she returned, Monsieur Albert was dead and there was no sign of the nun. Natalie didn't dare speak about it. She was afraid that no one would believe such a peculiar story and point the finger of blame in her direction. What do you think of that, Claire?"

The woman opposite him lowered her eyes.

"And then there's the bizarre death of de Cassagnac," the commissioner continued. "A man violently cut and dismembered until he took the form of a woman. The work of an angry and confused child? A child intent on paying tribute to a father who glorified evil? Or the child of a mother with physical deformities that made her look half like a man?"

The muscles in Claire's throat swelled up. "You don't know what it was like," she screamed. "To be birthed by monsters!" She buried her face in her hands.

A long silence followed.

"Do you know why I still believed you, against my better judgment?" The commissioner's voice sounded old all of a sudden. "Because you understood me. I told you what happened in my youth and what it did to me. You described similar symptoms when you talked about your own childhood: reality always on the verge of collapsing into a restless dream, people seeming to change shape in front of your eyes, glances that took on satanic significance, the feeling that someone was standing behind you all the time. You abused my *faith* in you. I don't know what truly motivated you, but hatred, greed, and insanity must have had a part in it. So what's the problem? We're all the same, aren't we? But that means we're all *out for revenge*, Claire, and the strongest wins, that's the law, and there isn't a curse in the world that can change that."

The woman sitting opposite the commissioner shivered from head to toe and lifted her head. "You've come to kill me, haven't you? I can see it in your eyes. Paul Lefèvre, officer of the law."

"There is no law, not anymore."

"I may be an irrational woman, but I did love you, Paul, really love you . . ."

"That reminds me of the day we first met, Claire. In hindsight, a truly meaningful encounter. You accosted me in the Rue

Notre-Dame-des-Petits-Champs with a timid look in your eye and a story about being chased by a couple of villains. I did the gentlemanly thing and accompanied you to your boudoir. Don't misunderstand me when I say that I'm pretty sure you had planned the encounter. Do you know what I think, Claire? I was the instrument you used to deal with your mother, the woman you hated but feared even more."

"You don't understand, Paul. You're blinded by—"

"There's only one way to save yourself."

"I don't believe you."

"*Gamble*, Claire."

"You can have the money!"

Lefèvre smiled and waved his hand in the air in a tired and limp gesture. "What are you waiting for?"

Claire de La Lune got to her feet, her head hanging, and made her way to her secretaire. Suddenly she was holding a small revolver in her hand, a Belgian six-shooter favored by ladies. She pointed it at Lefèvre. The commissioner fired the one-shot Remington built into his walking stick. The bullet penetrated Claire's heart and she fell to the floor.

She tried to get up. The commissioner stood and pushed her back with his right foot. He watched her choke on her own blood. When he was sure she was dead he stripped her naked, his hands exploring every millimetre of skin. He searched again and again, but there was no trace of the syphilis that had consumed her mother.

75

IT DIDN'T TAKE LONG TO find the money. The gold francs were stashed in a hatbox in the colonial wardrobe next to the bed. It was much more than he had expected. She had been busy in recent months. He was never likely to encounter such a shrewd and merciless killer as Claire again. He briefly regretted not having asked her which parts of her mother's memoirs really happened and which were figments of her imagination. Maybe she no longer knew. Every family has its secrets. A cheerless smile appeared on the commissioner's face: Every family has its skeleton in the closet.

The hatbox also contained pages that had been torn from Simone Bourbier's notebook. The commissioner examined them and started to read, the corpse of the woman he had once loved at his feet.

76

LITERATURE IS INFERTILE; NOT HIM. Back in Paris, I discovered that Charles had given me a venereal disease to complement the child in my belly. I cherished the first ulcer on my vagina as if it was a precious gem. He and I were now united by the same curse, which only death could eradicate.

We were twenty-five. Baudelaire didn't know he had a daughter, by this time three and a half. He had grown accustomed to our regular encounters in Paris, when I would dress as the diminutive Belgian Camille Poupeye. The herbal concoctions I had given him had wiped out every memory of that night in Oualata.

I quickly learned why Baudelaire could be cheerful one day and miserable the next. His "black angel" Jeanne Duval was an unpredictable vixen: Time and again she would sever their relationship and force my twin to jump through the most embarrassing hoops to put things right. As we listened to a mazurka in Café Tabourey, he gave me the first draft of a poem he had written for his quadroon to read, as she sat beside him bored and listless. Her profile betrayed the lazy pride of her race. Her salamander eyes had a velvety sheen;

deep beneath the sparkle of cruelty. She's probably like a corpse when they're doing the deed, I thought to myself. And he enjoys it! I would teach her some manners with that tail of mine.

Jesus, the man had a way with words, but he was hopeless when it came to reciting them.

Your hips are amorous of your breast
And of your back: your languorous pose
Enchants the cushions where you doʒe
When in their depths you make your nest.

And all she could do was pout and complain about Paris, "that center of universal stupidity." He kept calling her "my pretty" and even "angel" at one point. And what did he get for all his efforts? Flickering arrogant eyelashes. She scanned the café as if she was looking for a better aimant.

I saw through her. She had to play his Muse. He loved marble goddesses, lifeless, cold, and indifferent. I told him his verse had its merits, but would be better if he'd found a more appropriate subject. His eyes filled with anger. I bought a round of absinthe and patted him on the back like a man. He was the best; he just needed time to mature. That did the trick. What would be an appropriate subject?

I whispered in his ear that Evil might be a daring subject, certainly modern. Jeanne intervened, turned sweet all of a sudden, laughed at me, the putain. "A poet like you should be capable of letting himself be ruined by a woman and then writing about her. That's what I would call divine poetry!"

⚬⚭⚬

When you pass thirty, your memory becomes a clock that measures time in leaps and jolts. Charles had left Paris, disappointed by the 1848 revolution. But before long he returned grovelling. He proclaimed to all and sundry that he had fought on the barricades. In reality he had been drunk, staggering around asking anyone who would listen where his stepfather the General was, "so I can shoot the cowardly bastard."

But fortunately he didn't stop writing. His poems evolved more and more into a pure incarnation of Art. The musicality of his sonnets was phenomenal! He even managed to publish a few here and there. But his impossible character attracted so many enemies among the literary popes of the day that he didn't do particularly well. The artistic elite mocked him as "the dandy who thinks he rediscovered the art of writing." He reacted with sarcasm, but I could see how the lack of recognition hurt him.

As a result I too started to hate those who had treated him with such disdain. I made sure we "bumped into each other" every now and then. You could count the cafés he visited on one hand: Hôtel Pimodan, La Tour d'Argent, Café Duval, the kinds of places that never changed, places where he was free to rave in a drunken stupor, "I am a cemetery abhorred by the moon!" He was too drunk to notice, or pretended to be, that half of those present were sniggering behind their hats or veils.

He couldn't write a word without opium. When he had smoked the tears of the poppy he would call me his little forest sprite. Indeed, he was thinking of me when he wrote a short story he called "Little Sorcerer." It was a failure. He swore by all that was holy that the novel was a hackneyed genre, worn to shreds. But on the quiet he had dozens of ideas for stories he never wrote.

I was also absent from his life for long periods of time. It was good for the image of travelling salesman I had carefully projected for so many years. I was often convinced that my "profession" interested him more than I did. At such moments I felt like cutting his throat, but instead I glared at him roguishly to conceal the fire of love in my eyes, and dished up passionate stories about my adventures in far-off places.

He couldn't get enough of them. He kept coming back to the monumental book he planned to write about a poet who had turned his back on art and left for the Orient, where he grew rich on the sales of a magic perfume that drove women insane with desire. When the local sultan found out that the poet had seduced the most beautiful woman in his harem with the perfume, he took him prisoner and subjected him to "unutterable torture." He died in misery. I encouraged him to turn his story into a novel and took great pleasure in the anxiety and desire in his face.

Sometimes I whispered in his ear when his head was filled with opium and was lolling back and forth like an automaton: "A poet has to give voice to the demons inside us. Give them the freedom to speak. They will complete the work of which you dream with unheard-of magnificence."

He looked at me long and hard. I caught a glimpse of doubt in his bloodshot eyes. "Who are you? Really?"

"I'm your little forest sprite, the delicate monster you need to help you complete your masterpiece."

"My youth prevents me from writing a masterpiece. Loss! What prevents you from living as you would?"

I smiled. "Not my youth. J'ai eu une enfance qui ne fut rien moins que néant."

My words made him smile.

"Will you stay with me forever?" he asked a few moments later, barely comprehensible.

"Till the devil us do part."

—◦⊚◦—

Fate is eternal, immutable, they say. There's no such thing as accident. The entire world can fit inside a human head, but what goes on in it is beyond our control.

I thus became the very devil that was to drive my twin and me apart.

When I was thirty-six I opened a luxury brothel on the Chaussée d'Antin. One day Mylène warned me with a giggle that there was a gentleman in the salon who had asked for a girl with whom he could indulge in some "animal gymnastics." I asked Mylène if the man was drunk. He had "flat lips," she answered, and "melodramatic eyes." Melodramatic eyes? I marched to the salon, and there he was, my twin brother.

In spite of my diminutive stature, I was pretty sure he wouldn't recognise me as Poupeye in my frock and with my crimped hair. That wasn't my immediate problem. Charles was under the influence of opium. He behaved like an oaf and mumbled that he wanted "to soil himself with every whore in the place, as long as he could inspect them in advance."

At that moment Claire arrived. She was fourteen, an awkward but pretty young filly with luminous eyes. She had grown used to men selecting one of her "girlfriends" and disappearing with their choice for a while. She told dockworkers' jokes about it when she was with my girls. But this time she was uncharacteristically shy and remained at my side.

Charles doffed his hat and continued where he had left off, as if taking pleasure in the use of such language in the presence of a child. He wanted "a formidable whore." For the sake of decorum I asked him to temper his words. He winked at Claire and said aloud for all to hear: "The evil that does not recognize itself is infinitely more malicious than those who recognize themselves and are willing to admit it." He then let off an explosive and arrogant fart. Claire melted! Giggled behind her hand.

He continued as if he was taking us into his confidence: "The 'poet of evil' stands before you! A collection of my verses will be published in a month's time. I'll make sure you get a copy. But let me say this first: The religious exactitude with which I portray the malignant soul of humanity does not prevent me from being a mild-mannered chap in everyday life who lets people walk all over him. Without opium and wine I would never have the courage to appear in public and expose my deepest passions. So let me have a cocotte on the double or this craving will be the death of me!"

"My father is also a—" began Claire. I glared at her and she immediately held her tongue. I chose Justine for him. She had tender juicy breasts, which he quickly styled "pomegranates."

I looked on as his daughter watched him leave the room, and how he looked back over his shoulder like a man waking from a vivid dream.

When he had disappeared into one of the rooms I winked at Claire. "Don't talk to strange men about your father, certainly not if he's also a poet," I said. "Poets are exceptionally jealous types."

⁕⊚⊚⁕

Less than a month later he was back, in a terrible state, worse than the first time if that be possible. But there was nothing wrong with his memory. He had two copies of his collection with him. There was an engraving on the cover reminiscent of a Caduceus—the staff of Hermes. "I'm a man of my word," he effused. "Hot from the press of my publisher Poulet-Mallasis!"

His entire being trembled from the excitement of it all. "Think carefully before you accept my gift," he continued archly. "Literature isn't suitable for women. It rots their minds, makes them shallow, frivolous, licentious, capricious." He tossed back his head and laughed exuberantly.

An hour later he was still in the salon. He didn't ask for Justine. Instead he discussed the contents of his book with Claire. They sat with their heads together; their hands—the Baudelaire hands, delicate, refined, like the hands of a priest—almost touched but didn't.

I served my best wine and insisted that Claire drink along. She sipped at her glass with her eyes closed. Her blushing cheeks were alluring. When Charles was about to leave a couple of hours later for an important appointment with Gautier, I took him by the arm. "My daughter Claire is much taken by your work," I said.

"She is a pearl in your crown, madame."

"You did not indulge in la jouissance today. You were too excited, weren't you?"

He leaned toward me. "May I confide in you about your splendid daughter?" There were familiar traces of bitter almond and Havana tobacco on his breath.

"Let me guess, monsieur: You are a libertine with a longing for the forbidden." I was taking a risk, but I enjoyed it.

He bowed wittily. "True, madame. You must be clairvoyant. The desires of the flesh are often tainted with a sliver of sorrow. Every caress is imperfect, every longing bears the mark of its own inadequacy."

"How true. And how well put."

He stared at me. I nodded and invited him to continue.

"Only the transient purity of a young girl can comfort this incomprehensible heart of mine. Do you believe that art imitates reality? No, reality imitates art. If I may have the privilege to introduce this frail faun to the art

of love, I am certain it will inspire immortal verses. I'm happy to pay whatever you ask, of course."

"Come back next week, monsieur," I said. "Let me think about your proposal."

I tried to cool myself with my silk fan; the heat in that part of my body Sister Wolf used to call my devil's tail was close to unbearable.

⚬⊙⚬

That body part has governed my entire life and been a source of heart-rending doubts about my identity.

But it has also granted me the pride of a devil compelled to challenge every god.

When I opened the concealed peephole I had installed in each of the love-nests in my bordello and saw my daughter naked in the arms of her father, I couldn't help touching myself. Always moist and sensitive to pressure and rubbing, the organ quickly became engorged.

My daughter exhibited a mixture of attributes, the kind associated with foreign women and so highly thought of these days: she had the skin and hair of a Japanese geisha, Creole eyes, the breasts of a young Negress, and the hips of an Arabian belly dancer. Her father, by contrast, had developed rickets over the years, had an oversized angular head on narrow shoulders, a barrel chest, knobby knees, an excess of pubic hair, and a short stump of a penis. He examined her with a vaguely mocking smile on his face, but his right hand was resting on his heart and his left on his hip, in a pose reminiscent of a dancer.

He looked rather ridiculous, but Claire seemed impressed nonetheless. She looked away timidly from his body and obeyed his slowly pronounced commands: "Turn around . . . take your time. Lift your hands above your head. Lie down on the bed like la femme piquée par un serpent.*"*

She didn't understand what he meant. He explained, arranged her head and limbs in the correct positions. He referred with reverence to the sculptor Clésinger who had shaped a woman from marble who indulged in des délices inavouables, *as he himself had written in one of his critical pieces, concluding: "Only hypocrites conceal the true nature of the snake that makes this naked woman hoist her breasts heavenward."*

He ordered Claire to close her eyes and remain still. First he caressed her, his fingers like feathers, then he kneaded her flesh in round movements, faster and faster, like a man possessed. He crouched over her and mounted her. At the slightest movement he insisted she lie still. I noticed a tiny flow of blood between her thighs, but she didn't make a sound. Sweat poured from him and I saw the muscles in his neck swell up. He found no release. The tiniest deviation from the fantasy he was chasing was enough to transform her into a woman of flesh and blood and not the ideal marble statue he desired.

He tried again. Claire complied without complaint. Her cheeks were red. It annoyed him for some reason; I could see it in the way he looked at her. He redoubled his efforts, his face twisted, like that of a madman.

The roar of release did not come from his throat but from mine.

77

HE HAD LOST TRACK OF time as he wandered through the city. *En Joue*—
Take aim! The command resounded through the streets, followed by
salvos from Marshal Thiers' firing squads executing droves of communards. A tremendous thirst, reminiscent of his years in the desert, forced
him after a while to visit a cabaret that had apparently been spared by
the shelling. The fever in his head raged like a sandstorm. Oil lamps
illuminated the room. A giant stuffed catfish had been suspended from
the ceiling. On the walls: sea views and paintings of oriental women
with pitchers of water on their heads.

A small bas-relief of a winged lion graced the wall above the fireplace.
Almost all the tables were busy. National Guard members thundered to
and fro, making a racket on the wooden floor as they filled themselves
with Dutch courage before returning to the battle. The landlord, a bald
phlegmatic type with heavy whiskers, winked in his direction and pointed
in the chaos to a free chair. The man already seated at the table wasn't
particularly accommodating and didn't respond to the commissioner's
polite nod. A group of soldiers got to their feet, put on their berets, tossed
their rifles over their shoulders and marched to the door. Lefèvre took a
closer look at his table companion and raised his eyebrows.

The man's mouth appeared to form soap bubbles instead of words, just like the bubbles Hélène used to make when she played with soapsuds as a child. "Poor commissioner. When the sickness that has taken hold of you jumbles dream and reality into a maze with no exit, that's when you realize you're suffering from the curse of Baudelaire."

With beads of sweat forming on his forehead, Lefèvre leaned closer. "What was that? What did you say?"

The man looked up, his face expressionless. "I said nothing, monsieur."

Lefèvre stared at him. "You remind me of someone. You're the double of . . . Aren't you Castellani?"

"No, monsieur."

"I'm . . ." The commissioner bit his lip. "It's slipped my mind for the moment. I'm also very . . ." He dabbed the sweat from his cheeks with the back of his hand.

The other smiled. "Tired? Confused? Sick? I understand. Some call me Le Maçon, but my real name is Cagliostro, Guiseppe Balsamo di Cagliostro, at your service."

Lefèvre pointed at the book lying in front of the man on the table, his finger trembling. "What are you reading?"

"Shall I read it aloud?"

"Please, yes."

The man smiled, shook his head slightly, and opened his mouth, which was black as night:

> *I am the wound, and yet the blade!*
> *The smack, and yet the cheek that takes it!*
> *The limb, and yet the wheel that breaks it,*
> *The torturer, and he who's flayed!*

THE END

Endnotes

1   Roy Campbell, *Poems of Baudelaire* (New York: Pantheon Books, 1952)
2   Ibid.
3   Ibid.
4   Ibid.
5   Ibid.
6   Ibid.
7   From *The Mirror of Art: Critical Studies by Charles Baudelaire*, translated and edited with notes and illustrations by Jonathan Mayne (Garden City, NY: Doubleday, 1956)
8   From "Harmonie du soir", Roy Campbell (tr.), *Poems of Baudelaire* (New York: Pantheon Books, 1952)